LISBON '41

Malcolm Havard

Oakbrook Press

LISBON '41

Malcolm Havard

Oakbrook Press

Copyright © 2024 Malcolm Havard
All rights reserved

The characters and events portrayed in this book are fictitious. Any similarity to real persons, living or dead, is coincidental and not intended by the author.

No part of this book may be reproduced, or stored in a retrieval system, or transmitted in any form or by any means, electronic, mechanical, photocopying, recording, or otherwise, without express written permission of the publisher.

ISBN: 9798323295111

Cover design by: Malcolm Havard

Lisbon '41

An Inspector Lopes novel

MONDAY 12 MAY 1941,

LISBON 10.05 PM

The fog might be unseasonal but rolled up the Tagus with intent. It was more like October than Spring. The chill grey blanket crept up between the warehouses, hiding the cranes and softening the few streetlamps that the port district possessed.

The policeman scowled at the mist and swore to himself but the single word; 'Wonderful,' was all he said outloud.

'What's up Sarge?' said his young companion who strolled with an easy arrogant swagger that the sergeant found irritating. 'Old bones feeling the cold? You should stay indoors with your old lady. Put your feet up. Leave the street for us young'uns.'

'Watch your cheek, Da Silva,' growled the older man. 'You'll be cursing nights like this when you've lost that peach fuzz on your chin and that puppy fat round your ribs.'

'Yeah, yeah,' smiled Da Silva, showing no sign of being at all admonished. 'Whatever you say, old man.' He grinned slyly and the sergeant knew more was coming. 'Shall I have a word with my mum? Get her to knit you a scarf and mittens to keep those old fingers warm?'

'Enough of your lip. It's not the cold. This weather brings out the rats and I don't mean the grey ones.'

'Yeah, yeah,' laughed Da Silva.

'Look, kid, these are the kind of nights which can end up with your throat slit.'

The younger man laughed again but, at least, didn't come back with any smart backchat but fell into step with his superior. The sergeant silently cursed his luck to be paired with this cocky little sod, then moved on to his former partner for asking for a transfer. They'd worked well together but now… Da Silva badly needed taking down a peg.

They'd reached the river. The fog was worse down here, much thicker than at the top of the hill, but it didn't hide the dark bundles huddled in every doorway.

'Gah, it stinks here,' said Da Silva. 'Sodding dirty Jews, we shouldn't have let them in.' He kicked out at one of the nearest bundles. There was a yell of pain, the blanket was thrown off and a man, bearded, unkempt, eyes gleaming in what little light there was, sprang to his feet, fists raised-until he saw the uniform. Immediately he mumbled an apology and shuffled away into the fog, head down.

Da Silva laughed.

'That's right, you bloody Yid, you know your place, don't you?' Da Silva took a step after him, reaching for his truncheon but the sergeant grabbed him and pulled him back.

'Enough,' he said. 'What are you, some bloody animal?'

Da Silva shook himself free. 'Didn't have you down as a Jew lover, Jorge.'

The sergeant grabbed the younger man by the lapels and pushed him roughly against the warehouse wall.

'Who the fuck do you think you are? Shits like you don't get to use my given name. My name's Sergeant or Sir to you, Da Silva, get it? Well, do you?'

'All right, all right,' muttered Da Silva. 'I was only joking.'

'Joking? This beat isn't a joke. As for these poor sods, I don't care if they are Jew, Christian, Mohammedan or Chinese, they're refugees, that's all As long as they're not committing any crime I'm going to leave them be and so will anyone I work with - understand? Well, do you?'

The sergeant slammed Da Silva hard against the wall so his head made contact with the brickwork.

'Yes, yes, I do. For God's sake.'

'Yes what?'

'Yes, sir.'

The sergeant held him there for a few more moments, then let him go. His anger was fading now and it was replaced by a feeling he'd had before, too many times; shame that he'd lost his temper.

'Right, let's get on — .What the?'

There was a splash from somewhere ahead of them, deep in the fog, out of sight.

'What the hell?'

'Come on Da Silva, don't just stand there.' The sergeant started running but Da Silva easily overtook him, not having the older man's disadvantages of age and a lifetime of cigarettes and pastries.

Da Silva had vanished into the fog but the sergeant heard him shout:

'Hey, hey you!'

'Shit, it's the cops.'

'Las mich los!'

'Erschieß den Bastard.'

Who were the other voices? The sergeant redoubled his efforts to catch up.

Another shout. Then the crack of a gun. One shot, then two more in quick succession.

'Da Silva. Da Silva, where are you?'

There was no answer, just the sound of running feet fading into the fog.

He reached the quay where the ships rode at anchor, the chains gently clinking as the vessels swung with the tides. His chest heaving, gasping for breath and looked desperately about, where was the constable? He couldn't see a damned thing down here by the wharf side, not with the fog and…

He could hear something. A sound that was all too familiar from his service days on the western front. Gasping, rattling, bubbling.

Moments later he was cradling Da Silva in his arms as his young colleague, shot through the lungs, painfully breathed his last.

WEDNESDAY 14TH MAY 1941,

LISBON, 7.45 AM.

Dinis Lopes sighed to himself. The blue skies, the morning light glinting off the small patch of the Tagus he could glimpse from between the buildings hinted at a gorgeous, warm, spring day. It was unlikely he'd enjoy it, however.

He'd always enjoyed this view from the balcony. Lupa might be a little chaotic, rather too hilly for comfort and a little shabby but it both suited him and reflected the nature of his adopted home, Lisbon. Personally he'd have preferred to be in the even more chaotic, hilly and rundown Alfama but there was no way his wife would have accepted that. At least here he could argue that the presence of a number of foreign embassies gave the area some status that she could bask in. Still, it often wasn't enough.

It certainly wasn't enough now, not after yesterday.

The moment could not be put off any longer. He took a deep breath, steeling himself before going downstairs. Spring might be here with the promise of warmth and new growth but in the Lopes house the season was still winter, frigid, cold, barren, gloomy.

And it was his fault.

He sighed. He was never one to flinch from danger, or unpleasantness or confrontation, hell, which was precisely why he was where he was, so why should he start now?

He went down the stairs and into the breakfast room.

'Good morning, my love.'

His wife lowered the corner of her paper and stared back at him, her look one of loathing than love.

Sighing to himself, Lopes helped himself to meat and cheese from the breakfast that their maid had put out for them. The maid that would probably have to go given their new, straightened, circumstances.

He sat down at the table at which point his wife rose, put her napkin down on her plate and walked out of the room.

He had barely had a mouthful when the pounding on the front door began.

'PVDE, open up.'

Lopes felt his stomach tighten, his thoughts started to race. The Polícia de Vigilância e Defesa do Estado, the State Surveillance and Defence Police - basically his country's equivalent of the Gestapo! Why? What did they want? Wasn't his dismissal enough? Had he been framed for something? Or informed on? Had he said something careless? If so, what? He couldn't think of anything specific.

But did they need specifics? This was the PVDE.

Keep calm, he told himself, but his hand was shaking as he dabbed his mouth with his napkin. He rose from the table and threw it on his plate, taking one last look around the room. Would he ever see it again?

In the hallway the maid had opened the door. Four men stood there all dressed in the uniform raincoats that was the PVDE motif. One stepped inside.

'Dinis Lopes?'

'Yes.'

'You're to come with us.'

There was a half-stifled scream from the stairs. He turned to see his wife stood there, clutching the banister and was able to see her shock turn to anger.

'What have you done now?' she hissed. 'Look what you've brought us to. You've ruined us! Ruined me.'

She turned away as the PVDE man took hold of Lopes' upper arm and firmly guided him out of the house onto the street and into the waiting car.

WEDNESDAY 14TH MAY 1941,

LISBON, 8.35 AM.

They drove in silence to the PVDE headquarters on Largo Adelino Amaro da Costa. Lopes' mind was racing but he had reached some kind of peace, an acceptance that this was his fate and there was nothing he could do to change it. He'd seen so many others go through this realisation from the other side of the process; the ones who had had generally dealt with their situation far better.

The car pulled up outside the white, four storey building.

'Come on,' said the PVDE man alongside him, getting out and dragging Lopes out with him. They didn't dally on the street, hurrying inside. Lopes had been here a few times before as a visitor, providing information on a suspect, once delivering a foreign national for interrogation. That was bad enough, the atmosphere inside was oppressive and terrifying, almost certainly by design, everyone regarding visitors with suspicion and disdain. Lopes had been convinced that, if he was brought in for interrogation, he'd fold immediately and tell all he knew, true or not.

And now here he was, in just that situation.

To his surprise he was not led through to the rear of the building where he knew the holding cells and interrogation rooms were but upstairs to the second floor, then along a couple of corridors until they reached a door. This was opened and he was pushed inside, alone, the men leaving him there.

This was no austere interrogation room. It was a nicely appointed office. A secretary was at her desk, typewriter in front of her. She looked up at him.

'Inspector Lopes?'

He chose not to correct her as to his title.

'Yes?'

'You can go through now.'

Bewildered, he hesitated. 'Who is it I'm seeing, er, senhorita, please…'

But the assistant had gone back to her typing. Lopes had no choice but to go in blind. He knocked at the office door.

'Enter.'

He did as he was told.

The man inside was younger than Lopes, slim, with a narrow, almost petite face and slicked back, dark hair. He was sitting behind a large desk, a file open in front of him and a cigarette in a long holder in hand. He only barely glanced up as Lopes came and stood in front of the desk. There was a chair, should he sit? He wouldn't have if he was visiting a senior officer in his own service…correction, a senior officer in his *former* service, but he didn't work here, he was a visitor.

But this was the PVDE. The secret police. An organisation that worked in the shadows, one that was literally a law unto itself and not averse to acts that struck fear into people's hearts.

He remained standing.

The man behind the desk flicked ash from the cigarette into a crystal ashtray then looked up again.

'You may sit, Lopes,' he said.

'Thank you, er, sorry I don't know who you are.'

'My name is Oliveira, Tenente Oliveira. This file is interesting, Lopes.' He removed the cigarette from the holder and stubbed it out in the ashtray.

'Mine, I presume, sir?'

'Yes, of course it's yours,' said Oliveira. 'A full, successful career. Until…'

'Yes sir.'

Lopes knew exactly what Oliveira was talking about. He knew only too well. His last case: a young mother strangled during a tryst, a tryst that she had been paid for, which, it seemed, changed her status from a victim of crime to someone who'd got what she'd deserved. This was bad enough for her but made worse because the perpetrator was the son of someone important in the administration. He'd been told to drop it, but felt it was his responsibility as a policeman, a homicide detective, to push for justice for her. That was what the police were for, wasn't it, to protect the poor, the powerless?

Which was why he was now out of a job.

And now, apparently, that wasn't enough. They, whoever 'they' were wanted to punish him further with some trumped up crime.

'What have I done?' he said. 'What are the charges?'

Oliveira smiled. 'Do you have a guilty conscience, Lopes? Is there something that should be in the file which we don't know about?' The man's small dark eyes staring at him were unnerving, even for Lopes despite his years of experience with interrogation. But then Oliveira laughed and closed the file. 'Don't worry, we know all there is to know about you, and there are no charges.'

'So why—?'

'We are offering you a job.'

WEDNESDAY 14TH MAY 1941,

LISBON, 9.21 AM.

It took Lopes a few seconds to recover enough to speak.

'A job? Me? But I'm…' Lopes' voice trailed off.

'Non-political? Not the usual type we take on in the PVDE? Not some mindless thug? Is that what you were meaning?'

'I didn't say that.'

'You didn't need to,' said Oliveira. 'We know what we are. That you are not like that is, my dear Lopes, the point.' He smiled. 'You know what our organisation does…of course you do, you're an intelligent man, but humour me, tell me in your own words.'

Lopes looked quizzically at Oliveira but he seemed to genuinely want him to do this. Was it a trap? Whatever, he had to play along.

'You protect the Estado Novo from opponents within the country and threats from outside agencies.'

'Very succinct and correct. We are structured how?'

This was starting to feel like a cross between an examination and a test of loyalty but Lopes did not feel like he had the ability to protest.

'You are divided into two main sections; the Social and Political Defence section which acts to prevent crimes in these areas and -'

'Which means in practice?' prompted Oliveira.

'Stopping individuals and groups plotting to undermine or overthrow the Estado Novo, particularly connected with the Socialist and Communist movement.'

Oliveira smiled, clearly pleased with the answer of his 'student'. 'Indeed, carry on.'

'The second section is International. It deals with the control of immigrants and acts to root out spies and other undesirables.'

Lopes couldn't resist adding a closing coda. 'Have I passed, Tenente?'

'This was no test, believe me, you would not have even been in this room if I didn't know all there was to know about you, Dinis Lopes.'

All, thought Lopes. They knew everything?

But Oliveira continued. 'We are good at what we do, even if I say so myself. That is why we are equally hated and feared, something that you were diplomatic enough not to mention, that is a price we quite willingly pay, it shows how effective we are. But being good in these areas mean we are lacking in one particular other; in investigative skills, particularly where a crime has occurred.'

Again, Lopes took a few moments to take this in.

'But surely that is what the normal police are for?'

'Not always. Sometimes the cases are so sensitive we cannot allow them to leave our jurisdiction. We must investigate ourselves and not leave it to others. That is why we want you, Lopes, now that you have unexpectedly become, er, available. You'll head up a new office, the Office of Special Investigation.'

Lopes was silent for a few moments. His mind was racing. He could imagine what this job was going to be like; a separate investigation branch within the PVDE, already an organisation that trod on the toes of the Polícia de Segurança Pública, his former employers, and the Guarda Nacional Republicana. He, himself, had silently cursed (and sometimes not so silently) the PVDE for interference, for heavy handedly snatching contacts and suspects, for ordering the ending of investigations and, by adding to the disappearances and the body count, increasing his workload. He wasn't popular with his political masters already, now he'd add many others to the list. And the PVDE itself had a reputation for being pulled this way and that, supporting Salazar and the Estado Novo but with factions within it leaning towards (and being funded by) the Germans whilst others favoured Portugal's oldest ally, the British.

He was conscious that Oliveira was waiting. He had to say something.

'I'll need some time to think about this.'

Oliveira's fierce gaze did not weaken.

'No. You haven't got time. I want a decision now, before you leave this room.'

'Pardon, but…'

'Come on Dinis. We know your situation. You have a wife whose family thinks she married beneath her and who appears to now think the same herself, and this was whilst you were developing your career in the PSP. What will she and they think now that career has come to an end? You have a nice house, don't you, paid for by Maria's family, with servants—'

'Just a maid and a cook,' muttered Lopes.

'With *servants*,' Oliveira continued. 'That's still a long way to come for a boy from a little mountain village, however bright he was. It would be a shame to lose all that, wouldn't it? Taking this position with us would help to prevent that. It would be something for Maria to tell her friends about, wouldn't it?'

Lopes nodded. Waiting.

'And, of course, there are other, er, complications in your life, aren't there? Ones that have to be supported. How are you going to do that without your salary?'

That was it. They did know. He had no choice.

'Very well,' he said. 'When do you want me to start?'

Oliveira opened one of the drawers of his desk and pulled out a slim file. He passed it over.

'Now,' he said. 'Your office and your assistant are waiting for you. You'll find them both in room B12.'

WEDNESDAY 14TH MAY 1941,

9.50 AM.

Still clutching the file and in a daze, Lopes took the stairs down from the second floor to the ground and then looked for a way into the basement.

He found a set of narrow stairs at the back of the building. Descending into the gloom it seemed as if he was walking into the depths of Hades. *This was the PVDE headquarters,* he kept telling himself, *people came into here and never came out. He hated what this organisation did, here he was, working for them. What would happen if he didn't satisfy Oliveira?* His mind went off into all sorts of imagined disasters.

He shook himself. He made the most of things, always had. It had got him out of his village all the way to the big city, a career and a good marriage. Yes, the last two had soured and he was in a place he didn't want to be but that was not the first time in his life, was it? He would knuckle down and find a way out of this basement.

It was gloomy, light fittings scarce and those that were there gave off little light. The corridors were littered with boxes and other unwanted items; a broken chair here, a blackboard leant against a wall there. It was also stuffy and airless. None of this improved his mood as he searched for room B12.

He found it beyond the boiler room. The door was open and a young, dark skinned man in shirtsleeves was moving boxes and stacking them at one side of the room. He was perspiring heavily and his white shirt was grubby, presumably from the dust from the boxes. Seeing Lopes, the man put the box he was down and came to attention.

'Sir,' he said. 'I was told to wait here for someone. Is that you, sir?'

'I think it might be. Are you my assistant?'
'I think so, sir.'

'Good, good,' said Lopes looking around at their dismal surroundings. He sighed.

'I'm sorry for the mess,' said the young man. 'I wasn't given any instructions but the room was in such a state I felt I should at least try and tidy it up.'

'That's all right, it is what it is,' said Lopes. 'I'm inspector...' He paused. 'Actually, I'm not exactly sure what my rank or title is now. My name is Dinis Lopes. And you are?'

'Costa, sir, Alvares Costa."

Lopes held out his hand. Costa looked surprised, almost alarmed but, after a pause in which he wiped his hands on the front of his shirt, took the hand and shook it.

'Cape Verde?' asked Lopes.

'Yes sir.'

'You look familiar. Have we met before?'

Costa looked embarrassed. 'I was in the police, sir.'

Lopes nodded, trying to remember. 'The murder of that French refugee, last October?'

'That's right, sir. You interviewed me because I was the first on the scene. I'm amazed you remembered.'

'Your observations were good, and you secured the evidence. You did well. I don't think we'd have found the culprit without you.'

'Thank you, sir.'

'But what are you doing here? You said you *were* a policeman.'

Costa looked down.

'I was dismissed. It was my fault. My sergeant said everyone was doing it.'

'A bribe?'

Costa nodded. 'Yes. I didn't want to take it but I thought 'why not?' Now I know why not.'

'You were the only one dismissed?'

'Yes sir. Sir, I understand if you don't want to work with me.'

Lopes smiled, 'Everyone deserves a second chance, Costa. I treat people as I find them.'

'Thank you, sir.'

'Let me down and I'll change my mind but I don't think you're going to do that, are you, Costa?'

Costa returned the smile. 'No sir, Thank you.'

Lopes looked around. 'We need a couple of chairs, Costa.' He held up the file. 'For better or worse we have our first case.'

'Yes sir. At once. what is it.'

Lopes had opened the file and scanned the contents.

'It's a murder. Of a policeman.'

WEDNESDAY 14TH MAY 1941,

1.20 PM

Costa looked uncomfortable. He was hunched up, tense, unwilling to look up, probably afraid of making eye-contact with anyone. Lopes could sympathise.

He guessed the experience was rather like what an antelope or other small animal must feel drinking at a waterhole on the savanna in Africa, that strange, uneasy truce that he'd read about that falls in an evening whilst predators and prey slake their thirsts together.

They were not at a waterhole but in the building's canteen, surrounded by their new PVDE 'colleagues'.

In Africa there would be safety in numbers; a handful of big cats and scavengers amongst a multitude of herbivores; here he and Costa were two amongst a pride of lions - or rather a clan of hyenas.

'We've every right to be here,' he murmured, though whether this was for Costa's or his own benefit he wasn't entirely sure.

'Yes, sir,' muttered Costa but he remained hunched up, staring at his plate.

Lopes forced himself to look around. It was a small act of defiance. It was still chilling; the reputation of this organisation was so bad. His mind kept going over the same thought; these men make people disappear, or, even worse, send them to Tarrafal, that stinking, fly-ridden hellhole, the 'slow death camp' on the northern tip of Santiago in the Cape Verde islands. Horror stories came out of there but very few men that were sent there ever did.

He turned back to his table companion. Of course, Costa was from the islands, maybe from Santiago itself. He'd know better than most.

Yet here they were breaking bread with them - literally.

'Nearly done, Costa,' he said. 'We can soon get back to work.'

Costa nodded.

'You must be our new recruits.'

A stocky, sweaty, mustached man in a brown suit at the table next to them had pushed his plate back and was in the process of lighting a cigarillo. There were three others with him and Lopes knew that this man was their superior as the others kept glancing at him, taking their cues as to how to behave as dogs in a pack watch the lead hound. There certainly raised no objection to the noxious, acrid smoke produced by the cheap brand that the man had lit and was now puffing on.

'Yes, I'm...'

'I know who you are, Lopes,' said the man. 'And what Oliveira has brought you in to do. "Office of special investigation" indeed. What a joke.'

'I...er...'

'God alone knows what he thinks he's going to achieve with a washed-up ex-cop and a darkie crioulo with sticky fingers.'

His acolytes laughed as he rose.

'Lopes, a word of advice. Make sure you keep your nose out of my business,' he said, puffing smoke out in Lopes' direction.

'Now, now, Da Souza, that's not very friendly.'

Another man, tall, slim, with slicked back neatly cut hair, had come over. The cigarillo smoker looked as if a nasty smell - other than his foul cheroot - had been pushed under his nose.

'Colleagues - hah! That's a good one, Jose. Come on boys, we've got real work to do.'

Da Souza led his men out of the canteen.

'You'll have to get used to Da Souza and his like, I'm afraid. We are a bit...er...factional here,' said the newcomer. 'I'm Jose Dos Counha - International Section. I also report to Tenente Oliveira.' He held out his hand to Lopes who shook it. 'I, for one, think it's good to have you with us.'

'That's good to know,' said Lopes. 'This is my assistant, Costa.'

Dos Counha nodded but did not offer to shake Costa's hand.

'May I sit?' he said and did without waiting for affirmation. He looked towards the door that Da Souza had left by. 'You've not accepted an easy job, I'm afraid.'

Accepted, thought Lopes. It was hardly acceptance, more like being press-ganged, but said nothing.

'You are an intelligent man,' Dos Counha continued. 'You know our country's neutrality requires us to tread a narrow, often precipitous path. Those from both sides are keen to pull us either from one side to the other and, to do so, they seek to recruit friends and agents to achieve their goals. Some of these agents fall within my sections remit to watch and sometimes take action against.' Dos Counha looked straight at Lopes. 'And some of their friends are within this organisation.'

'And who are you friendly with, sir,' said Costa.

Lopes couldn't help but smile. The young Cape Verdan had both brains and guts. But perhaps he was too bold for his own good. It was time for an intervention.

'Yes, well, I think we both realise that this isn't going to be easy. However, we will work to the best of our abilities fairly and impartially - neutrally if you like - in carrying out our investigations. Perhaps this will reduce any opposition to us.'

Dos Counha smiled. 'Perhaps, perhaps.' He reached into his pocket and brought out two badges. Lopes could see they had the PVDE insignia on them. 'Tenente Oliveira asked me to give you these. They will certainly help you as you go about your business.' He pushed them over then stood. 'Good luck, gentlemen,' he said.

After he'd gone, Costa picked up his badge, looked at it for a second, then put it in his jacket pocket. Lopes just stared at his.

'Boss?' said Costa.

This broke the spell and Lopes picked his up and pocketed it as well.

'Right,' he said. 'Let's get started.'

'What's first, boss?'

'Let's start with the police investigation of the murder. The files will be held by homicide at the Central Station. We'll go there first.'

WEDNESDAY 14TH MAY 1941,

2.15 PM

The central station of the Municipal Police was set behind high walls in its own grounds. The gatekeeper, although he recognised Lopes was reluctant, at first, to let him in.

'I thought you'd left, sir,' he muttered.

'I had, but now I'm back,' said Lopes.

'Yes, sir, I'm sorry but we've had instructions not to let you in. It's from on high.'

Already? Lopes puzzled over this; why? Unless they knew already where he'd ended up and considered him a threat. That was possible, Lisbon was a big city but the circles he moved in were small, word could - would have got out. Whatever, he had backing now. He took out his PVDE badge and showed it to the gatekeeper. The effect was as he'd expected - and dreaded. The man's eyes widened when he saw it, then his gaze flicked briefly to Lopes' face then away, unwilling to make eye contact. Yes, he was now feared because of whom he worked for.

For all the success of using the badge this was not a feeling that sat well with him.

'Please, go in,' said the gatekeeper.

It almost sounded like a plea.

Inside the main building, Lopes led Costa up to Homicide.

The desk officer looked up at his old colleague in some surprise. Lopes flashed the PVDE badge before the protest even started.

'The young policeman who was murdered, Da Silva. Who is the investigating officer?'

'Inspector Ribeiro, sir. Shall I call him?'

He reached for the phone.

'Wait. Who is his assistant?'

'I think it's Sargento Ajudante Cruz, sir.'

Lopes nodded. 'Call him please and ask him to bring the files.'

As the man made the call, Lopes murmured to Costa 'Ribeiro and I have never got on. He's a creep, in the pocket of certain groups, which, thinking about it, might be why he was given the case in the first place. He's not the brightest either, normally an important case like this wouldn't get anywhere near him. It's interesting that he's got it.'

'You think there's been someone manipulating the investigation?' Costa whispered back.

'It could explain why this is our first case.'

Costa nodded. 'And Cruz? You know him?'

Lopes nodded. 'I trained him. He was my assistant for a couple of years, ah, here he is. Pedro, how are you?'

It had been a year or so since their paths had last crossed. Cruz was still youthful looking but his hair had started to have flecks of grey in it at the temples. Cruz looked surprised to see Lopes but he wore a wide smile. 'Hello, sir, it's good to see you. I'm sorry about the…well, it seemed unfair.'

'That's in the past now, it is what it is. How's Ana?'

'She's fine. We're expecting our second.'

'That's wonderful. This is my new assistant, Costa.'

Cruz and Costa shook hands but Cruz was frowning. 'Assistant?' he said.

'We're in the PVDE,' said Costa.

'Ah,' said Cruz. Lopes knew he was too polite to say anything else.

'Which, in truth, is why we're here,' he said. 'We've been asked to look into the murder of constable Da Silva. Can we see the investigation files?'

Cruz bit his lip thoughtfully. 'That's…er…difficult.'

'Why?'

'The case has been closed. The files have been sent to storage.'

'Closed? Already?'

'Yes. The culprit was identified.'

Lopes stared at Cruz. It was obvious that he was unhappy about what he was saying.

'Identified but not arrested?' he said.

Cruz nodded. 'A small-time crook, a Spaniard, Santiago.'

'Santiago? The house breaker?'

'Yes, sir.'

'But he's just a burglar. He'd never been involved in anything like this before, has he?'

Cruz pulled a face. He looked distinctly unhappy.

'It seems he was this time, sir. An informer identified him as being involved. The boss went to bring him in for questioning and he pulled a gun on him. Ribeiro shot and killed him.'

Lopes nodded slowly. 'Were you there when this happened?'

Again Cruz looked downcast.

'No,' he said.

'Why not? You were the second investigator, weren't you?'

'Inspector Ribeiro instructed me to stay here.'

'And this man was identified by one of Inspector Ribeiro's own informers?'

Cruz nodded. Lopes saw his eyes flit nervously across the room. He followed his gaze to find that Ribeiro had arrived and was heading in their direction, his face distorted in anger.

'What the hell is this man doing here?' he demanded from Cruz. 'And why are you talking to him about?'

'The Da Silva murder, sir,' said Cruz.

'That case is closed. Anyway, what business is it of yours, Lopes? You've been sacked, and not before time. You've no business being here. Get out before I have you arrested.'

Lopes let a couple of heartbeats pass before reaching into his pocket and pulling out the PVDE badge. 'I have every right to be here and if you choose to obstruct me, I'll have *you* arrested.'

Ribeiro stared at the badge for a few moments, then lifted his head and stared straight into Lopes' face.

'Found a rat's nest to scurry into, have you, you sad, pathetic little man,' he said. 'I don't care what bullies and thugs might be protecting you, you'd better watch your back, Dinis.'

Lopes smiled. 'Was that a threat, Alex?' he said. 'No? Well, we need to see the files on the Da Silva case. You can refuse of course, but you know I'll be back with more of my new colleagues, don't you? So, you might as well let us have them.'

Ribeiro glowered at him. 'The files shouldn't leave this building,' he said.

Lopes was about to object but Costa interrupted.

'We can look at them here, sir,' he said. 'Make notes. If it's easier.'

Lopes smiled inwardly. It looked like he'd fallen lucky with his assistant. He was a bright one; yes, that was a compromise that allowed Ribeiro to save face.

'Well?' he said to the policeman.

'Very well,' said Ribeiro. 'Cruz, sort them out - but keep an eye on them. Not one piece of paper leaves here.'

'Yes sir.'

Ribeiro took his leave, but not without giving Lopes one last deadly stare.

'I'll get the files for you, sir,' said Cruz.

Lopes looked at Costa when he had gone. 'Well done,' he murmured. He checked his watch. Hell, it was getting late and he'd not had a chance to call Maria to tell her what had happened.

'I can do the note taking, sir,' said Costa. 'If there's somewhere you need to be?'

It was tempting - as tempting, in a way as using the PVDE badge and the power and fear that came with it. He'd not wanted to take it but he'd used it twice already and it felt good, too good. He should take the penance, at least for a while.

'Let's start together, Costa,' he said. 'At least at first.'

Was this penance though? Wasn't he just putting off the moment he'd have to face his wife? Wasn't he making it harder for Maria Sofia, letting her worry more?

Yes, he decided, he was right on both points.

The latter was just a bonus.

WEDNESDAY 14TH MAY 1941,

6.15 PM

Lopes took the tram back home. He always liked to travel this way, even when he had use of a police car, it felt right, travelling amongst the working people, it made him more a part of the city and not someone above it.

That was especially important now, given the badge he carried. It weighed next to nothing but he was well aware of its weight. It could drag him down.

Riding the tram also allowed him thinking time. He'd used it throughout his career to process his day. Today there was a lot to process.

He'd landed on his feet again - sort of. This job was his saviour but was it a poisoned chalice? He'd been picked to do this investigation, someone high up wanted him to do it. Why? Well, probably for the reason that Ribeiro had been picked; because they, whoever they were, wanted a certain outcome. So, what outcome did *they* want? Why had there been a cover-up?

His eyes were drawn to the headlines of the newspaper read by the man opposite:

**HESS FLIES TO BRITAIN: DEPUTY FUHRER
'MENTALLY ILL' - BERLIN**

Lopes smiled to himself. At least someone else was having a worse time than him. Briefly he wondered why Hess, given his position, might have done it but then he dismissed it. He had other things to puzzle out. His thoughts moved back to the other, more pressing, things.

Costa was proving useful, useful and bright. But was he too useful and too intelligent? He knew nothing about him and this was the PVDE, it paid to be suspicious of everyone, its nature was to be underhand. So, was Costa a spy?

Lopes mentally shrugged. What did it matter if he was? The PVDE knew everything about him anyway. Including the situation at home.

Which he was about to experience for real as the tram was coming up to his stop.

*

'What have you brought to our house? The police coming and arresting you!'

'It wasn't the police,' he muttered.

'No, it was even worse, it was the PVDE. What will the neighbours think?'

'I'm sure the neighbours didn't notice, and they weren't arresting me…'

'I didn't know that. And you didn't think of ringing to tell me, did you? I've stayed in all day worrying.'

'I was busy…with the job,' Lopes muttered.

'And what do we gain by you working for them? Nothing. It will be worse than being a policeman, no status, no prospects.'

'I was a policeman when you married me.'

'I didn't think you'd stay as one. Father could have -'

'Don't tell me what your bloody father would or wouldn't do!' he yelled. 'Yes, your precious father could have used his money to buy me a position in politics and what would I have been then? A poodle of whatever company director he was seeking favours from. That was and isn't inviting, Maria Sofia.'

He hadn't meant to snap, but this was a familiar refrain and his shield of tolerance that had stopped him from rising to it had long since been eroded. Anyway, the argument was only heading one way, down a long-trodden path. Already Maria Sofia had tears coursing down her cheeks, he would soon feel the guilt and hurt the tears always created in him. She knew what she was doing, she knew him and his character and was able to flick the right switches. This well-worn path; a one way tirade, a barrage of disappointment, scolding and disdain and goading that extracted one, usually small, rejoinder by him which produced more than tears but near hysterical sobbing caused by the apparently mortal hurt to her feelings he'd delivered.

Sometimes took it took days of apologising and kowtowing for things to settle down again.

Today, though, he'd reached a limit. He wasn't staying for the final act.

He turned and walked out of the house, only pausing to collect his hat and coat.

There'd be hell to pay for this.

He'd pay that bill tomorrow. There were others that were more pressing,

*

He took his glass of fiery Aguardente de Medronho from the bar and searched in the gloom for a free table. He spotted one over against the wall. He was just in time, the guitarist had taken his seat and was doing some last minute tuning. In a few moments she would be there, in the spotlight, where he had first seen her, what five years ago? No, nearer six.

Six years. Six occasionally wonderful but mainly painful years.

He glanced around the room. There were some couples but also several single men like him. Where they also former lovers? Or want to be ones? He would not put anything past Margarida.

One table, towards the back of the room, was occupied by two men, leaning in close to each other as they conversed in whispers. Lopes frowned, quiet conversations in the shadows were a feature of wartime Lisbon but something had attracted his attention to these men in particular. What was it? Did he know them?

Yes he did.

With a smile he settled back.

The man nearest to him was Sir Simon Hazelwood, of the British Embassy. Lopes had met with him a couple of times over issues with ex-pat British citizens who's found themselves in trouble. The other man he's only met a couple of times and never in an official capacity. His name was Von Wernsdorf, someone who occupied a similar position to Hazelwood but in the German embassy.

Only in Lisbon, thought Lopes. Yes it was well known that the German Ambassador Hoyningen-Huene was no Nazi but this was still the representatives of two countries currently engaged in an existential struggle on the world's stage and there were Nazi and Abhwer agents (not necessarily the same thing) in the German embassy and spies and SOE terrorists and saboteurs in the British. Yet here the two diplomats were quietly meeting. That they were not unhappy to be seen together was evident when Hazelwood spotted Lopes, smiled and raised hi glass in greeting then murmured something to his table companion. So what was the reason for their meeting?

Who knew? Lopes dismissed the need to speculate. He had his own problems and, in the meantime, the reason why he was here was about to make her entrance.

To a smattering of applause she came out of the wings and stood by the stage. Lean, her face almost gaunt, framed by her dark, gypsy curls, her lips a dark scarlet. The master of ceremonies exchanged nods with her and made his way to the centre of the stage. He waited for quiet, though, in truth, this midweek night was not busy and the customers had already stopped talking. They were all as expectant as Lopes and, in Lisbon, everything stopped for Fado. No bar service, no talking. It was that important and revered.

'Ladies and Gentlemen, we have come to the highlight of our evening. Accompanied by Tiago Santiago, I give you…' He swept his hand towards her. 'The queen of Fado, the nightingale, Margarida Rodriguez.'

The applause was stronger as she walked to the centre of the stage. She looked at the ground, her face set, waiting until it had died down. When it did the guitarist started to play.

Margarida raised her head and started to sing.

*

'Noutros tempos, os fadistas
Vinham, já grossos das hortas
Pra o teu balcão returrar
Os fidalgos e os artistas

> *Iam pra aí, horas mortas*
> *Ouvir o fado e cantar.'*

The last notes of the song died away and the people in the room rose as one in applause, Lopes included. Some were even wiping tears from their eyes, affected by the sentimental lyrics of the song. Margarida was soaking up the acclaim until her gaze fell on him. Then her face hardened and her smile vanished.

Once the applause had stopped she stepped off the stage and headed towards him, though her progress was hampered by the other customers seeking to shake her hand, to heap praise on her and offer her drinks. She accepted one, her usual Ginja with fruit, shook off the last of her admirers and sat at Lopes' table.

'Where have you been?' she muttered.

'I've had a few problems, with work.'

'So?'

'So?'

'So why should your problems affect me and my son?' she said, her dark eyes smouldering with anger.

Lopes stared at her, well aware that many others in the room had at least half an eye on them. There was nothing he could do about that.

'My son too,' he murmured.

Margarida shrugged. 'Real fathers would have sought to have actually been in his life rather than treat him as a dirty secret.'

'That's not true,' he said, though he knew it was.

'Pah, You let us live in squalor yet I don't see you giving up that palace you live in.'

Lopes sighed. This was also a path well-trodden. 'You know my wife would never divorce me. And us living together? How would that work? There's too much passion, too much anger. We'd kill each other.'

Margarida gave a snort of disgust. 'Ah, passion, yes, you wanted that, didn't you, just as much as you wanted my body. You wanted the excitement, the thrill of the affair. You didn't really want me and certainly not my child.' She sipped her drink, then took one of the cherries floating in it and sucked the juice out of it before swallowing. It was electric, delivered to perfection, pure sensuality, a deliberate reminder of a moment they'd shared before.

It worked. He felt the old stirring of desire.

He shook himself, this wouldn't do. 'That's not true. I want to be in his life. I want to see him,' he said. 'He's my son.'

'I don't care. I want my money. It's two weeks late. I have the rent to pay.'

She held out her hand. Lopes took the cashed stuffed envelope from his jacket pocket but didn't hand it over.

'I want to see him,' he repeated. 'I need to see João.'

'No,' she said.

'Then why should I pay you?'

'Because if you don't I will come to your house and shout out everything until the whole world knows the truth.' She pushed her hand closer. 'Your wife would love that, wouldn't she? Embarrassment in front of the neighbours?'

He'd lost, he knew it. All he had left was pleading.

'Please, I want to see João,' he said. 'It's been so long.'

Margarida sighed. 'I'll think about it,' she said.

He knew that was a lie but it was the best he was going to get.

He gave her the envelope. Immediately she was on her feet. She drained her glass and slammed it on the table before heading swiftly to the wings.

There were some fragments of fruit left in the glass. Lopes stared at them, the torn remains of a past sweet harvest now long past.

Another singer had come on but Lopes put his hat on and headed home ignoring the glares of the audience at this breach of protocol.

THURSDAY, 15TH MAY, 1941

8.25 AM

Despite his efforts to avoid it by employing his usual precautions (shallow breathing and drinking honey and hot water before he'd left the house), he couldn't stop coughing.

He'd been expecting it, his chest had tightened in the night, he'd felt the pressure like a belt around his ribcage. It was familiar, an old friend, an unwelcome visitor. The first time he'd felt it he had been terrified; he was sure he was having a cardiac arrest, Maria Sofia, who he was still sharing a bed with then, had called for a doctor. The diagnosis was both a relief and a blow. It was the after-effects of being gassed in Flanders in the Spring of '18, that his lungs had been permanently damaged and were still susceptible to irritation by smoky or polluted atmospheres.

In other words, exactly the conditions found in his beloved Fado bars.

He should stop going. But he couldn't. Like the other things he should stop, he just wasn't able to.

So he had mornings like this when he coughed and coughed until he felt faint, when the blood flecked the handkerchief pressed to his mouth and the other passengers on the tram tried as best they could to move away from him fearing he had something contagious.

He was still wheezing when he made his way down to his new basement office.

Costa was already there.

'Morning, Boss,' he said but it was what he *didn't* say that Lopes found most significant; he didn't ask about his chief's breathing problems. It might have been politeness but Lopes guessed there was another reason; he knew. He'd been briefed before taking the job.

So what if he was a spy, sent to watch Lopes? As long as he could do the job it didn't matter. He was a good assistant, much better and brighter than most and Lopes was just going to do his job anyway, as he saw fit.

'Morning, Costa.'

'What's the plan for today, sir?'

He couldn't resist a little test. 'What do you think we should do?'

'Look at the crime scene?'

That lad *was* good, thought Lopes.

'Yes, we will do that but I'd like to review the notes you made on the police file first,' he said.

'Yes, sir,' said Costa, pulling out his notebook.

'Have you got the report written by the other patrolman?'

'The sergeant?'

'Yes,'

Costa flicked through the pages. 'Ah, here it is. Do you want me to read it out?'

'Yes, please.'

'"We were three hours into the evening patrol of the port area. We had just finished a short break at the cafe Tavares and had headed towards the Santa Maria warehouses, Da Silva said he needed to relieve himself so went to find a quiet spot. The fog was very thick so I was unable to see what happened next, but I heard a shout followed by a shot. It took me a few minutes to find Da Silva by which time the perpetrators had gone and my colleague was dead.

It is my opinion that Da Silva stumbled across a break-in and that the perpetrators panicked and shot him."' Costa looked up. 'That's about it, sir.'

Lopes nodded thoughtfully.

'Da Silva was a probationer, wasn't he?'

'Yes sir, been in the force three months.'

'Who was the sergeant, do we have a name?'

Costa checked through his notes. 'It just says Gomez, Sergeant J Gomez.'

Lopes laughed. 'Jorge Gomez. The old sod is still on the beat then? Good on him. But that makes sense, Gomez is old school, rough, tough, takes no nonsense, an irritable old sod. They him all the wet-behind-the-ears new recruits to knock some sense into them and show them the right way to do things..' He looked up at Costa. 'Including me, when I came out of the army in '19.' He stared at

Costa's notebook. 'That's why I know that report is a fake. I know the way Jorge writes and that's not it. Gomez also wouldn't let a three month probationer wander off alone around the docks under any circumstances, not even to relieve himself. And that's a lot of hogwash too; they'd just had a break, why didn't he go then? No, this is all rubbish.'

'We need to talk to Sergeant Gomez?' said Costa.

'Yes,'

'Before we go to the crime scene?'

'The station where he's based is only about a mile from the Santa Maria warehouses. We can go on the way.'

'Sir.'

THURSDAY, 15TH MAY, 1941

10.05 AM

'He's not here, he's been transferred.'

The desk officer had displayed the now familiar reaction to the PVDE badges, fear and a desperate eagerness to help - much to Lopes' disquiet, using the badge was getting too addictive for his own liking - and was now showing discomfort at his own answer. Lopes understood why; it was unbelievable.

'Jorge Gomez has been transferred, from *here*?' he said.

'Yes sir, I'm afraid so.'

'But Jorge has been here for what, 20 years? He's a fixture.'

'I know, sir, but…'

The desk officer's words trailed away. He clearly didn't know what to say.

'Where's he gone?'

'I don't know, sir.'

'Then get someone down here who does,' snapped Costa. 'And do it quickly.'

As the man hurried away Costa caught Lopes' eye. 'Sorry, sir. I just didn't think we were getting anywhere.'

'Perhaps. Whatever, you certainly got their attention.' Once again Lopes found himself wondering about his new deputy. His musing was interrupted by the arrival of the station commander. It was someone Lopes knew.

'Dinis. What are you doing here? I thought you'd left us.'

'Hello, Gustavo, I had but the powers-that-be seem to think I was still useful.' He took out his badge and, rather apologetically, showed it to his old colleague who gave a grunt of laughter.

'At least those thugs have got a real policeman in their ranks now,' he said, then gave a nervous glance at Costa. Lopes knew why; careless words uttered in the wrong company could ruin a life in the

Estado Novo. He though he should give some solace. If it acted as a warning to Costa too, so be it.

'Costa here is also ex-police. Maybe it's a step in the right direction.' He frowned. 'You've had a bad week. A probationer murdered and your senior sergeant transferred away.'

Gustavo looked troubled. 'Yes,' was all he said.

'But the perpetrator was caught.'

Gustavo's ghost of a smile showed what he thought of that.

'Where has Jorge Gomez been transferred to,' said Lopes. 'Which station?' He nodded to Costa to take out his notebook.

Gustavo scowled. 'He's not in the city. He's been sent up to Porto.'

Lopes was genuinely astounded. 'What? Jorge? In Porto? His whole life is here. He's a born and bred Lisboa.'

Gustavo shrugged. 'He was told he had to go.'

'By whom.'

Gustavo didn't answer, short of a brief shake of the head.

Lopes stared at him for a few moments, then checked his watch.

'Thank you, Gustavo,' he said. 'Come on, Alvares. We might as well go. There's nothing to be gained by staying here.'

He turned and walked out, Costa behind him.

'What the hell have we been dropped into?' he said. 'What sort of fool's game is this? Lied to, hindered at every step, and this is before we've even got started.'

'Yes, sir,' said Costa.

'But you probably know that only too well.'

'Sir?'

Lopes stopped walking and looked at Costa. He seemed genuinely confused. Perhaps he was, perhaps he wasn't a plant.

Or perhaps he was just a good actor. Agents would have to be. He saw the best in everyone, he trusted people; that was both a benefit and a character failing. It made no odds, all he could do was do his job, play the hand he'd been dealt.

'Nothing,' he said. He checked his watch. Early, too early for what he needed to do. 'Let's have a look at the crime scene,' he said. 'At least that can't lie to us.'

'Yes sir.'

In a black mood, Lopes headed towards the port buildings.

THURSDAY, 15TH MAY, 1941

11.26 AM

Lopes walked back to the place they'd first gone to. There it was obvious that someone had cleaned the cobbles with water and stiff brushes. This was where the young policeman had lain and where the lifeblood pumped out of his dying body pooled. That an effort had been made to sweep away the evidence seemed appropriate.

Costa came over to join him, notebook out. He'd not been behaving like someone who had a mission to watch Lopes. He'd been concentrating on the job, making a sketch of the site, pacing out the distances from key features; the warehouses, the wharf side, cranes where people could have hidden in the shadows, the doors to the buildings.

Lopes nodded to himself. The lad *was* good. Why would they set a spy on him who was this competent at police work? Yet, how did someone who was a lowly beat officer pick up such skills?

He dismissed these thoughts. What did it matter? He either was a spy or he wasn't. It wasn't going to change how Lopes did his job.

So, to the case.

'What do you think, Costa?' he said.

Costa looked up from his notebook clearly startled to be asked a question.

'Sir?'

'What does your sketch tell you?'

'I was just doing this to get things straight in my own mind, sir,' he mumbled. 'I wouldn't presume to put my views in front of yours.'

'We need this case straightened out, Alvares. Go on, please,' said Lopes.

'Well, sir, I think Da Silva must have first run into whoever shot him down there.' He pointed towards the water. 'Then they ran up here, between the two warehouses.'

Lopes nodded. 'Why do you think that?' he said.

'Because of where we are.' He nodded towards the two huge buildings that they were between. 'Da Silva and his murderer or murderers could only have got into this passageway from one end or the other. It doesn't really make sense that, if they were disturbed during a crime, they would have run away from the city and further into the port. The best way to escape would be into town.'

Lopes nodded again. 'I think that too. Anything else?'

'It's just speculation on my part, sir. It might not be worth anything.'

'Go on, please.'

'Well,' Costa frowned. 'I did wonder what they might have been doing if Da Silva disturbed them. The wharf here is being repaired so there are no ships tied up within a hundred metres, maybe further, so they probably wouldn't have been picking up contraband, therefore the only thing I can think of that they'd be doing down here is a break-in.' Costa stared down towards the water's edge. 'But…' He shook his head.

'But the main doors to the warehouse are down there, as you'd expect, facing the wharves, and there's no sign of any break-in,' Lopes said.

Costa nodded. 'Nor on any of the other doors and the windows are too high.'

'So not a break-in,' prompted Lopes, encouraging Costa to go further.

He obliged.

'They might not have started when they were disturbed.' Costa himself looked dubious. 'Perhaps they had tools with them. But then they could have just claimed they were workers on the dock repairs. So…'

'So?'

'So why shoot a uniformed officer? It's a huge step, unnecessary, especially for a career burglar like Santiago, the man who they blamed. Why do it? Why not accept the arrest like he had many times before? It makes no sense.' Costa looked back at his boss. 'But I'm just guessing, sir.'

Lopes sighed. 'I'm not surprised you are, Costa, because none of what we see here, nothing which we've heard makes sense.' He looked at his watch. 'There's somewhere I need to be and it's best if I go alone.'

'Sir?'

'If I'm going to get people to talk I can't take anyone else with me. Sorry.'

'Yes sir,' said Costa. 'What would you like me to do?'

Lopes had expected more of protest from Costa; if he was a spy, which surely he had to be, he'd have wanted to stay with Lopes, see who he was meeting, what he wanted. It was confusing.

'I'd like you to go to the central station, to records, and see what files they have on Santiago.'

'Look at what he'd been arrested for and if he ever carried a gun?'

'Exactly Costa. From my memory of him he never had but let's be sure. I'll meet you back in the basement this afternoon.'

THURSDAY, 15TH MAY, 1941

12.45 PM

It was a warm day so Lopes ordered a beer rather than his usual de Medronho. It helped also that the beer was a weaker drink; he didn't want a sleepy afternoon.

He found a table in the corner where he could keep an eye on the patrons coming and going. He knew most of them and most of them knew him, giving him a nod of acknowledgment - or sympathy - but generally leaving him be. That was because the clientele were mostly uniformed police, this was their bar, their place. Lopes had frequented it when he was a beat officer, after his shift and before heading home, which is exactly what most of these men would be doing.

It was one of the things he missed about his uniformed days; the camaraderie, the shared experience, the tall stories and the gossip. Even when he became a detective this still felt like home even though his rank built a wall between him and his former colleagues.

They'd know what had happened to him, of course they would. The grapevine meant that they'd know the facts even better than him.

Whatever, he wasn't here for sympathy, he wanted to find someone, he wanted to use that grapevine, tap into the gossip.

He didn't have long to wait.

The man who came into the bar was one of several who could have provided the gossip Lopes was looking for but, in fact, Alfonso Martinez was perfect. A sergeant, like Gomez, and friends with each other, often taking a boat together to go out fishing. As Martinez stepped up to the bar Lopes was on his feet and went over to him.

'Alfonso, can I buy you a drink?'

Martinez turned in surprise. He broke into a smile.

'Dinis…what are you doing here? I heard you…well…'

'Fell foul of my own pride, yes, I'm afraid so,' laughed Lopes. 'I think we all knew it was bound to happen sooner or later. What can I get you?'

'De Medronho.'

Lopes ordered. 'Can I have a quiet word,' he said.

'Of course,' said Martinez. They took the drink back to the table where Lopes' beer still stood.. Lopes noted that the sergeant was looking, if not worried then perplexed.

'What is it, Alfonso?' he said. 'Come on, spit it out.'

'I'd heard a rumour,' he said when they'd sat, 'About who you're working for now.'

Lopes pulled a face. The grapevine had been working overtime.

'The PVDE, yes that's true,' said Lopes.

Martinez pulled a face. 'Look, Dinis, We go back a long way so you know I'm not going to be informing on anyone. Forget it if you think I would. I don't care if I get into trouble, I'm no snitch.'

'I know that, and I'd never ask. You know me, I wouldn't work that way. They've recruited me to do basically what I did before; investigate crimes, not to snoop on people.'

Martinez grunted a reply, suggesting he was not convinced. Lopes continued nonetheless.

'I'm investigating the death of that young probationer on the docks a few days ago; Da Silva.'

Martinez nodded. 'A bad business. Poor lad, though he wasn't the nicest. Still, he was a cop and he didn't deserve that. But why are you investigating? They got the shit that did it.'

'So they say.'

Martinez frowned.

'What do you mean by that?'

Lopes didn't enlighten him. 'Your old fishing buddy, Jorge Gomez was with him, wasn't he?'

Martinez took a sip of his drink. 'Yeah.' Lopes could see he was looking wary.

'And now he's gone, left Lisbon after 20 years service, suddenly up sticks and goes. Him and his wife too. How did that happen? And why?'

Martinez stared into his glass.

'Why you asking me? You should know the reason,' he said.

Now it was Lopes' turn to frown.

'Me? Why should I know?'

'Because it was your lot who told him to go.'

Lopes stared at him. He had a nasty feeling that Oliveira's job offer was not a lifeline but was instead him being tossed into a stormy sea to either sink or swim.

'The PVDE told him to go?'

'Who else has that sort of clout? Look Dinis, what's going on? Is this some kind of trap? Are you trying to get me to say something that will get me locked up, because if you are I'm not going to play that game.'

Martinez downed his drink and stood up.

'Please, Alfonso, sit, I really didn't know and I'm not playing any games.' Martinez stayed standing but stayed where he was. 'Alfonso, you know me, I wouldn't do things like that. I'm not in the PVDE by choice, believe me, I'm not out to persecute people. I just want the truth, and to put the right people behind bars. You know me, Alfonso, that's how I've always been, haven't I?'

Martinez nodded. 'Yes you have. But…'

'But nothing. I'm not going to change whoever I work for. Look, I've only been in the PVDE for a couple of days but I've already seen that it's riven by factions pulling one way and another. I'm guessing that's what's happened with Jorge, and, for that matter, with young Da Silva. It's not the organisation itself that's behind it all it's someone or some group in it that's pulling the strings.'

Martinez stayed standing, still looking deeply unhappy. 'And that makes it better? That it's not the Novo Estado but it's politics? Shit, Dinis, what have you got yourself into?'

Lopes laughed. 'Alfonso, I attract trouble. Whatever, I've been given this job and I'll do it. Something stinks about the investigation, stinks worse than the fish market on a hot afternoon. I'm going to get to the bottom of it.' He waved at the barman, indicating that they wanted another round. He was pleased to see Martinez take the bait; he took his seat again.

'You don't think the man who they say killed that young lad really did it, do you?' he said.

'My guess is not.'

'So the real killer is still out there.'

'Yes,' said Lopes, as the second round of drinks arrived. 'Did you see Jorge after the murder?'

Martinez took a sip of his De Medronho and nodded. 'He was in here, the lunchtime after. He was shaken up.'

'Did he tell you what happened?'

'It'll be in his report, won't it?'

'It should be, but what I read didn't sound like one of Jorge's reports. Tell me what he told you.'

'That they were on patrol, that they heard the splash and Da Silva, being younger and a lot fitter than him, got ahead. There were shouts, then shots. By the time he found the lad he was beyond help and the bastards that did it long gone.'

Splash, thought Lopes, what splash? That wasn't in the report.

'Right,' said Lopes. 'The shouts, did he say anything about them? What did they shout?'

'He couldn't understand them,' said Martinez. 'He said he thought they were German.'

THURSDAY, 15TH MAY, 1941

2.30 PM

Costa was waiting for Lopes in their basement 'office'. It looked like he'd been back for a few minutes because he was back in shirtsleeves and he'd done some more tidying. The place was looking a lot more presentable. Spy or not, Costa was proving useful.

'What did you find out about our Spaniard, Santiago?' he asked.

'I went back through his arrest records, sir, and you were right, there's absolutely nothing about him ever carrying a gun.'

Lopes nodded. 'Of course that doesn't mean he didn't own one nor that he was carrying one the day he was arrested.'

'No sir.'

Lopes smiled. 'But it's damned suspicious.'

'There's more, sir,' said Costa. 'It's circumstantial but I think it's telling.'

'What's that?'

'Santiago only did housebreaking, sir. His arrest record shows nothing else. He was a burglar, always worked alone and he only took valuables, jewellery, cash and the like, though he was accused once last year of stealing documents.' Costa paused, suddenly looking uncertain. 'So…'

'So what was he doing on the docks? It's all big stuff. Not his style at all. You're right, Costa, it is telling, it just doesn't make sense.'

Costa shyly acknowledged the praise. He looked to be delighted with it.

'What did you find out, sir?' he asked.

Lopes told him.

'A splash? And men talking German? That wasn't in the sergeant's report,' he said, frowning.

'No, it wasn't. To be honest, that doesn't surprise me, I did say Gomez hadn't written it.'

Costa nodded. 'Germans?' he said. 'More than one?'

'Yes, that was what my contact said Jorge told him.'

'Again that doesn't fit Santiago's record. He spoke Spanish and Portuguese, there's no record of him speaking any other language.' Lopes nodded. 'And the splash, what was that about?'

'It looks like total hogwash. Someone is trying to cover something up. And we can guess at what; The Germans were throwing something into the harbour,' said Lopes. 'Something they needed to dispose of and big enough to make a splash that could be heard from what, fifty, a hundred metres away?'

'A body,' said Costa. 'They were getting rid of a body.'

Lopes nodded.

'It's a leap of the imagination, I admit, but it makes sense and it fits the facts. There was no sign of a break in, they weren't after something on a ship because there were none tied up anywhere near them, in fact that was probably why they chose it, it was quiet, with the fog they were unlikely to be either seen or heard.'

'Except they were,' murmured Costa.

'Except they were,' Lopes nodded grimly. 'By two poor bloody cops on duty who were in the wrong place at the wrong time. It cost Da Silva his life and buggered up Jorge's retirement plans. And it meant that things had to be covered up, and quickly.'

Costa nodded.

'So,' he said. 'Why have we been put on this?'

Lopes stared at his assistant. He looked genuinely perplexed. If he had been put in place to spy on Lopes he hadn't been briefed on the case.

'I don't like to think why, Alvares,' he sighed. 'It's a decision made by someone above us.'

'But why us?' said Costa, then clearly the conclusion that Lopes himself had himself made revealed itself to the younger man. 'Oh, right,' he added.

'Yes, it's our job because we're expendable, Alvares. It's not too late for you, I wouldn't blame you if you wanted to go. I'd support you.'

Costa shook his head. 'No, sir. I want to help you.'

'Thank you.' Lopes swallowed. He found he was surprisingly affected by this conversation.

Costa interrupted his train of thought and brought him back to business.

'So what do we do? Find out what, if any, bodies have been washed up since Monday night?'

'There will be bodies, Costa, there always are. More than ever since the refugees arrived.' Lopes thought for a few moments. 'I'm pretty sure it was close to high tide at midnight on Monday, but we'll need to check the tide times. The body will have stayed close by for a while in the slack water then taken downstream as the tide went out. If it wasn't found in the city then it might have washed up further down the coast.' He looked around the office and murmured. 'We could do with a telephone in here.'

'I'll see what I can do about that, sir,' said Costa. 'For now I'll go upstairs and ring around the morgues in the city and beyond.'

'Thank you. I will…erm…what shall I do?'

'You could go home, sir, you look tired.'

Lopes shook his head. That was the last thing he needed but he wasn't going to tell Costa that. 'No, I want to keep going. I'll look into Santiago. Do we have an address for him?'

'Yes, sir, I found it in the files.'

Costa flipped through his notebook until he found it, then told Lopes who noted it down.

'Alfama, of course. Good, I'll go over and see if I can find anything there. They'll probably be nothing but let's leave no stone unturned.' He looked up at Costa. 'Especially as someone has gone to so much effort to pile them up on the evidence.'

Costa smiled at this.

THURSDAY, 15TH MAY, 1941

3.19 PM

Lopes took a deep breath at the top of the stairs that was a short-cut between two of Alfama's notoriously steep, narrow streets. He'd taken the tram as far as he could but the last section had to be on foot. The sun was high overhead and reflected off the house walls, tiled, whitewashed or bare stone alike, magnifying the effect. He took advantage of the shade before continuing his trek upwards, taking off his hat and allowing the breeze funneled up the stairs to cool his sweat-damped hair. The rest of the city was in bloom, other parts of the city had trees offering welcome shade but not here in Alfama. It was a tightly packed, cramped, poor old place, there was hardly room for nature for the space taken by humanity. Most of the time Lopes loved the place, it was dark, dangerous, chaotic but alive.

Today, though, he cursed its oppressive heat.

He put his hat back on and continued his climb. Not far now.

It took another ten minutes. He sighed when he looked up at the apartment block, then checked his notebook. Yes, this was the address Costa had given him for Santiago. Five floors, possibly a garret above the last one he could see. It was a warm afternoon and he was pretty sure that Santiago's place would be somewhere towards the top.

It was inevitable.

Still, a long climb up the stairs that would strain his gas-damaged lungs was preferable to going home.

The door from the street was locked. Of course, there would be a caretaker, these buildings usually had them, old men or women in general, paid with a roof over their head and what pittance they could cadge from the tenants. That worked fine in an affluent area but here?

It wasn't Lopes' place to worry. He needed to get in. He knocked at the door.

There was no answer, not at first at least. He wasn't giving in so pounded harder, the booms from the door echoing up the inside of the building. Surely someone would hear?

Someone did, and by the swearing Lopes could hear as they came to the door they weren't happy about being disturbed.

'What the hell do you want, why are you making this racket?' The man who had opened the door was small, perhaps in his fifties, unshaved, unwashed and disheveled, and was blinking sleep from his eyes. He also carried a truncheon which he brandished menacingly. 'I should -' he said as he raised it, then stopped as Lopes pulled out his badge, the man's anger rapidly turning to fear.

'You should let me in,' said Lopes. 'That is what you were about to say, yes?'

'Yeah…er…sorry…I didn't mean anything.'

Once again Lopes tried to bury his own distaste at the power of the PVDE badge. He never in his life or career was comfortable with being feared.

'I've come to look at Jose Santiago's rooms. He was a tenant here?'

His intention was to calm the man by telling him that he was interested in someone else and not him but his words just seemed to magnify his anxiety.

'We never knew what he did, sir,' the caretaker stammered. 'Honestly, sir, on the veil of the Virgin Mary, we didn't know. The building owner would have had him out if he'd found out.'

'Yes, yes,' Lopes found the stench from the man's body almost unbearable. 'I want to see his rooms.'

'But the police, they came, they searched…'

'Forget the police, this is PVDE business.'

'Of course, I'll take you up there.' The man opened the door fully and beckoned Lopes inside.

Lopes was wrong about the floor, it wasn't the fifth but it was almost as bad, the fourth, and he was in a pretty bad way by the time they'd toiled their way up the stairs.

'Are you all right?' asked the caretaker.

Lopes was able to mouth the word 'Gas'.

'You were in Flanders?'

Lopes nodded.

'Poor sod,' said the man. He unlocked Santiago's door and was about to go inside but Lopes stopped him. He had recovered some breath so was able to speak a little.

'No, wait downstairs,' he said.

The caretaker didn't argue, though Lopes saw him glance up the stairs.

Lopes dismissed this but gave himself a few more seconds to recover before heading inside.

It was a single, sparsely furnished room and had been trashed. The bed had been overturned, the sheets and blankets torn off it and the mattress had had a knife taken to it, horsehair stuffing protruded from it like intestines from some disembowelled creature. The same had been done to the pillow, the floor was covered with a downy blanket of feathers which set off Lopes' coughing again. He blundered to the window and opened it, pushing the shutters open to let light and air into the room.

He stood at the window for a few minutes, gasping for breath whilst tears coursed down his cheeks. Eventually the coughing subsided and his breathing returned to normal. He wiped his face with his handkerchief then turned back to the room.

The police could make a mess when carrying out a search but this went way beyond what he'd ever seen them do. Someone had been looking for something, they'd been looking very hard, why would the police do that in this case? Santiago was wanted for murder, he'd been identified by an informer - supposedly at least, yet this room had been ripped apart.

'So what were they looking for and did they find it?' he murmured to himself.

He picked up an upturned chair and set it the right way up. Sitting on it he examined the wreckage. Unless the searchers were incredibly unlucky and they'd found whatever they were looking for in the final possible hiding place there would be a place where they had stopped, which would be relatively undamaged. This would be where they had found it.

There were no such signs in Santiago's room. The search had gone on until the bitter end.

Something caught his eye on the floor. Brushing aside the feathers he uncovered the item. It was what he thought, a coin, the colour unmistakable; gold. He picked it up and examined it. A

German gold 20 mark piece; the head of Wilhelm II on it. Nearby was another, and next to that was a smaller 10 Mark piece, also gold.

Lopes went and sat back on the chair and back to scrutinizing the wrecked room. Not only did this not look like a police search it didn't look like looting either. Santiago's friends/rivals in the criminal world would have stripped the place to make a few escudo whilst they could - there was no respect in the criminal world, it was dog-eat-dog. Unless they were rushed and extremely careless, why did they leave the coins? Lopes looked around the room again; this search wasn't rushed, it wasn't careless, it was thorough.

It didn't add up.

He looked at the three coins in his hand. They were worth a small fortune. German, so probably stolen from desperate refugees. This was their portable wealth. It hadn't done them any good, and it certainly hadn't helped Santiago.

He should put them back. But they'd end up in the pocket of some lowlife. Probably the caretaker, thinking about it.

Lopes frowned, then put the coins in his pocket before rising and heading down the stairs.

'You finished? Can I lock up?' said the caretaker.

'In a moment.' Lopes paused , framing the question in his own mind. 'This place is full, isn't it? No spare rooms?'

The caretaker laughed. 'Of course it's full, the city's packed, has been since last year. The landlord, rot his soul, is making a fortune.'

'So why haven't you cleared out Santiago's room, got a new tenant in?'

The caretaker looked awkward. 'I was told not to,' he muttered.

'Who by?'

The caretaker shook his head. 'Just someone. I can't say.'

'Not the police?'

'No. Look, please, I'm just doing as I was told.'

'Who told you?'

The man didn't answer, so Lopes sighed and took the badge out again. 'You'd better come with me, we'll have a word down at headquarters.'

'No, it's not my fault, they said…'

'Who said?'

'The men. The Krauts.'

'Germans? Did they do the search?'

The man looked miserable but nodded. 'Yeah,' he said. 'Look, please, don't tell the boss. I'll lose my job.'

Lopes stared at him for a few moments. Then he nodded towards the upstairs. 'Clean it up. Anyone who objects tell them it was on orders from the PVDE.'

'But…'

'Just get on with it.'

The caretaker reluctantly headed up the stairs. Lopes took his leave, deep in thought.

What the hell was going on? Germans at the dock, Germans here, searching through the belongings of someone who was supposed to have been involved with the shooting there, but who probably wasn't, not directly anyway. A small-time crook and a dead policeman. How were they connected, or, more accurately, what was their *real* connection?

Lopes was so deep in thought that he almost missed them. He'd left the narrow alleyways and chaotic layout of Alfama and had reached Pombal's Baixa with its grid-plan streets. He was lucky, he glanced back as he crossed a busy junction to check that he was clear to walk into the road and saw a man react, and do so in an odd way, stopping mid-stride and turning to look in a shop window.

Lopes tried to act like he hadn't seen. He just kept walking but now had more than half an eye behind him, turning his head to look left and right as if taking in the scenery and the goods in the shops but using his peripheral vision to watch for the signs he was being followed.

He was. There were two of them, one on either side of the street, one better than the other in being able *not* to stand out. Lopes uttered a silent prayer for the man's ineptitude; without it he wouldn't have known, but he also recited another one for himself; he was alone, unarmed, being trailed by God-alone-knows who or why. What did they want? To find out where he was going to lead them? Or to snuff out the investigation by snuffing out him?

His heart thumped harder, his throat was dry. There were plenty of people in the street but would that stop them? Probably not, if they wanted to kill him they would and could, it would be easy to escape. He rarely carried a gun, after Flanders he hated them, but sometimes, in the early days of his service, he had been required to if it was known they were going in somewhere dangerous. After his promotion to inspector he never carried one, leaving that to his juniors. Whatever, in nearly 20 years of service, he'd never fired a gun in anger, rarely had he wished he had one.

This, though, was one of those occasions.

They were closing in, yes, they were definitely closer. Lopes started to walk faster, looking for somewhere to duck inside.

Abruptly a car pulled up alongside him, the rear door opened. Lopes was about to run when he saw who was inside: A stocky, sweaty, mustached man in a brown suit.

'Lopes,' said Da Souza. 'Get in.'

THURSDAY, 15TH MAY, 1941

4.35 PM

Lopes sat in silence for a few minutes whilst the car made its way through the sparse late afternoon traffic. Da Souza was smoking one of his foul-smelling cheroots and the smoke was getting to Lopes' damaged lungs, already stressed by the anxious climax to his pursuit by the men who trailed him, he could feel his chest tightening, from experience he knew he would be wheezing all night.

If Da Souza noticed he was struggling he disregarded it, if anything he puffed harder on his cigar and emitted great clouds of smoke that filled the rear of the car. Lopes tried not to cough, knowing that when he started he was not going to be able to stop but he couldn't help it. As he did he saw Da Souza's driver look at him through the rear-view mirror. He, at least, looked sympathetic.

Da Souza wasn't.

'Well, Mr. Special Investigator, what a state you've got yourself into,' he said. 'Dashing about the streets like that. It was a good job I was passing, you looked in distress. Is it all getting too much for you? Perhaps you should give it all up.'

Lopes had pulled out his handkerchief and had covered his mouth and nose with it, trying to not cough by pure willpower.

'Why were you hurrying?' Da Souza went on. 'A man with your problems, you should be taking it easy. Let that little negretto do your legwork. Actually, you shouldn't be doing this job at all. It's obviously too much for you.'

Anger helped Lopes to at least a partial recovery.

'I was being followed,' he said. 'They were closing in.'

Da Souza's eyes widened. He looked amused. 'Followed? Really? I didn't see anyone, did you driver?' The driver said nothing. 'Oh, dear, Lopes, it seems you are adding paranoia to your physical problems. Sad, very sad. And, of course, you're not armed are you. A policeman who won't carry a gun. Yes, I know you Lopes, I know all about you.'

Lopes sat back. 'I know what I saw,' he said. 'And I'm guessing this is exactly why you've turned up.'

Da Souza smiled, took one mighty puff on his cheroot then stubbed it out.

'Paranoia, pure and simple, Paranoia, Lopes. Sad, very sad.' He peered forward. 'This is your street isn't it?'

Lopes looked out. Da Souza had indeed driven him straight to his house in Lupa. The fact that not a word of instruction had been passed to the driver was significant, underlining his suspicions.

'Yes, it is,' he said.

The car pulled up to the kerb. Lopes started to open the door but Da Souza put his hand on his arm.

'You need to watch yourself, Lopes,' he said. 'Look after yourself. You're on your own. Anything could happen to you. You wouldn't want that wife of yours made a widow, would you? Or, some of your other complications causing you problems? No, I thought not.'

Lopes tugged himself free and got out. He watched as Da Souza's car pulled away.

'Great,' he muttered to himself. 'This is worse than he thought.'

He looked at the house. He was tempted to walk away, find a bar. But that wasn't him, he didn't walk away. Not from anything.

Lopes went inside.

FRIDAY, 16TH MAY, 1941 8.43 AM

'So you think Santiago is actually connected to the case, Sir?' Costa was looking thoughtful, which was not surprising given the tale Lopes had just related.

'Absolutely. Whoever did the search was looking for something specific and they didn't find it, I'm pretty sure of that.'

'I wonder what it is.' said Costa.

'I wonder whether we'll ever be allowed to find out. Da Souza made it clear sticking our noses in was unwelcome.'

'But we're not going to stop, are we sir?'

Lopes smiled, 'Of course not. Now, you've heard my story. What did you find out?'

Costa took out his notebook.

'There have been four bodies pulled out of the Tagus in the last few days but I think this one is the most likely. It's in the morgue at Alges.'

'Why do you think it's this one?'

'From the description of the condition and where it washed up,' said Costa.

'Go on.'

'The others seemed to have been in the water much longer. This one had only been immersed for a couple of days at most and was found just down the coast by a fisherman. It's where I'd expect a body going in the water at the docks to end up.'

Lopes nodded. 'I'm impressed, Costa,' he said. 'I wish all my deputies were as efficient,'

Costa shrugged. 'I was just doing my job, sir,' he mumbled and turned away.

He's actually embarrassed, thought Lopes, then remembered his suspicions.

'Well, I'm sure you're right. Let's go and have a look at it, shall we, before we work out what to do next'

'Yes sir. I'll get the car.'

'We have a car?'

'Yes, sir. Tenente Olivera sent it with his compliments. He says we're going to get our own telephone too.'

Lopes preferred the trams but could see the logic of having the car. It was also considerably safer. Yesterday had proved that.

'Let's go then.'

*

The morgue in Alges had many of the characteristics that Lopes expected; in the basement, the temperature cool, the walls and floors tiled and it smelt of formaldehyde that did not quite mask the smell of death. There was one thing he didn't expect; a three-way argument going on between the morgue attendant and a pair of men, both blond and bulky in smart suits, and a small, dark-haired young woman.

'I'm sorry, madam, but you're mistaken. These gentlemen have provided Herr Baumer's identity papers and—'

'He's not Baumer,' said the woman, 'He's Uwe Vogel.'

'This has gone on long enough,' said blond man number one . 'We are here for the remains of our uncle. We have the correct paperwork. Please hand him over,'

'Uncle,' laughed the woman. 'Don't make me laugh. Relatives? You look nothing like Uwe.'

Blond man number two spat on to the tiles. 'Why should anyone believe anything you say?'

'What do you mean by that?'

'Exactly what I said you lying Jew bitch,' he muttered.

The woman took a step towards him, fist balled, ready to strike. Costa stepped in front of her.

'What do you want?' she said. 'Get out of my way.'

'That's enough,' said Lopes pushing his way to the counter, taking his badge out and showing it round. 'Now what's going on here?'

'What's going on is that these apes are trying to take the body of my friend,' said the woman. 'And I don't know why or why they'd say he was someone else.' The woman was still in the full flow of her anger and hadn't looked at Lopes' badge. Then she did and went quite pale. She stopped talking immediately.

'Because he *is* someone else,' said Blond number one, 'We have the papers to prove that he's Paul Baumer, our uncle. we're here to take him back to Germany for burial.' He waved a piece of paper at Lopes who glanced at it briefly but shrugged.

'I'm sorry, that's irrelevant.'

'But—'

'We can't let you do that until we have completed our investigation,' said Lopes.

'We have received permission from your state to repatriate him. I do not see why this is a PVDE matter. you should keep your noses out.'

Lopes stepped right up to the man so their noses were almost touching, though Lopes had to tilt his head back as the German was considerably taller than he was. 'It's not for you to say what is or is not a PVDE matter, that's my decision. It's also my decision whom to arrest and you seem to be a prime candidate for that right now.'

The man stepped back.

'I presume from your accent you are German?'

'Yes.'

'Do you have diplomatic status?'

Blond man number one started to say something but the other coughed and Lopes saw him give a little shake of the head.

'No,' said Blond One. 'we don't. We're just ordinary citizens of the Reich.'

'Family members,' said Blond Two.

'Good, well in that case I suggest you leave here right now. When we've concluded our investigations, then you can have your uncle's body. Unless, of course, this young lady's claim is... where has she gone?'

Lopes had had his back to the woman whilst he faced off against the two men so had not seen her leave. One of the blond men laughed and muttered something.

'I'll see if I can find her,' said Costa hurrying out of the room. Lopes turned to the two men.

'Gentlemen, please leave.'

Staring daggers at Lopes they did and Lopes turned to the mortuary attendant. 'Let's look at our mystery man,' he said. "Take me to him,'

Ten minutes later he stood and looked down at the body on the gurney, whoever this man was, Paul Baumer or Uwe Vogel, he had clearly enjoyed good living. The pale, naked body was very overweight, and the flesh flabby . The immersion in water for several days had not improved his looks but he had clearly not the most handsome of men in life. He had thin, receding hair which appeared to have been dyed given that some had run and had stained the skin. Lopes put his age at somewhere between 40 and 60, a wide range certainly but it was hard to say given both the condition of the body and also by the aging effects of the high life he'd enjoyed. Lopes suspected he was actually towards the younger end of the bracket.

'I see no autopsy has been carried out,' he murmured to the mortuary attendant.

'No, sir.'

'Why not?

'It's just a downing. We get three or four a week, there's no call to...' he broke off at the sound of raised voices outside. 'What the hell is happening today? This is intolerable,' he grumbled. As he went to investigate, Lopes laughed to himself; mortuary attendants normally had a much quieter life with a clientèle who didn't talk back. The man would need a stiff drink after today.

He went back to examining the body. He nodded to himself, one thing was clear; the man had been badly beaten before death.

The mortuary door opened and the attendant put his head around it.

'It's your assistant,' he said. 'He's caught the woman.'

'I'll be right out. Would you mind laying out this man's clothes and possessions for me to have a look at.'

'Can 't. Sorry.'

'Why not,'

'He didn't have any. Came in like that, stark naked.'

Lopes looked in astonishment at the man, then back at the body on the slab.

'Organise an autopsy,' he said, 'Get it done as quickly as possible. I will give you my details. Contact me when it's done.'

'But, I don't have...'

'Just get it done. Right, where is Costa?' A pounding started, echoing off the tiled walls and floor. 'Never mind, I'll work it out.'

Lopes found Costa outside of the morgue, leaned up against a robust looking door, an amused look on his face with a trickle of blood running from a small cut on his cheekbone.

'Our little wildcat do that?' said Lopes, pointing at the blood. Costa touched the cut with his fingertip and nodded.

'Yes, sir, she was…er… reluctant to come back with me.'

'This a store room?'

'I thought it was the best place for her. It had the strongest door and no windows.'

'Good plan.' The banging, if anything, increased in volume and frequency, 'Let's get her out.'

Costa nodded and turned the key in the door. 'Ready,' he said. Lopes nodded.

Even so he wasn't prepared for the girl darting for freedom like a rat released from a trap.

Fortunately Costa was quick. He took hold of the woman's arm then pulled her to him and held her in a bear hug.

'Let go, let go, you fucker.' The woman fought to free herself.

'Language, Miss,' said Costa. 'There's no need for that.'

'Let me go. I've not done anything wrong.'

'Then why did you run?' said Lopes. 'Actually, I know why you did; because you saw our badges. you know who we are.'

'Yeah, you're the Gestapo,' said the woman. 'Let me go.'

'Please, stop it. Listen, we're not interested in you. we're investigating a murder, actually, two given the state of that body. As far as we're concerned you can go - but only after you've answered our questions.'

'Why should I believe you?'

'We'll prove it. Costa here will let you go. But first, please, in turn, promise not to run. I'd rather not have Costa here have to shoot you.'

She swore under her breath but nodded.

'Let her go,' he said to his deputy.

Costa let go. He was pleased to see she didn't try to run though she looked suspiciously at both of them..

'Good,' said Lopes. 'Thank you. We just need to talk to you to find out what all that was about,' he waved at the mortuary.

The woman glanced at the doors, then down at her feet. 'I don't like it here,' she muttered. 'It smells of death.'

'Come on,' said Costa, 'It's a morgue. What did you expect? Answer the inspector's question.'

She glared at him. Lopes smiled to himself, she was a fierce one.

'I was here looking Uwe. He's been missing for days now. I'd searched the hospitals, then I heard a body had been washed up. It was obvious it would have been brought here.'

'That's reasonable,' said Lopes. 'What's this man's full name?'

'Vogel, Uwe Vogel.'

Costa noted this down. 'So why do you think the man in there is this Vogel?'

'They showed me his picture. It's definitely him.'

'Those other men were sure it was their uncle,' said Lopes.

The woman gave a bitter laugh. 'Ah yes, the mythical Paul Baumer. That's a load of hogwash. The body is Uwe's.'

'Can you prove it?' said Costa. 'It's your word against theirs.'

'Prove it? Why would I want a body? Do I look like I could pay for a funeral?'

'There are all sorts of motives for falsely claiming a body,' said Lopes.

'Like what?'

'Inheritance, insurance fraud, possibly just insanity.'

'Are you suggesting I'm a criminal? Or insane?' said the woman.

'No,' sighed Lopes. 'Miss...I can't keep calling you that, what is your name? It would be easier to know.'

'Easier to deport me you mean?'

'We could do that if we wanted to without a name,' said Lopes. No, to make it easier to talk to you rather than just calling you Miss.'

'Maria Del Santo,' she said.

Lopes sighed. 'Please don't bother giving us a false name, that would just make it worse.'

'It's not...'

'Don't take us for stupid,' said Costa. 'It's obvious you're not Portuguese.'

She gave him a black look. 'Katz. Elena Katz.'

'That's better. Miss Katz, I am Inspector Lopes and this is my colleague Sargento Costa.'

'I'd like to say it's a pleasure to meet you, but it's not,' she said.

Lopes smiled. 'We're not suggesting anything about your motives. As I said before, we're not interested in you. We are investigating a murder that happened on the docks in the city a few days ago. We think it may have been connected with the dumping of a body into the Tagus.' Lopes nodded towards the doors to the mortuary. 'We think it might have been that body. That's why we need to find out who it is for sure.'

Elena's eyes had widened at the word murder. but Lopes noted that she didn't seem that surprised.

'It's definitely Uwe,' she said. 'And I can prove it.'

'How?'

Lopes saw Elena redden giving him a clue to the nature of her relationship with Vogel.

'He has scars on the inside of his right knee and on his thigh,' she said. 'They're shrapnel wounds. He got them at the front in 1918.' She looked at Lopes. 'Can I get out of here please?'

'Costa, there's a cafe across the square. Take Miss Katz there, get her whatever she wants. I'll join you shortly.'

'But I want to go. I told you what you wanted to know,'

'Miss Katz, we can still arrest you and take you back with us to headquarters. I don't think you want that, do you?'

She looked sullen and shook her head.

'Good. Costa, if you wouldn't mind?'

After the pair left Lopes went back into the mortuary. Vogel's naked body lay on the slab looking for all the world like a big white fish in a fishmonger's window. Ignoring the stench of decay he leant over it, scrutinising the knees and right thigh. He nodded to himself. She was right. This was Uwe Vogel, not Paul Baumer. Baumer was a fake identity, it was the Germans who'd lied.

A fake to hide the identity of the real body. Why? That was easy: because Uwe Vogel was central to their case. But how exactly was he was involved?

They were questions he needed answers to.

And that meant starting with Elena Katz.

*

Costa looked questioningly at Lopes as he walked towards the table where the pair sat, Lopes gave the slightest of nods, hoping that she wouldn't see however it was clear she had. Elena looked away and Lopes was sure she wiped a tear from her eye.

Interesting. She cared. But was it out of affection or the loss of a meal ticket?

'Have you ordered,' he asked Costa, trying to forget his harsh judgement on the young woman.

'No sir.'

'What would you like, Miss Katz?'

She shook her head. Lopes didn't want to push her too much just yet. He was sure there was a better way of getting her to talk.

'Costa, go and order us some coffees. And get a brandy as well.' He saw her glance at the Pasteis de Nata that the diner on the next table was tucking into; despite her upset there was a hunger there. 'And some of those too,' Lopes murmured.

Costa nodded and went to the counter.

'Are you alright,' Lopes kept his voice quiet.

She sighed. 'Yes.' A few moments later she added. 'Thank you for asking.'

'I'm sorry about your...er...friend.'

She pulled a face at his clumsiness but just shrugged but, despite her apparent indifference she looked away, composing herself.

Lopes used this chance looked her over. She was young, he placed her in her early twenties, no older, with dark, shoulder length, wavy hair and dark eyes. Her hair partly covered one cheek, at first he assumed it was some style trend, perhaps copying some Hollywood starlet, but then she brushed it aside briefly revealing she had a scar that started by her ear and ran straight down to her jaw. It was well disguised by make-up but it was clearly either a knife or glass wound. Still, she was very pretty, there was no doubt about that.

Young and pretty. The contrast with the body on the slab was stark.

She looked up and met his gaze defiantly.

'Go on then,' she said. 'Ask me.'

'Ask you what?'

'The question gave been wanting to put.'

'What's that?'

'Am I a whore? Is that why I was with Uwe?'

Lopes frowned. 'I never thought that.'

'Liar,' she said.

'All right,' he said. 'You are young and attractive and Vogel was. ...'

'Old, and fat.' she smiled, 'Yes, that's right. Poor Uwe, he always worried about his weight and how I was only with him for his money and protection.'

'And you weren't?'

She smiled. Costa came back at that moment.

'Of course I was,' she said. 'In this world, at this time, you have to use the assets you have to survive. I have my looks, Uwe had his money. But it was more than that, he was kind, he could have... Others did...' Her voice trailed away as the waiter brought coffees and pastries. Lopes pushed one of the Pasteis de Nata towards her, as well as the brandy,

'You are a refugee?'

She started to pick at the custard and nodded.

'From France? Jewish?'

Again a nod.

'A French national? You have a French accent.' .

She shook her head, 'No. I'm German. My father was a professor. He decided we should leave in '34 before those bastards really started to crack down. He moved us to France. When the Panzers came we tried to get south.'

'Tried?'

'We were in a refugee column. Some Stukas attacked. My parents were killed.'

'I'm sorry.'

Her mouth was now full of pastry. She shrugged. 'Worse things have happened since,' she said.

Lopes nodded. 'Until Uwe Vogel came along.'

'Yes.'

'How did you meet him?'

She looked fiercely at Lopes. 'Are you trying to trick me into telling you I'm an illegal, Mr. Secret Policeman? Bribe the little girl with cake and then ship her out to the concentration camps? That's the way of your lot, isn't it?'

'We can do that if you don't co-operate,' said Costa

Lopes held his hand up to his deputy.

'We're not trying to trick you into anything, Elena. Other than to get to the bottom of these murders, we've no interest in you, or any refugee.'

She gave a snort of derision. 'Really?' she said.

'Yes. I find the idea of sending anyone back to face persecution disgusting. I'd never be a part of that.'

She stared into his eyes. 'You work for the PVDE?' she said.

'Yes.'

'Then don't be so naive. You *are* a part of it.'

Lopes took a slow, deep breath, then nodded. 'Yes,' he said, 'I am. But will you answer my question anyway?'

'Why?'

'Because I need to know a lot more about Uwe Vogel. I need to understand why he ended up in the Tagus and why a certain country's agents tried to cover up that up by claiming his body.'

Elena finished her Pasteis, wiped the last crumbs from her mouth, then took a sip of coffee. Only then did she answer. 'Alright,' she said. 'We were smuggled across the border into Portugal in small groups. When we got to Lisbon we heard on the grapevine that Uwe was one of the people who could help us get papers and a ticket out to America. He had connections, he could get things done.'

'At a price or out of conviction?'

She gave a little smile. 'At a price of course, what else? Many of the refugees had gold and jewellery on them, they'd prepared to flee, it was their survival money.'

'What did you have?' said Costa.

She gave him a withering look. Lopes felt it important to move things on.

'Tell me about Uwe. What was he doing in Lisbon? What was he like?'

Her face softened. There was clear affection.

'What was he like? Hopeless but brilliant in his own way, that was Uwe. Do you know what I mean? Sometimes those weaknesses got the better of him.'

Lopes nodded, 'Maybe I know that only too well.'

'He'd been in Lisbon for years. He'd come as the agent for some big German company and then just stayed. I think he had a wife and family back in Berlin who he was glad to be rid of.'

'He was a salesman?'

She shook her head. 'No, an engineer. He was good, he was always tinkering with some radio or other stuff. When he wasn't hitting the bottle.'

'Which he did a lot?'

'Which he did too much.'

Lopes nodded to himself. 'I'm going to play devils advocate here, so don't take this the wrong way, but could that be what happened to him?'

'What do you mean?'

'That he got drunk, got in a fight with the wrong person and ended up dead?'

'No. Uwe was a friendly drunk. He was more likely to fall asleep that get into a punch-up. He wasn't a fighter.'

'Sorry, I needed to ask.'

'When did you last see him, Miss?' said Costa who was making copious notes.

'Monday night, he was meeting someone. I wanted to go with him. He said no.'

'Was that unusual?'

'No. It did happen from time-to-time. Monday was different though. He'd been on edge. Something had happened a couple of days before. It had shaken him, badly.'

'What was it?' said Costa.

She shook her head.

'It was a break-in, wasn't it?' said Lopes.

She looked surprised. 'How did you know?'

'Never mind that. You said Uwe was shaken. Why?'

'Uwe's place was like a bank, it had to be, he had a lot of... Well, you know.'

'Gold? Jewellery?'

She nodded.

'The stuff he stole from the refugees?' said Costa

Elena's dark eyes suddenly flashed with rage.

'Uwe didn't steal. He did things that he was paid for, 'she said.

'Yeah, right,' said Costa. His voice was dripping in sarcasm.

Elena was on her feet her instantly, her hand raised. Lopes rose too and grabbed her arm before she had time to strike. 'That's enough. Costa, there's no need for that.'

'Yes, sir. Sorry sir.'

'And Miss Katz, please, calm yourself. We're just trying to find out what happened to Uwe. You can help us.' She fought to free herself for a moment then the fight seemed to go out of her. Lopes let her go and she took her seat again. 'Thank-you,' said Lopes. 'So, did they take everything?'

She shook her head. 'That was what shook him. He said it looked more like a search than a burglary, though they took a few things to make it look like one, coins and stuff.'

'What were they looking for?' Lopes asked.

'I don't know. Uwe didn't say.' She looked into his eyes. 'Can I go now?'

Lopes saw Costa frown. 'We should take her in, sir,' he murmured.

'On what grounds? She's not the murderer is she?'

'No, but she's not got papers.'

'I have papers,' said Elena.

'Forged ones, I'll bet,' said Costa.

Elena started to answer but Lopes held up his hand. 'I really don't care about your status here. It's not an issue for me.' He glared at Costa who sullenly nodded.

'So can I go then?' Elena repeated.

'In a moment,' said Lopes. 'The coins that were stolen, were they German? Pre the Kaiser's war?'

Elena nodded. 'Yes, Gold German crowns with Wilhelm's head on it.'

Costa wrote this down.

'Is that it?' she demanded.

'Yes, but we may need to talk to you again.' He waved away Costa's protest. 'Where are you staying?' asked Lopes. 'At Vogel's apartment?'

'That's the plan but…' She sighed. 'The landlord seemed to know Uwe wasn't coming back. He'd been in - well, he claimed he hadn't but he had - and stripped everything out, everything of value.

Then he asked for the rent. The bastard. I've probably got a week then I'll be out.'

'Give us the address, please,' said Lopes, which Elena did. 'Thank you. If you do move please let us know.'

'I will,' she said and rose.

FRIDAY, 16TH MAY, 1941

12.50PM

After she had gone, Lopes sat contemplatively at the table, whilst Costa flicked through his notes.

At last Lopes looked up and at his assistant. 'What did you make of her?' he said. .

'She's a feisty one,' said Costa. 'And pretty.'

'I didn't ask whether you'd like to go out with her. I meant do you think she's telling the truth?'

'Sorry, sir.' Costa bit his lip. 'I think so, sir but she's a clever one, a survivor. it wouldn't surprise me if she was keeping something back.'

Lopes nodded, flicking the crumbs of pastry on the table cloth. 'Yes,' he said. 'Sorry I snapped, she *is* pretty *and* feisty.'

'That's alright, sir, I should have stuck to the job.'

'It's just that we've been lied to so much over the last few days. I'm getting a bit sick of it.' He swirled the remains of his coffee round in his cup. 'So we have a name, Vogel, a German. There were Germans on the dock, when Da Silva was shot and we had more here trying to claim the body and throw us off by claiming Vogel was someone else.'

'Is it worth talking to their Embassy?'

Lopes shook his head. 'I doubt it, They'd deny everything. We need to know more before we even think of that.'

'Like what they were to looking for by taking Vogel?'

'Exactly.' Lopes put the cup down. 'No point sitting here moping. Let's do some digging into Herr Vogel. Find out what he was about, Whom he met, who his contacts are. If he was sailing close to the wind he must have files on him, either with the police or with the PVDE, possibly both. If you do the police I will do some sleuthing around the PVDE files. I could do with knowing about them anyway.'

'Yes sir.'
'Good. Let's go and do it.'

*

There was a surprise waiting for Costa and Lopes when they returned to their basement 'office'. On Costa's desk was a telephone. And before they had time to even comment about it, it started ringing.

Costa picked it up.

'Office of special investigations? Yes, yes of course, I'll tell him.' He put the phone down. 'That was Tenente Oliveira's office. He wants to see you straightaway.'

Lopes raised his eyebrows and sighed. 'Right, I'll do that. You head out to police headquarters and get the files on Vogel whilst I find out what this is about.'

'Yes sir.'

A few minutes later he was in Oliveira's outer office. 'He asks if you'd wait, he's with someone,' said his secretary.

He didn't have long to wait, The door to Oliveira's office opened and a small, uniformed man with dark hair and a dark moustache strode out, prompting the secretary to leap to her feet and Lopes to do the same, The man strode out without looking at either of them. Lopes thought he recognised him but before he had time to ask the secretary said 'You can go in now.'

'Close the door,' said Oliveira as Lopes stepped inside. Oliveira looked pensive, more than pensive, worried. 'Sit. You saw who was with me?'

'Was that...?'

'Capito Agostinho Lourenco in person, yes, the head of the PVDE. He's taking a special interest in this case.'

Lopes swallowed. 'He is?'

'Yes, and he wants results, which means I want results too. How are you proceeding with your investigations?'

Lopes found his throat was dry and forced himself to swallow again. The states were suddenly very, very much higher than he'd realised. If the big boss was involved that meant the State and Salazar were too. He was carrying out an investigation of national importance.

Despite his mind reeling he managed to summarize his and Costa's findings to date.

Olivera listened, expressionless.

'That fits with what we know,' he said.

Lopes waited, expecting his chief to elaborate on what that was. Nothing was offered so Lopes decided to risk a prompt. 'Which is, sir?'

Oliveira gave him a fierce glare.

'That I cannot disclose,' he said.

Again Lopes waited. Again nothing more was forthcoming.

'There must be something you can tell me, Tenente,' he said. Oliveira stayed silent. 'This is more than a murder investigation, isn't it?'

After a few moments Oliveira simply said, 'Yes.'

'Then you have to give me something, sir. Give me some idea of what this is all about.'

Oliveira sat back in his chair and looked at the ceiling, then closed his eyes. He was clearly trying to decide what to say.

After a few seconds Oliveira started to speak still with his eyes closed. 'We have been told by certain... er... friends of ours that another country's agents are looking for something that is critical to their interests. It is also critical to the interest of those friends too. They need to find it.' Oliveira straightened up, opened his eyes and stared intently at Lopes. 'Time is of the essence, Lopes. We need progress. we need this brought to a conclusion.'

Lopes returned the gaze.

'How exactly?' he said.

'Pardon?'

'How am I to bring this to a conclusion when I don't know what that conclusion is?'

'You are the investigator. That's up to you.'

'Yes, but what am I looking for?'

Oliveira continued to stare at Lopes, his face inscrutable.

'An object not a person?'

Again Oliveira didn't even blink.

'So you're not going to even give me a hint as to what it is I'm looking for? For God's sake!' Lopes got to his feet.

'Where do you think you're going, Lopes?'

'I can't go on like this. I quit.'

'Your resignation is accepted,' snapped Olivier.

'Good.'

'So a certain package of information, including photographs and a copy of your son's birth certificate, which has your name on it, plus the address of where he and his mother can be found will be sent to your wife this evening.'

'What? Why?'

Oliveira suited. 'Because you've made your choice, Lopes. There are consequences.'

Lopes set his jaw. 'I don't care. Maybe it's best if it's out in the open.'

'And maybe if it was you've had done it yourself already. But no, you stay and enjoy the luxuries of life your wife's wealth brings, Dinis. And why is that? Because you can't do without them, because you are weak.' Oliveira bit his lip, Lopes could see that, behind his temper, he was worried, under pressure. 'I'm sorry, Lopes, that was unnecessary.'

Lopes nodded but smiled. 'It's probably the truth.' He sat down again. 'All right, what do you need me to do, if, and it's only an if at the moment, I stay on?'

Oliveira sighed. 'I need answers. I need ... whatever it is you need to find.'

Lopes nodded. 'Do you actually know what it is? This thing I'm looking for?'

Olivera swallowed and tapped the desk with his fingers. 'No, not really. Only that it's damaging. Damaging to our allies. Potentially damaging to everyone.'

'I thought we were neutral.'

'We *are* neutral. You're not naive, Lopes, you know it's complicated. Neutrality is nuanced.'

'You mean we must keep our old friends happy, whilst not upsetting our newer ones. The ones who might take over if it all goes wrong.'

'Either side could take over. Yes, it's more likely that it would be the allies of Franco at the moment but who's to say what will happen in the future once the Yankees get drawn it - which they will, Lopes, which they will,' He looked at his watch, a Rolex, Lopes noted. 'I have other meetings,' he muttered. 'And you, Dinis Lopes, need to get back to work and get this matter closed off. Quickly.'

Lopes stayed where he was, 'I resigned,' he said. 'And you accepted it.'

'So what? I recruited you once. I've just done it again. And anyway, you really don't want to bring things to a conclusion with your wife, do you? She'd bankrupt you. That would make your position even worse, wouldn't it?' Oliveira rose. 'So, get on with it, Lopes. I suggest you succeed.'

FRIDAY, 16TH MAY 1941

3.30 PM

'How does he expect us to do that, sir, if he won't tell us what we're looking for?'

Costa had just returned from police HQ and Lopes had filled him in on his meeting with Oliveira.

Lopes shrugged. 'Who knows? But we've been told to get it done so get it done we must. What did you find out about this Vogel?'

Costa pulled out his notebook and flicked through it until he found the right page.

'Uwe Vogel is — was I mean — a German national and a permanent resident. He had a record.'

Lopes nodded. 'Well, that's no surprise. Anything major?'

Costa shook his head. 'Not really. Until last year it was minor stuff. Drunkenness mainly, in…' He flicked back through the pages of his notebook. '1932, twice in '34 and so on.'

Lopes nodded again. 'He's been in Lisbon that long?'

'It seems so though the earliest arrest describes him as being on a sales visit from Germany so he may just have been here temporarily. That one, back in '32, was just for causing a disturbance. He was singing outside some woman's house at 3 am.'

'Miss Katz did say he was a happy drunk. What else was there?'

'Two more arrests for much the same thing in March '37 and August '39. Both times he got off with a fine.'

'Was he a resident by then?'

Costa nodded. 'Yes. He was described as being the local representative for his company in Lisbon both times.'

'What was the company?'

Costa flicked back through his notes. 'Telefunken AG. Do you know them?'

'I think they make radios, something like that. You mentioned something about last year being different. was he involved in something more serious?'

'Yes, he was arrested for burglary.'

Lopes stared at his assistant in surprise.

'Burglary? When?'

'July of last year. He was caught in a hotel with tools with someone else, and you'll never guess who.'

'Our conveniently dead thief and supposed murderer Santiago by any chance?'

Costa smiled, 'Yes, sir.'

Lopes sat back and nodded. 'Well, well, well, so the little monkeys in my head were right.'

'Yes sir, it seems so.'

'So, it's all connected, Santiago, Vogel.'

'And Da Silva too. We mustn't forget him.'

Lopes nodded. 'Yes, yes, you're quite right, though it looks like he was collateral damage.' He sighed. 'But our lord and masters clearly aren't interested in the poor lad, are they? That's not why we were put onto this job.

'No, sir.'

'But that doesn't mean we won't try and bring them to book for that. Let's go and do some more digging. Find out who Vogel and Santiago associated with.' He smiled, 'And the best place to start is with Miss Katz.'

*

'We're being followed, sir.'

'Who is it? Can you tell?'

Costa looked in the rear-view mirror.

'Looks like a PVDE car.'

'That's no surprise then. The only thing we don't know is whether it's the good PVDE or the bad PVDE.'

'Is there much difference, sir?'

'Good point, Costa, good point.'

'Should I try and lose them?'

'No. What's the point? Let them have their fun.'

They pulled up outside the address that Elena had given and Lopes looked up at the building. It was in a prominent position on the Largo Barão Quintela, four storey, with a facade of high-quality blue and white tiles, small cast iron balconies giving a view over the square which was shaded by mature trees in full spring flower.

'Very nice,' he said. 'Crime clearly pays.'

'Indeed, sir. Though it didn't in the end.'

'What do you mean?'

'He's on a slab.'

'True, Costa, very true.' He nodded at the bell, 'Let's see if we can raise someone!'

It took a full five minutes for the bell to be answered by a rather grumpy building superintendent.

'What do you want?' he snapped. His expression and attitude changed as Lopes showed them his badge. 'Sorry, sir. I want no trouble. How can I help you? '

'And I'm not here to give you any, we want to see Herr Vogel's apartment.'

'He's dead. His apartment is being cleared out.' '

'Why? I'd heard his rent had been paid?'

'He'd paid up to the end of the month.'

'Then why are you cleaning it out?'

The superintendent shrugged. 'Got to make a living. Can't have his place going empty. The city is full. Ain't you noticed?'

'Who's cleaning it out?'

'Some friends of his.'

'Miss Katz?'

'Who?'

'Small, dark girl, young and pretty?'

'Oh her? No, I threw that little bitch out. She wasn't on the lease. She'd no right to be there.'

'So, who are they?'

The superintendent shrugged. 'Ask them yourselves. They're upstairs now. Third floor, front, Apartment 3A.'

Lopes exchanged dances with Costa, then nodded and headed upstairs,

The door to apartment 3A stood open. Voices could be heard inside.

'This is where I wish I was armed,' he whispered to Costa,

In reply Costa opened his jacket and showed Lopes he had a holster under this armpit with a small pistol in it.

'Where did you get that?'

'Tenente Oliveira sent it down to me, sir. Thought it might be wise after what happened to you.' He gave a little smile. 'The Tenente said you never carry one, sir, so I should.'

Lopes stared at Costa for a few moments. "…the Tenente said…". So, Costa, the disgraced junior was somehow on speaking terms with their head? Of course, he thought, that explained a lot. He shook his head; it really didn't matter.

'Right, 'he said. 'Let's do it.' He rapped on the door. 'PVDE. Open up.'

The conversation inside stopped, then Lopes heard a few words being exchanged, not, as he expected German but in English.

The door was opened, cautiously from within.

Two men stood inside the apartment. One was middle-aged and paunchy the other young, sleek and smartly dressed.

'You're not PVDE,' said the older man. 'Where are your macs?'

His Portuguese was fluent but there was a hint of a British accent.

'Contrary to popular opinion, we don't all dress the same,' said Lopes, sharing them his badge. Costa did the same. 'Now you know who we are, what are your names and what are you doing here?'

'Clive MacDonald, I'm a friend…sorry, I mean I was a friend of Uwe,' said the older man. 'We're just sorting through his things, making sure everything's in order.''

'We?' Lopes turned to the younger man. 'Who are you?'

In reply the younger man reached inside his suit jacket. Lopes saw Costa move his own hand towards his holster.

'Easy,' said the young man, his eyes fixed on Costa. 'I'm not armed. I was Just getting my documents out.' Exaggeratedly slowly and using two fingers he extracted a passport then showed it to Lopes. There was a CD on the front. Corps Diplomatic.

'As you can see, I have diplomatic immunity so I'll be going now,' he said. 'I'm sure you two gentleman would not want to interfere with diplomatic business?'

He moved to put the document away but Lopes stopped him. 'Wait,' he said. 'I have a right to look at the documents to verify they are genuine.'

The young man smiled. 'Of course you do,' he said and passed over the passport.

Lopes could see instantly that the photograph inside matched the man.

'Henry Armstrong?'

'At your service. And you are?'

'Lopes. Dinis Lopes.'

'Ah, so you are Lopes. We meet at last,' said Armstrong holding out his hand for his passport. 'I'll be getting back to the embassy. MacDonald, be sure to let me know if you have any issues with the inspector here.' He touched the bin of his hat. 'Good day to you both.'

He stepped across the room and picked up a smallish, beige-coloured, fabric-covered suitcase.

'Wait,' said Costa. 'Where do you think you're going with that?'

'It's mine. I brought it here with me,' said Armstrong.

'That's right,' said MacDonald. 'He did.'

'We can't let you take it,' said Costa. 'We want to see what's inside.'

'Well you can't, it's private and. I would remind you, I'm a diplomat. The inspector here will tell you what that means, won't you?'

Lopes sighed. 'We can't carry out any search of his possessions,' he said.

'But we don't know if it really is his,' Costa protested.

'We have to take his word for it.'

'Thank-you inspector. MacDonald, I'll see you later.'

Armstrong pushed past them and descended the stairs. Lopes watched him go then turned to MacDonald. 'Let's go inside,' he said.

The hallway led to a lounge area. A door to one side revealed the bedroom. Everywhere things were disturbed. Cupboard doors were open, drawers pulled out and their contents strewn over the floor.

'I thought you said were packing Vogel s things.'

MacDonald shrugged. 'We are.'

'Really? What are you packing them up into?' Lopes looked around. 'Come on, MacDonald, you're looking for something, aren't you? What is it?'

'What if we were? Why should I tell you? It's none of your business. I'm a private individual, and a citizen of His Majesty's —'

'You're a resident of Portugal, MacDonald, and there are no private individuals where there are threats to the state, as I believe there are grounds to suspect here,' snapped Costa. 'I'd suggest you open up and tell us or you'll find yourself locked up.

Lopes looked at Costa is some surprise but it seemed to have had the desired effect on the British man.

'All right, no need for that, I was just telling you who I was, I didn't say I wasn't going to help.'

Lopes chose not to point out that MacDonald had suggested exactly that. 'What are you looking for?'

'Nothing in particular. Vogel and I were in business together. I was looking for anything that might be connected with that.'

'What kind of business?' said Costa.

MacDonald looked shifty. 'You know, this and that,' he muttered.

'That's not helpful. Can you give us a few examples?'

'Buying, selling, imports and exports, things like that.'

'Importing refugees and exporting them out of the country by any chance?' said Lopes,

MacDonald was silent. He looked down, clearly not wanting to make eye contact.

'Where is the young lady who lived here?'

'Which one?'

'What do you mean?'

'There were so many. Uwe liked his women.'

'The one who lived here. Elena.'

'Oh, her. Who knows? Who cares?' said MacDonald. To Lopes, the man's demeanour said something else, something quite different from the words he'd uttered.

Lopes was tired of it all.

'You're being obstructive, MacDonald. You can come with us.'

'You can't, I'm a respected businessman.'

'Yes, we can, and you know we can. Costa, cuff him.'

'But…I've got things to do. You can't hold me.' He tried to push his way out but Costa pulled out his automatic. It was small but the effect was immediate. MacDonald stared at it like he was hypnotised.

'Please don't,' he said, 'I'll help.'

'All right,' said Lopes. 'One last chance. What were you looking for? Really?'

MacDonald fell silent.

'Where's Elena Katz?'

He shrugged. 'I don't know. I really don't.'

'Not good enough, Costa.'

Costa snapped the cuffs on the protesting Britain.

'Let's see if a night in the PDVE cells improves your memory.' Lopes nodded at Costa. 'Put him in the car,' he said. 'I'll join you in a few moments.'

After they'd gone, MacDonald protesting all the way down the stairs, Lopes examined the apartment. It was just like Santiago's, a thorough search — probably more than one in fact — had been carried out. And had been carried out to a conclusion; nothing had been found. Lopes sighed. Progress but no progress. More evidence but no clues.

At least they had MacDonald. Perhaps he could tell them something. Time would tell.

FRIDAY, 16TH MAY 1941

6.05 PM

Back at HQ, Lopes went to use the toilet, leaving his deputy to process the prisoner. When he returned, he found Costa in the middle of an argument with Da Souza. Tempers were clearly hot.

'Who do you think you are? You're a no-one. You can't clutter up our cells with anyone you drag in off the street.'

'He's not anyone. He's a suspect in a murder case.'

'Then he should be in a police station. Not here. Our organisation is for enemies of the state,' said Da Souza. 'Lopes, did you tell your man here to do this?'

'Yes, of course I did.'

'Why? Don't you know your standing here? It's less than the janitor's. You're nothing, an embarrassment. And this Office of Special investigations set up for you, what rot. It's window dressing.'

'Really?'

'Yes, really. Window dressing led by a washed-up failure with a shrew of a wife. And as for him,' he jabbed his finger at Costa. 'We all know why he got sacked by the police.' He turned to the custody officer. 'Get that man out of here,' he said.

'Don't do anything of the sort,' Lopes said.

The man glanced anxiously at Lopes and then back at Da Souza.

'You know me, don't you?' said Da Souza to him.

'Yes, sir.'

'But you don't know these clowns, do you?' He jabbed his index finger at Costa and Lopes.

'No, sir, I don't.'

'Good, so if you know what's good for you, do as I tell you.'

The custody officer stepped towards MacDonald's cell, keys in hand.

'I'm sure Capito Lourenco will be fascinated to hear about it if you do,' said Lopes. The custody officer stopped immediately. 'Oh, didn't you know, Da Souza? We're working on this case with the full knowledge of the head of the PVDE. And, of course, if we're working with the blessing of Lourenco that means we are also doing so at the behest of Dr Salazar himself.'

Lopes was pleased to see the colour drain from Da Souza's face. Unable to fully suppress a smile he turned to the jailer. 'Give our prisoner something to eat. We'll be back later to talk to him. Come on, Costa, let's get something ourselves,' He nodded to Da Souza. 'See you around,' he said.

'You'll pay for this, Lopes,' said Da Souza. 'Just you wait.'

'Yeah, yeah,' muttered Lopes but he couldn't help but think he'd have to watch his back over the next few days.

*

'So, when do we talk to him, boss?' said Costa. 'Now or let him stew?'

Lopes leaned back in his chair. 'There's a chance that someone will let him go whilst we're away,' he said, almost to himself.

'I could stay, sir, though I'd have to go home and tell my wife first.'

'You have a wife, Costa?' said Lopes. 'You never said.'

'You never asked, sir.'

'No, you're right, I didn't and that's remiss of me.'

'You have been very busy, sir.'

'But still... Children?'

Costa blushed. 'Three, sir. All girls.'

Lopes laughed, 'Ah, Costa, you'll have so many problems ahead of you!'

Costa grinned. 'I know, sir but I wouldn't have it any other way.'

'Good, but you're not staying here tonight. Go back to your wife and kids. Now we've put the fear of God in them, I don't think they'd dare let him go. An overnight stay should loosen his tongue.'

'Yes, sir. Goodnight.'

'Goodnight, Costa.'

*

There were perhaps twenty people waiting at the tram stop. Lopes checked his watch, of course, the city's shops and offices would be emptying at this time. It would be a squeeze to get on the first tram, if he could at all.

He smiled to himself, why should he worry about getting home quickly? Certainly not to discuss his day with his wife. She was still avoiding him; they had barely passed two words to each other in the last few days. Perhaps he should stay in town, find some Fado, perhaps somewhere new he hadn't been to before?

He was musing on this as the first tram approached rattling up the tracks. It was packed, yes there would be no room, indeed the driver was ringing the bell in warning and gesturing to these waiting that he was going straight through.

The woman alongside him sighed and muttered something in her frustration. Someone had stood right behind Lopes, so close that he felt their breath on the back of his neck. That felt strange, the waiting passengers-to-be had spread out along the pavement, there was no need to be so close. He was about to turn to find out who was there and to, perhaps, glare at them in the hope that they would move away when he heard them whisper something; only barely discernable above the rattly clank of the approaching tram.

'Drop the case, Lopes. Remember, this could have been you.'

Lopes turned, but the man had stepped to one side, behind the woman who'd muttered and pushed her hard. Unprepared, she fell, right in front of the approaching tram.

Her scream was brief, cut off as swiftly as the tram's metal wheels cut her in half, carrying away her mangled trunk, head and one arm. The other was left, palm open, at Lopes' feet.

The scream from the queue went on longer, mingling with the squeal of brakes as the tram driver applied the emergency stop.

Lopes was momentarily frozen, staring at the arm, barely able to process what had happened. Too late he turned to look for the assassin, someone he'd only got the briefest glance at. There was a man hurrying away, about to turn the corner, hat pulled down over his eyes. That had to be him. Lopes followed, pushing his way through the people who'd come to gawp and, eyes fixed on where the man had disappeared, ran as fast as his gas-damaged lungs could manage.

He was too late. As he rounded the corner, he saw the man getting into a car and the car speeding away.

He tried to get the registration number but he couldn't make it out.

They'd gone. He swore in frustration.

*

It was hours later when he finally got home.

He'd had to wait until after the ambulance had come, after talking to the police and giving a statement, after witnessing the woman's husband arrive to identify the body. The look on the man's face had been heartbreaking, there had been hardship in the couple's life, clear from the man's dusty clothes, but genuine love too.

Love that had been snuffed out. And for what? To deliver a warning to him, Lopes. He didn't care about the warning but the woman was different. Her life had been reduced to nothing, someone thrown away without regard, unimportant, trash. That he cared deeply about.

'What time do you call this?' said his wife. 'Are these the hours you're going to keep now? Is this what I have to put up with?'

Lopes didn't answer. He just stared at her, thinking of the widower, of his lost love.

Then he went into his study and poured himself a brandy.

He hadn't told the police about what the man had said. But he wasn't going to stop. Not after the woman's death.

She *was* important, she wasn't rubbish to be discarded, she would be revenged.

He wasn't going to stop.

SATURDAY, 17TH MAY 1941

8.25 AM.

Costa could tell something had happened the moment Lopes walked into their office.

'Sir, are you alright? You look like you've been up all night.'

'I have, just about,' said Lopes and told Costa about the woman at the tram stop.

'Mother of God, sir, they'd go that far?'

'Apparently so. Whatever, we are not stopping. The bastards are not going to get away with this.' He nodded towards the cells. 'MacDonald still here?'

'Yes sir,' said Costa. 'And not in the best of moods.'

'He's not the only one,' said Lopes. 'Let's go and see what he's got to say.'

'Before we do, sir, this came down from the morgue.' Costa picked up a file from the desk. 'Vogel's autopsy.'

Lopes took the file and flicked through it. 'Poor bugger,' he murmured. 'They really put him through it.'

'It was heart failure though that killed him,' said Costa. 'His arteries were clogged.'

'Yes, but you only had to look at him to know that he wasn't fit,' said Lopes. 'And, if what Miss Katz said about him was right, he wasn't brave. This looks like a punishment beating as much as anything.'

'Perhaps they went too far,' said Costa.

'Possibly, possibly,' said Lopes, closing the file and tossing it back on the desk. 'Let's go and talk to our guest.'

*

'About bloody time,' said MacDonald as he was brought into the interrogation room. 'Have you come to your senses? Are you going to release me?'

'Sit down, MacDonald,' said Lopes.

'No, I want-'

'Sit down. Now!'

Lopes rarely raised his voice but when he did people took notice and obeyed. MacDonald did as he was told, but didn't stop grumbling, 'I'm a British citizen, you have no right to do this.'

'You are in this country,' said Lopes. 'That means you are bound by the laws of Portugal.'

'I follow this country's laws,' said MacDonald.

'Your record suggests you don't.'

'I've never been convicted of anything,' muttered MacDonald.

'Yet. Your record says different. You've been arrested, what, four…no, five times.' Lopes looked up from his notes straight at the man sitting opposite him. 'I believe you British have a saying, "There's no smoke without fire?" .'

'Sometimes the record is wrong.' MacDonald lifted his chin defiantly. 'Over the years I've been picked on by either overzealous or corrupt policeman.' He smiled. 'I'm sure, inspector, you know some of both.'

'I do, but that's irrelevant here.'

'I disagree…'

'Because' Lopes interrupted. 'As much as I find it distasteful, the PVDE treat cases very differently from the State Police. Smoke is enough. suspicion is enough. If the PVDE don't like your face then that's quite enough. So, Mr. MacDonald, if you don't want to find yourself ejected from this country tonight, I strongly suggest you start to co-operate.'

MacDonald looked sullen and Lopes could tell he had a beaten man in front of him.

'Good,' said Lopes. 'I can see the truth of your situation is sinking in. So, tell me what you know about the murder of Uwe Vogel.'

MacDonald reacted. 'Murder? They said —' Quickly he looked down, not willing to make eye contact with either Lopes or Costa.

'Who said?' said Costa.

'Nothing. Just people, he had a weak heart, everyone knew about it.'

Lopes pulled a face. 'Do you want to know how he died? I've just seen the autopsy. He was beaten, tortured in fact before he died. That in my book, weak heart or not, is murder.'

MacDonald just grunted a reply.

Lopes decided not to push it.

'Tell me how you knew Vogel,' he said.

'We moved in the same circles, shall we say?' said MacDonald.

Costa gave a little laugh. 'You mean you were involved in the same crimes,' he said.

MacDonald was on his feet in an instant. 'I don't have to listen to that sort of talk,' he said.

'Yes, you do. sit down,' said Lopes. After a few seconds MacDonald did as he was told. 'Good. Now when did you meet?'

'Uwe was posted here by his company. To be honest I think he volunteered. He and his wife didn't exactly get on.'

'His company? That would be Telefunken?'

'If you knew that why ask? Yes, he was the rep for Telefunken. Well, more of an engineer actually, making sure all the radios his company sold worked properly.'

Lopes nodded, 'An engineer,' he muttered. Something was niggling at him. He reached for the tiles and leafed through it.

'Why didn't he go back to Germany? ' Lopes said a silent thank you to Costa for filling in the void whilst he thought. 'When he stopped working for Telefunken?'

'Who says he stopped working for them? 'said MacDonald. 'Alright, Yes, he left their employment in the middle of '38. Some mix-up in the accounts department but poor Uwe got the blame. As to why he didn't go back, why should he? He was happy in Lisbon. And his wife wasn't here. The two facts may be connected.'

'Tell me exactly how he made a living,' said Lopes.

MacDonald just smiled. 'As we all do. Doing this and that, you know.'

'Smuggling, fencing stolen goods, bribing officials to get visas and berths on ships and generally fleecing refugees,' said Costa.

'I told you before, we ran an import/export business,' said MacDonald. 'And as for our other activities, we meet a need. People are willing to pay for our services. They are in demand.'

'And if they can't pay?'

MacDonald shrugged. 'We're not a charity.'

'Indeed,' said Lopes. 'Let's get back to Herr Vogel's demise, which is the reason you're here.'

'I had nothing to do with Uwe's death.'

'I don't think you killed him but you do you know who did and I'm sure you know why.'

MacDonald shook his head. 'Not a clue old chap.'

'You're lying,' said Lopes. MacDonald just shrugged. 'Would it surprise you that the men who dumped his body in the river were German?'

'No, but there's your answer,' said MacDonald. 'What we do can be contrary to the policy and beliefs of certain countries. It can upset people.'

'Helping Jews you mean?' said Costa.

'Of course.'

'Something you have done.'

'I said so, didn't I?'

'Yet you seem to be not worried about your own safety,' said Lopes. 'In fact, you seem totally unconcerned about it. Why is that the case, Mr. MacDonald?'

MacDonald held Lopes' gaze, 'I'm more careful than poor Uwe was. Remember that Uwe was German himself. I'm not, the locals we work with aren't but Uwe was. He was stupid, like taking up with that Jew girl. Besotted he was. I'm sure that didn't go down very well with his compatriots.'

'Vogel and Elena were close? I thought it was a… er… business relationship?'

MacDonald laughed.

'Not for poor Uwe. He was a sucker for a pretty face and a nice figure and, I have to admit, she had both. He had a blind spot as to where she was concerned. He trusted her too much. He did what she asked…' MacDonald suddenly looked uncomfortable. He bit his lip.

Lopes frowned. What was that about?

'Anyway,' MacDonald found his voice again. 'Uwe couldn't see he was being played. He couldn't see that, to her, it was just business.'

Lopes nodded thoughtfully, thinking about the morgue and in the cafe. There Elena seemed genuinely upset, and she'd sought out answers to what had happened to Vogel. Did that really show someone who wasn't concerned, who didn't really care? Mind you, she could just have been worried about the loss of her protector and meal ticket.

'Come on, I've helped you, haven't I?' MacDonald interrupted his train of thought. 'Can I go now?'

Lopes made MacDonald wait before he responded. It was a tactic he'd used many times in interrogation. He used it before asking critical questions, silence was unsettling, and he had one to ask now. He let the moment drag before speaking.

'Your businesses were going well, this time last year?' he said. 'Your's and Vogel's'

'I said that, yes, this war has its benefits, for the right people, in the right places.'

Lopes nodded, letting the moment stretch into seconds. Then he delivered the follow-up question,

'Then why did he turn to burglary?'

MacDonald's confidence was clearly knocked.

'What? I…er…'

'He was caught, wasn't he? In the middle of a burglary.'

'I don't know, was he?'

Lopes opened the file and pushed it towards the man, turning it around so he could read it. 'You read Portuguese, don't you?'

'Yes.'

'Tell me what that says there.' Lopes pointed at the page.

MacDonald squinted at the page. '"items in possession of suspect Uwe Vogel at time of arrest; One pair of pliers, one small pair of wire cutters, a screwdriver, electrical wires, associated items, possibly for a radio."' he read, 'So what?'

'So what? So what, Mr. MacDonald? So what was your business partner accompanied by a known thief, Santiago, doing in a city centre hotel last July with that equipment? July, last year at a time the country was being flooded by refugees, when your joint businesses were booming? What possessed him to do something like that?'

The silence from MacDonald's side of the table was telling. Lopes stared at the Briton. He could see the man was desperately trying to frame an answer.

'I don't know, do I?' he muttered at last. 'I was his business partner, not his keeper.'

'I put it to you, Mr. MacDonald, that you *do* know.'

'And I tell you again, I don't.' he said, 'I wasn't there, was I?'

Lopes stared at him for a moment then took the file back and flipped a page. 'Whilst I've no proof you were, indeed, not there when the burglary took place, you certainly were at the police station at 7 am the next day, weren't you? That was some three hours after the arrest, a short time yet there you were standing bail for your partner, weren't you?' Lopes turned the file around and pushed it back towards MacDonald. 'That's your signature on the bail form, isn't it? You paid a substantial sum to secure his release, didn't you?'

MacDonald was staring at the page as if wishing the signature was a mirage that would disappear if he looked hard enough. They remained stubbornly where they had been put.

'I wasn't at the hotel,' he muttered.

'I never said you were,' said Lopes. 'But, clearly, you knew about it.'

MacDonald shook his head. 'You can't say that. You've no proof.'

Lopes knew that line of questioning had reached a dead end. He had to find another way in.

'Tell me what happened.'

'I was just told of Uwe's arrest and asked to help out.'

'Who told you about it?'

'What?'

'Who told you Vogel had been arrested?'

'I can't remember, it was over a year ago.'

'But this was your friend, your business partner. This wasn't an everyday event, was it? Vogel didn't get arrested every day, did he? Surely this would stick in your memory?'

MacDonald was sweating. Good, thought Lopes, the pressure was telling. 'Come on, man, don't insult our intelligence by saying you don't remember. It's obvious You do. I suggest that, if you want to stay in the country, you tell us, now.'

'He shouldn't have done it,' Macdonald muttered.

'Done what?'

'They made him do it, said that it was his duty.'

'To do what?'

MacDonald opened his mouth to answer but there was a knock at the door of the interrogation room. Lopes frowned at the interruption and nodded at Costa to go and see who it was.

It was the custody officer. He looked nervously at Lopes and then at the prisoner then gestured to Costa to step outside. Lopes waited whilst the muttered conversation at the door continued- all the time cursing; MacDonald was being given time to frame an answer, to wiggle off the hook. This was a potential disaster. Then Costa came back though and turned the potential into reality.

'I'm sorry, Boss, but we've got to let him go.'

'What? Is this Da Silva again? He has no right—'

'It's not Da Silva. They are Tenente Oliveira's instructions.'

Lopes was so stunned he couldn't speak.

'What? No, why?'

MacDonald was already on his feet. 'At last,' he said. 'Someone has seen sense.' He held out his cuffed wrists. 'Take these off, Lopes.'

'Damn it, no, I'm not having this,' said Lopes. 'Stay here, I'll go and talk to him to find out what all this is about. You,' he said to the custody officer. have you got a phone?'

'Yes sir.'

'Good, take me to it.'

He got through to Oliveira straight away.

'Let the Britisher go,' the Tenente said before Lopes had chance to speak.

'But... he's our best chance of recovering... well, whatever it is you're looking for.'

'I'm sorry, Lopes. This is out of my hands. Pressure has been put on us. We've no choice.'

'Pressure? By whom?'

'Lopes, enough. No questions, just let MacDonald go. Oh, and don't try to resign again, it wouldn't be accepted.'

The line went dead.

Lopes held onto the instrument for a few moments, breathing heavily. He was so tempted to smash it down and keep smashing it until it was just fragments but he was better than that. He'd observed examples of petulance by his colleagues in the police over the years. It had always been embarrassing to watch, both during and afterwards when the shame had set in. This was bad enough without giving anyone else the satisfaction.

He placed the telephone carefully back in its holder then walked back to the interrogation room.

'Release him,' he said to Costa.

Costa didn't argue, he did as he was told.

MacDonald rubbed his wrists.

'I told you you'd overstepped the mark, inspector,' he said. 'I hope you've learned your lesson.'

'MacDonald, I would watch yourself if I were you,' said Lopes. 'I don't care what strings have been pulled for you, you're playing a dangerous game and you need to watch your step.'

MacDonald frowned. 'Are you threatening me, Lopes?'

Lopes smiled, 'Me? Hardly. I think you'll find your threats will come from a different source. You ought to reconsider and voluntarily tell us what we need to know, then we could protect you. Remember, Vogel died because of it.'

MacDonald stared at Lopes. His mouth opened and, for the briefest moment, Lopes thought that he might go along with it.

But then he shook his head and walked to the door, 'How the devil do I get out of here?' he said.

'We'll walk you out. It's the least we can do.'

'There's no need.'

'No, we insist, don't we, Costa?'

'Yes sir.'

'Come on, it's this way.'

He led MacDonald up and out of the basement interrogation rooms into the lobby and then outside, MacDonald blinked in the sunlight.

Lopes was not surprised to see Henry Armstrong get out of a black Citroen Avant and wave towards the erstwhile prisoner.

'I think that's your ride', said Lopes.

MacDonald just grunted a reply and headed over to the Citroen.

'Should I follow, sir?' whispered Costa as the man got in. 'I can get the car.'

'Forget it,' said Lopes. 'I'm pretty sure they'll just go to the British embassy. We can't touch him there.'

'No sir.'

They both watched as the car, with both men inside, pulled away from the kerb and disappeared into the traffic.

'Come on,' sighed Lopes. 'Let's get a coffee and decide on our next move.'

SATURDAY, 17TH MAY 1941

9.45 AM

They sat in the office together in silence, Costa and Lopes, the files strewn across the table. Neither had spoken for ten minutes. For want of something to do Lopes filled his pipe then felt around for his matches. Costa beat him to it, offering him his own box. After Lopes lit the tobacco, Costa took the matches back and lit a cigarette of his own.

'We're stuck, aren't we, sir?'

Lopes nodded slowly.

'Yes,' he said.' It looks like we are.' He stared at Costa for a few seconds, weighing up what to say. How much could he trust his assistant? Well, more and more each day was the truth. He needed Costa's help. ' So, although we're supposedly investigating the murder of a young policeman it's increasingly clear that we're actually looking for something. You realise that?'

'Yes, sir.'

'It's something that everyone seems to want —'

'— but we have no idea of actually what it is.'

'Indeed, Costa, indeed. And, whatever, we're stymied at every step, even by our so-called allies.' He puffed hard on his pipe for a few seconds. 'But I'm not giving up. This is just making me more determined to get to the bottom of it all. How about you?'

'Yes, sir. But how do we do it?'

'With good police work, Costa, damned good police work. Back to basics, we work methodologically through the evidence. ' He tapped out his pipe. 'Let's start with the hotel where the pair were arrested. Where was it?'

Costa checked his notes.

'The Avenida Palace,' he said.

'Of course, I should have guessed; nothing but the best. That's good for us. The Avenida is such a prestigious place to work I bet they don't have much of a staff turnover. Let's go and chat with some of them, see what they remember. Come on, Costa we'll crack this case yet.'

'Yes, sir.'

*

Lopes could feel many pairs of eyes on him as he walked into the hotel. This was no surprise; the Avenida had a certain reputation. It was the current world in microcosm, the place where spies from all nations, combatants and non-combatants alike rubbed shoulders with each other watching the other parties' every move whilst also casting a suspicious eye on any strangers. It was in a perfect location for intrigue, next to and virtually beneath the Rossio station, the main land gateway to Lisbon and looking out over a square full of cafes that themselves were the ideal spot for meetings and observing the comings and goings from the station and hotel. Lopes knew that the hotel was aware of this and had a secret entrance up in the station itself that the most security conscious of guests could use on special request.

The young man behind the check-in desk greeted them with a smile. 'Good morning, sirs. How can I be of service?'

Lopes showed him his badge.

'I'd like to see the hotel manager please.'

'Of course, sir, please take a seat.'

Lopes and Costa did as they were asked. One of their fellow customers lowered the corner of his newspaper to look at them briefly before going back to reading. Dotted around the lobby were tables where some intense whispered conversations were taking place, the atmosphere simply reeked of intrigue and secrets.

Absolutely appropriate for this case, Lopes thought.

The hotel also reeked of other things; wealth and luxury. cool marble was underfoot, the walls consisted of plaster panels, the inlay painted in an opulent deep red with the columns in white the details picked out in gold. Above was a stained-glass roof that cast dappled light in multi colours over the lobby and its inhabitants.

'It feels more like a cathedral,' Costa murmured.

'A cathedral to money,' Lopes replied.

The desk clerk had returned. 'The manager will see you in his office,' he said. 'Please, follow me.'

Both Lopes and Costa rose but before the latter could follow Lopes tapped him on the shoulder. 'No, let's work smart. Why don't you have a walk round the hotel. see if you can find some staff who remember the break-in.'

Costa didn't protest, instead there was a ghost of a smile on his face.

The areas behind the front desk were much less opulent than the public areas but still grand enough. This was also true of the manager's office, a medium-sized room dominated by a large, dark, quite ornate mahogany desk. The manager, a small, slim man in his mid-forties balding but with hair at his temples rose to greet Lopes as he came into this room. 'Inspector,' he said, 'I'm a busy man but always glad to help the PVDE with...' Abruptly he stopped. 'I thought there were two of you,' he said.

'My colleague is quite junior,' said Lopes. 'I've left him outside. There's no need to involve him in whatever conversations we have.'

'Whatever, I don't like the idea of him wandering around my hotel –' protested the manager.

'It is gratifying that you would like to help us,' Lopes interrupted. 'Inspector Dinis Lopes, Office of Special Investigation,' he added and thrust his hand towards the manager. After a few moments the man took the proffered hand and returned the handshake. The grip was cool, clammy, rather sweaty. 'May I sit?' said Lopes doing so anyway.

'Of course,' said the manager, with a nervous glance towards the door.

'Good,' Lopes took out his notebook. Working with Costa he'd got out of the habit of doing this but it was a useful ploy; it gave the impression that you knew more than you actually did, saying "Look, I've made notes on something before I arrived, your story had better tally with it". 'Now, Mr... er...?'

He waited expectantly,

'Gonzales. Juan Gonzales.'

'Ah, you are Spanish?'

'My father was.'

'I see,' said Lopes writing in his notebook.

'What is this about?' said Gonzalez. 'What are you writing?'

Lopes smiled to himself: the man was already rattled. He let the seconds stretch before asking his next question.

'I presume you worked in the hotel in July of last year?'

'Yes, I've been manager since 1938 Before that I was –'

'So,' Lopes interrupted again. 'You were here on the night of 1st July last year. Or rather the early hours of July 2nd.'

'That was, what, ten months ago? I can hardly be expected to remember my movements that far back.'

'I think you'll remember this. There was an attempted break-in that night. Two men were caught by some of your staff.' Lopes looked at Gonzalez and smiled. 'I'm sure that's not an everyday occurrence at a hotel as prestigious as this one.'

Gonzalez had looked instantly uncomfortable at the mention of the break-in. 'No, of course not,' he said, ruining a finger around the inside of his white, starched collar. 'We pride ourselves on looking after our guests, their possessions and their privacy.'

Lopes nodded. 'Were you on duty when the men were caught?'

Gonzalez shook his head, 'No, but I was in the hotel. I have a room in the staff quarters. I was in bed but was called straight away.'

'Did you see the men?'

'Yes.'

'What were they like?'

Gonzalez gave a description of them which, in outline, described Santiago and Uwe Vogel.

'Where were they caught?'

'On the sixth floor.'

'And what is located on there?'

'There are a number of suites.'

'Including the presidential suite, the one that is reserved for your most valued and prestigious guests?'

'Yes,' said Gonzalez, his voice low as if afraid someone might be listening and who would tell the other guests.

Lopes nodded and noted this down.

'Was this the suite that the two men were trying to break into?'

Gonzalez looked pensive. 'I can't answer that,' he said.

'Can't or won't?'

Gonzalez frowned. 'Inspector, as I said, we pride ourselves on giving our guests a comfortable, safe and secure stay here at the Avenida Palace. I cannot countenance anything being said that might prejudice that.'

Lopes stared at him, 'I see. So, it's won't say, is it?'

Gonzalez returned the stare. 'Take it how you choose, Inspector,' he said.

The impasse continued for a few more seconds until Lopes accepted that the manager wasn't going to willingly give up any more information.

'Very well, I have made a note of your obstructiveness,' he said. The manager started to protest but Lopes didn't give him a chance. 'Let's move on for now. Who was staying on that floor when the two men were discovered?'

'I'm not at liberty to tell you that,' said Gonzalez. 'We offer our guests confidentiality so I cannot –'

'That's enough!' snapped Lopes. 'This is a murder case I'm investigating, and not an ordinary one. Firstly, it's of a policeman but it's also one that has attracted the interest of the highest state actors.'

'What? I…'

'Yet you choose to be evasive.'

Lopes saw that this had struck home. Gonzalez swallowed. 'State actors? You mean...'

'I do.'

'I'm sorry inspector, I didn't mean to appear obstructive, not at all, it's just that I'm accustomed to offering the hotels' clientèle complete discretion.'

'So, you won't help?'

'I didn't say that.'

'Good. Now we've established that, answer my question: who was staying in the presidential suite at the time of the break in?'

Gonzalez took a deep breath. He seemed to be struggling with some inner demons. At last, he spoke. 'No-one. It was empty.'

This was unexpected and it took Lopes a moment to recover.'

'What?'

'It had been vacated that morning.'

'Who by?'

'I can't tell you that, but I can tell you he was a foreign businessman.' Gonzalez opened his hands in appeal. 'Please inspector.' Lopes scowled but noted this down.

'Who was booked into the suite next?'

'I'd have to check my records.'

'Senor Gonzales, I have already warned you not to withhold anything.'

'Inspector, please. It was nearly ten months ago; I really can't remember.'

'That's not good enough.'

The manager rose. 'Can I consult my files?'

'Please do.'

Gonzales went over to a glass fronted cab net and opened the door. After a few moments scanning the volumes on the shelves he pulled one down and returned to his desk. He leafed through it until he found the right page. 'Here it is. The next time the room was occupied was July 20th.'

Lopes leaned forward to take a look. Gonzales pulled the ledger away from him. 'This is confidential, our guest privacy-'

'Mr. Gonzalez, your privacy will be assured if you don't let me look because you'll be in a cell on your own,' Lopes snapped.

Reluctantly Gonzales pushed it back over towards Lopes.

It took a few moments to work out what it was showing. Down the left-hand side of the page were room numbers and names, one of which was the presidential suite. Across the page were dates and days, starting with Monday 1st July 1940. Ruled horizontal and vertical lines produced a grid and in the grid, boxes were hand-written around with names written above them plus a number in brackets. The arrows were terminated with a short vertical line. The information in the boxes was completed by either a tick or, rarely, a cross. So, he thought, the arrows indicated the duration of the stay, the names were the guests' and the number was the number of people in the rooms. The tick or cross showed whether the guests had turned up or not to fulfil their booking. Lopes estimated that perhaps ten percent of the bookings were a no show but, sometimes, replacement quests were pencilled into the rooms.

The presidential suite was in almost constant use in the month of June and was, indeed, due to be occupied by the businessman, Johansson, up to the 8th, after which there was a break of a day, when a new guest, an Arthur Zimmerman, described as a US citizen, was supposed to take it until the end of the month.

Supposed to because both Zimmerman's and the last eight days of Johansson's booking had been scored out in red with the words *'Keep free for special guest'* written above it with an arrow running to the end of July. In the end this 'special guest' can't have arrived because there was a pencilled amendment showing that Arthur Zimmerman had, indeed, eventually got the suite he'd booked.

'What is this?" Lopes said, 'Why were these bookings cancelled?'

Gonzalez leaned forward to look at the entry. He shrugged. 'It is as it says, we were told to expect a special guest and that we were to offer them nothing but the best.'

'But they didn't arrive?'

'Clearly not, so we were able to offer the suite to other guests.'

'Yes, so who were they?'

'As I told you before, our client's privacy is-'

'-and as I told you before, obstruct my investigation again and you'll end up in a cell. Who were you told to expect?'

Gonzales' face was set in a frown, for a few moments Lopes wondered if the man was going to call his bluff and make him arrest him. He could imagine how it would go down at the PVDE if he followed up on MacDonald's arrest with that of the manager of the finest hotel in Lisbon.

Fortunately, his bluff worked.

'The Duke and Duchess of Windsor,' Gonzales said, his voice barely above a whisper. 'The former British King and his wife.'

SATURDAY, 17TH MAY 1941

11.10 AM

'You'll never guess who was expected to stay in the Presidential suite,' murmured Lopes as they walked to the car.

'Actually, sir, I know,' said Costa in an equally low voice. 'I talked to some of the chambermaids, they knew all about the Windsor's visit. They were disappointed that the Duchess never arrived.'

Lopes gave a little grunt of laughter. 'So much for it being a big secret.'

'Indeed, sir.'

They reached the car and got inside, Costa in the driver's seat. 'Where to now, sir?'

Where indeed, thought Lopes.

'Nowhere for the moment. Let's just mull this over,' he said. 'So, Santiago and Vogel were arrested trying to break into the presidential suite where the ex-king of England was due to stay — but never actually did. Why did they do that?'

'To plant something incriminating?' said Costa.

'Or some kind of microphone? Remember Vogel was caught with wires and electrical equipment.'

'Possibly, sir, I wonder...'

'What do you wonder, Alvares?'

'It's possible that the evidence collected from the break-it was photographed. They've started doing that. It might be worth a check with the records office.'

Lopes nodded, 'Yes, please do that.'

'The king did come to Portugal didn't he. I mean the ex-king?'

'Yes, he did.'

'Where did he stay?'

Lopes frowned, trying to remember. 'Somewhere out of the city as far as I remember, somewhere on the coast. He was here about a month, him and his wife. He came into Lisbon sometimes, to go to the embassy and use the bank. There was always a fuss about security when he did.' Lopes bit his lip. 'I remember there being a lot of tension when he was here, even more than usual. It was a great relief when he and his wife left.'

Costa nodded. 'So that could explain what Vogel and Santiago were doing at the hotel.'

'It could,' said Lopes. 'But it doesn't explain why both men were murdered, does it?'

Costa frowned for a moment until the penny dropped. 'Ah, they couldn't have recorded them at the hotel because the duke never stayed there and they were caught.' He frowned again. 'You said *both* murders?'

Lopes nodded. 'Yes, I did. I think we have to assume the worst given all that has happened, that Santiago was deliberately killed by parties within the police to silence him.'

'Perhaps the two of them did succeed in planting microphones later?' said Costa. 'Perhaps at the house where he stayed?

Lopes nodded. 'It's possible.' He checked his watch. 'We need to investigate this more. I know the poor chap that got the short straw of organising the duke's security from the police side. He retired straight afterwards, probably because of the strain of the visit. It was hard for everyone.'

'Are you going to see him?' Lopes nodded. 'You go and investigate the situation with the photographs of the evidence. I'll go and see Alberto. see what he remembers.'

'Should we meet back at the office later?'

'No, it's getting late, it's the weekend. You go home and see your family.'

'Thank you, sir. you too.'

Lopes just nodded.

SATURDAY, 17TH MAY, 1941

12.30 PM

'Dinis, my boy, good to see you.'

Lopes grasped the older man's hand. 'You too, Alberto.'

Alberto kept hold of Lopes' hand and drew him closer, 'Though not to see you in such circumstances,' he murmured, 'You were a fool. Why didn't you just back down and let things go? That would have been the best way. Bend not break.'

'I know but...'

'And now you've ended up working for that bunch of thugs at the PVDE. I thought you were better than that, much better.' Alberto sighed, then released Lopes' hand and smiled. 'But you're still you, Dinis. How can I help you?'

He indicated the chair in front of the dark wood desk that formed the centrepiece of Alberto's study. His home was a comfortable one in a nice suburb. Retirement seemed to be suiting him, Lopes couldn't remember Alberto looking so relaxed. He felt a pang of envy.

'Thanks, Alberto,' he said. 'I'm investigating a murder - actually probably three murders that might be connected.'

Alberto frowned. 'That doesn't sound good. "Probably" and "might be"? It sounds like you're struggling.'

Lopes gave a wry side. 'You're not wrong there,' he said.

'So how can I help you?'

'The connection may be the visit of the former king of England last year.'

Alberto sighed heavily and shook his head. 'Oh, him,' he said. 'Good heavens, what a nightmare having him and his entourage in the country was. The Duke of Windsor and his wife are some of life's awkward characters.'

Lopes nodded. 'I'd heard he was difficult to deal with.'

'Difficult is not the word. He was like a sulky child, everyone around him was treated like servants, me included. I was glad when he finally got on a ship and left.'

'He wasn't staying in the city, was he?'

'No, he was out at the house of the banker, Espirito Santo. His villa is on the coast, at Cascais.'

'What day did he arrive?'

'It was early in July, the 3rd I think.'

'And he stayed about a month?'

Alberto nodded and gave a rueful sigh. 'But it felt a lot longer.'

'Because he was a difficult character?'

'No, I mean, yes, he was difficult, and that wife of his too, but the biggest problem was that he was the focus of attention of all the big players, the British on one side and the Spanish and Germans on the other. It was like wasps at a picnic, you couldn't keep them away.'

'Why were they so interested in him?'

'Because the man was a menace. He was forever talking down the British war effort, saying they were bound to lose and that they should do a deal with Hitler. He met Hitler before the war, did you know that?'

Lopes shook his head. 'No, I took very little interest in what he did. I suppose, given his background, the British wanted to shut him up whilst the Germans wanted exactly the reverse?'

'Exactly. up to the point of, if rumours are correct, kidnapping him and taking him back to Germany: Alberto shook his head. 'It was an utter nightmare, trying to keep him safe. Imagine the problems it would have created for the Estado Novo if anything had happened to him whilst he was here. There would certainly have been some local involvement which we couldn't have hidden. You must realise that there are factions pulling one way and the other?'

Lopes laughed. 'Indeed, I know that only too well.' He frowned. 'Was it widely known what the Duke was saying at that time?'

Alberto nodded. 'Oh yes. It didn't help that the man drank heavily and, when he was in his cups, it didn't matter to him what he said, who he was talking to, or who might be listening. The British were beside themselves; they couldn't wait to get him out of the country and away to his island exile where they could control him again. But the bastard didn't want to go. And the Nazi's absolutely didn't want him to.'

Lopes noted all this down. It was no real surprise; he'd heard rumours and listened to the gossip at the time but there was something that didn't add up. 'Alberto,' he said, 'I know that if I reveal something about my investigation it won't go any further, will it?'

'I feel a little insulted that you should even ask that,' said Alberto. 'But I understand why you had to.'

'Thank you. The man at the centre of the case, someone who is now dead, is suspected of trying to plant a microphone in a hotel room where the Duke of Windsor was expected to stay. Does that make any sense to you?'

Alberto frowned and nodded to himself whilst he thought about Lopes' question. 'In a way I suppose it does, as I said, the spies of the warring parties were stirred up by the duke's visit, it would make sense that they would try to listen in to his conversations. But,' he went on, 'If you were asking whether this man's death might be connected with this, I can't see it. As I said, the Duke was loose lipped, he didn't seem to care what he said, to whom, and this was widely known.'

Lopes used the pause whilst he wrote this down in his notebook to frame his next question. 'What if there was a recording of what Windsor was saying? Wouldn't that be embarrassing?'

'A gramophone record?'

'I presume so, I'm not an expert but it would have to be that I suppose. Something that the Nazis could use for propaganda?'

'Well, yes, that would be something that I'm sure the British would choose to suppress,' said Alberto. 'At least if it had come out at that time.'

'The British? Not the Germans?'

'No, of course not. Why would the Nazi's be concerned about suppressing it?' Alberto's shrewd old eyes regarded Lopes with some amusement. 'So you think there was German involvement in his death?'

'Possibly.'

'Then no, that makes no sense, does it? Was this man's death recent?'

'A couple of days ago, yes.'

'Then that makes no sense either,' said Alberto.

'What do you mean?'

'What the ex-king was saying last summer *was* sensitive at that time but only at that time. The Nazi's had knocked France out of the war and looked to be on the verge of sweeping across the channel. England could have chosen not to fight. The King's opinion could have swayed that. Now Churchill has rallied the country behind him and the threat of an invasion seems to have gone. You even get senior Nazi's like Hess flying to Britain on a peace mission.'

Lopes looked up from his notebook. 'Is that why Hess went?' he said. 'I've not been following the news.'

'That's what he said apparently. Berlin says he's crazy. He does look a bit touched, doesn't he?' Alberto smiled. 'But he's not important, your case is, and it looks like you might have reached a dead end on this lead.'

Lopes nodded. 'Yes, it looks that way.' He sighed. 'Damn, I really thought we were getting somewhere at last.'

Alberto rose. 'Sometimes I miss police work,' he said. 'Then I see former colleagues like yourself and am reminded of the frustrations of the job and am glad that I am retired. I'm sorry, my boy, that really must sound selfish?'

Lopes also had risen. 'No, it sounds an eminently sensible position and a very enviable one right now. Alberto, thank you. You really have been most helpful. Even if it means that I've reached a dead end.'

SATURDAY, 17TH MAY 1941

2.12 PM

Lopes strolled to the tram stop deep in thought. They had made progress, there was no doubt about that, but it seemed the case was like a pit; the deeper they dug the less they could see.

The tram arrived and he got on, paying for his ticket almost without noticing.

So, there *was* a connection to the former British King. Vogel and Santiago had been trying to break into the hotel room where he was expected to stay.

And there the light faded, expected to stay but didn't so the two men's efforts had failed. And what was the point in making a recording anyway if it was widely known what the man was saying? This was what, ten months ago? Why wait until now to create trouble? Did that mean there was no connection between the two men's deaths and the Duke of Windsor's few weeks in the country the previous year?

Lopes sighed. It was quite possible it wasn't connected, that they'd got on the wrong track that led to another dead end.

But something told him there was a connection and this shouldn't be dismissed. His instincts as a policeman had usually served him well, he'd learned not to ignore them.

The tram rocked and rattled as it passed over a set of points, bringing him back to the here and now. He'd almost missed the stop he needed to take to switch lines to take the one that brought him closer to home. The tram was already slowing, ready to stop. He rose, ready to alight.

But then a thought struck him; why was he going home? There was nothing there for him. If he stayed on then he would pass close to where his former mistress lived. The boy — his son — might be out playing. It was a long shot but it had been weeks since Lopes had seen him.

It might be a desperate, sad thing to do but that's exactly what he was: a desperate and sad burned-out man in need of a lift. He sat down again. Farther down the tram a man who had stood did the same. Lopes gave a little smile; he was glad that he was not the only indecisive person in Lisbon. He sought out the man's face, wanting to share a sympathetic moment but he was looking away. For a second Lopes wondered if he was avoiding eye contact but then dismissed the notion; his fellow traveller was just engrossed in his own thoughts, as, of course, Lopes himself was.

Yes, back to his conundrum.

The engineer, the thief and the king - the ex-king. Two dead and one exiled.

Connected but not connected.

He absently watched the street as the tram laboured its way up the hill. This was not an area he knew well but there looked to be some nice-looking cafés and bars. His thoughts went to Fado. Perhaps they sang it here? It was always good to find somewhere new.

Elena might like Fado.

He frowned.

Why had he just thought of her?

Yes, she was part of this but why had he thought of her now? The thought had been sudden, Clear, almost like he'd just —'

Abruptly Lopes rose and pressed the bell to tell the driver to pull up at the next stop. Impatiently he urged it to arrive. When it did, he didn't wait for the tram to come to a complete halt but jumped off when it had slowed enough not to risk a fall. As it was, he stumbled momentarily but quickly recovered and hurried back down the street which the tram had just climbed. He walked up to the café the tram had just passed and, standing beside the window out of sight, cautiously leaned across so he could see in.

The café was only half-full, it was, after all mid-afternoon on a Saturday, people had other things to do like shopping, going to football matches, and lunchtime was some hours ago now (something Lopes' stomach reminded him of at that moment; he eaten nothing since breakfast.). Whatever, he had a good view of Elena. She was sat with a man on a table at the back of the café, he with his back to the window. They were leant forward towards each other suggesting their conversation was taking place in whispers. The body language did not suggest an intimate conversation, no this looked more like a business transaction than one between lovers.

Although, Lopes mused, a transaction for an intimate act could not be ruled out.

He stepped away from the window, disgusted at himself for having that thought. Elena was a survivor, a refugee, an orphan in a world gone crazy, she did what she needed to do. He was the same, he was in no position to judge.

So, what was she doing now? Was this anything to do with the case? It seemed unlikely, a long shot.

Yet he had a feeling, deep down, that she was the key. His empty stomach rumbled again.

Well, there was only one way to find out. He could kill two birds with one stone. Also, it was getting darker, the clouds were gathering and their vigour suggested a thunderstorm. Shelter would be a good idea.

He went into the cafe and walked straight up to the couple.

SATURDAY, 17TH MAY 1941

2.36 PM

Lopes saw Elena react the instant she saw him. There was alarm in her eyes and she started to rise. Lopes guessed she had acted instinctively and then found some control because she sat back down and even forced a smile.

'Inspector,' she said. 'This is a surprise.'

'Miss Katz, indeed,' said Lopes. 'I was just passing and saw you and, as I'd missed lunch...' He smiled too, hoping to put her at ease but, in fact, she'd quickly regained the confidence she'd shown at their first meeting. Lopes glanced at her table companion. He was not someone he recognised though there was something about his dress and style that whispered 'American'.

'That was lucky then,' she said.

As Elena hadn't offered an introduction, Lopes thrust out his hand. 'Dinis Lopes, PVDE.'

The man had risen and, briefly, displayed some alarm at the mention of where Lopes was from, his eyes flicking to Elena and a quick, almost accusatory frown passed across his face before he, too, forced himself to smile and turn to Lopes. He put out his hand. 'Patrick Connolly, US Embassy.'

The accent confirmed Lopes' assessment even without the confirmation of the man's status, added, the inspector guessed, to point out he was a diplomat just in case this was a more official intervention than Lopes had suggested.

'If you don't mind, inspector, we're a little busy,' said Elena.

'Actually, we've finished,' said Connolly, getting up and putting his hat on. He nodded towards Elena. 'See you around, honey. I'll be in touch.'

'But…' said Elena, then seemed to bite her tongue.

'Please don't leave on my account, Senor Connolly,' said Lopes. 'I don't want to interrupt. I *really* did just come in for a late lunch.'

'That's fine, inspector, I *really* was leaving anyhow.'

Connolly turned and walked out of the cafe.

Elena glanced up at the inspector, pure fury burning in her eyes. 'Well? Don't Just stand there. Sit if you're staying.'

Lopes smiled at her less-than-warm invitation and did as he was told. It reminded him of his former mistress, overcoming the spikiness and the aggressive barriers to get close was strangely appealing. Did he feel the same way about Elena? She was attractive and –

'Are you just going to sit there and stare?' Elena's dark eyes flashed at him, like warning beacons. 'I thought you said you were hungry. Just damn well order something.'

He raised his hand to summon a waiter over. 'Can I get you something? Another coffee? A pastry?'

'I'm fine, thanks.'

'I can't eat alone. Please, take something.'

'Who said I was staying?' she said. 'I'll have my bill,' she said to the waiter.

A couple came in from the street, totally drenched. The waiter left their table and fussed around them, saying if they sat, he'd go and find some towels. The threatened rainstorm had clearly arrived.

'You can't go out in this,' said Lopes. 'Stay until it clears up.'

She puffed out her cheeks. 'All right. I'll have a coffee.'

Lopes placed the order when the waiter returned, adding another coffee and some salt cod for himself then sat back.

Time for business.

'Who is Mr. Connolly to you?' he said. Elena just crossed her arms. 'Your new protector?'

'None of your business.'

'Everything is my business. It's my job to deal with threats to the state from home and abroad. You in weak position. A refugee and one who has dubious status in Portugal, Miss Katz. I'd be very careful if I was you.'

She continued to stare at him defiantly. 'And here was me thinking you were better than that, inspector,' she said. 'It seems not.

You're just like the others; an officious bully, a coward using your badge for power.'

"The others?"

Elena shook her head. 'Forget it,' she muttered. The waiter brought the coffees and the food, giving Lopes a moment to regroup. He'd been clumsy; this wasn't the way to handle her. He took a sip of his coffee; it was a good brew, strong and fresh.

Another wet and miserable looking customer came into the cafe. Good, thought Lopes, still raining. He had time to recover this.

But something was making him uneasy, some instinct causing the hairs on the back of his neck to prickle. What was it? The man who had just come in. Did he know him? Someone he'd arrested? He couldn't be expected to remember everyone. Still, Lopes tried to recall where he'd seen him before. It was difficult though; the newcomer kept his head down and his hat shielded his features. He'd gone and asked the barman something who'd pointed towards the other end of the bar towards the telephone.

'So are we just going to sit here in silence like an old married couple, ones who can't stand each other anymore?"

Elena's words dragged his attention back to her. Was that a lucky guess about his life or was this young woman that astute? Possibly the latter, she'd needed to survive on her wits, after all.

'Please accept my apologies.'

'What for? For having a failing marriage?'

'For using my position to try to pressure you. I take it other policemen have used their power to get what they wanted?'

'Yes, they have. But then, don't we all use what we have to get what we want?'

'We do. Was that what you were doing with the American?'

He was still half watching the man at the bar who had finished his telephone conversation but had stayed close by it. What was he waiting for?

'I told you, that's none of your business.'

'And, despite what I said about not wanting to use my position, it still *is* my business, isn't it?'

'Still why should I answer? This was a private meeting with Mr. Connolly.'

Elena took a sip of her coffee whilst Lopes regrouped. She kept her head down and stared into the dark liquid.

'Come on, I'm sure there's a perfectly innocent explanation of why he was with you. You are, after all, a very attractive young woman.'

Abruptly Elena looked up at him and smiled.

'Ah, so that's it, is it?' she said.

'What is?'

'You're jealous. You think there's something between me and Connolly. You want me for yourself.'

Lopes actually felt himself blush.

'No, of course not.'

'Of course not? Oh, you don't think I'm attractive then?'

'No, I do but—'

'So you're not interested in me because I'm Jewish, is that it? So that's the way the land lies.'

'Miss Katz, please stop it. I meant that I wasn't flirting with you. I just want answers. Anyway, you're half my age.'

'That's never stopped any man ever, has it?'

Lopes couldn't help but smile.

'No, alright you're right on that last fact. But to be clear, the reason I'm not flirting with you is that I'm investigating a crime. A series of crimes in fact.'

Elena sipped her coffee and nodded thoughtfully. 'So, I'm a suspect?'

'I think you're involved, yes.'

'I didn't kill Uwe.'

'I know that,' said Lopes. 'But...'

'But what?'

'But you know more than you say you do; I'm convinced of that.'

Elena's face gave nothing away. 'Why would you say that?' she said. 'Have you got evidence?'

'No, but there's a lot circumstantial that points to you.'

'Like what?'

'You lived with Vogel. His activities, I believe, are the key to all that happened.'

'Lived with, past tense. Uwe is dead and I've been evicted from the apartment.'

'An apartment that shows signs of being thoroughly searched. Did you know that?'

Elena still remained impassive. 'That's no surprise. Uwe had many valuables. He was a wealthy man. People know he's dead. They want what he had.'

'Yes, but most of those valuables were ignored in the search. So they were looking for something else.'

Lopes watched Elena closely for a reaction. She sipped her coffee and gave none.

'What?' she said.

'What do you mean what?'

'What were they looking for?'

'I don't know.'

'Then how am I supposed to help you, inspector? You think I'm involved but you don't know how. You think someone was looking for something Uwe might have had but you don't know what.' She shook her head. 'Poor inspector. You're not getting very far, are you?'

'No, I'm damn well not, because people like you obstruct me at every turn.'

'Me? How am I obstructing you?'

'How? Because you know very well what it is I'm looking for.'

Elena smiled but said nothing.

'In fact I think it's something that you have. Something that you were using to barter with Mr. Connolly perhaps. For a passage to the States.'

There was a slight reaction. It was fleeting but that had hit home, there was no doubt.

'You think I'm bartering this unknown thing with a man I've just met for a way out of Lisbon?' Elena laughed. 'You have a vivid imagination, inspector.'

'I believe that's the truth,' he said.

'What could I possibly have that would interest someone from the US consulate?' she said. 'Apart from the obvious of course, the thing you so gallantly suggested. That I was whoring myself for a meal and a roof over my head.' She stood up. 'I've had enough of this.'

'It's a recording, isn't it?' said Lopes.

'What?' He saw her swallow. Again, this had hit home.

'Yes. Of the former British King.'

She said nothing.

'You have a disk or a cylinder somewhere.'

Elena laughed. Suddenly she looked relieved. 'A record, really? Would you like to search me for it? Perhaps I should take my clothes off right here so you can look for it? I may have a phonograph in my knickers too.'

She started to unbutton her blouse.

'Don't be silly,' he said. 'Stop it and sit down.'

Elena glanced outside. It had brightened up considerably.

'Thanks for the coffee. I'm going to take my chances with the rain.' She started to fasten her coat. 'Unless you have plans to detain me?'

For a moment Lopes considered doing just that. But then he noticed something. The man who he'd thought he'd recognised had reacted to Elena getting up. His eyes were on her.

'No? ' said Elena. 'Good. See you around, inspector." she headed for the door.

Lopes got it. He made the connection. He'd remembered where he'd seen him.

He swore under his breath, threw some money on the table and hurried after her.

She hadn't gone far. He took her arm and pushed her forward. 'Keep walking,' he said. 'We're in trouble.'

SATURDAY, 17TH MAY 1941

3.06 PM

'What? What are you doing? Get off me.'

She tried to wriggle free but Lopes ignored Elena's protests and hustled her down the street.

'I was followed,' he said. 'I was slow, it took me a while to realise. He was on the tram with me.'

'So? That's no excuse to - ow! That hurts.'

Lopes pushed her roughly into an alleyway. 'Be quiet!' he hissed.

'Who was? What are you hiding from?'

'The man from the tram, I told you. I saw him use the café's telephone. He was calling in the troops.' Lopes peered around the edge of the building back down the street. He'd seen a car coming towards them from the opposite direction, in a hurry. It had looked awfully like the one who'd followed him from Santiago's apartment.

'So what? So, they are after you, why is that my problem?'

She shook herself free and tried to walk away but Lopes grabbed her and pulled her back out of sight.

'Because they are not after me. They were following me and let me be. Then they saw you. Then it all changed.'

'But... how could they...' she began, then closed her mouth.

'How could they know what you have? Because Vogel told them, that's how. He told them what you have – Damn!'

The man from the tram was walking up the street, looking from left to right, obviously searching for them. A car pulled up alongside him, another was behind. That route out was closed.

'His reinforcements have arrived,' he said.

'And you've dragged us into a dead end! Brilliant move.'

He looked down the alleyway. She was right, there were houses on both sides, At the end of the alley there was a wall perhaps ten feet high and, in it, an old door. That looked like their best chance.

'Come on,' he said. 'We can't stay here.'

She didn't resist as Lopes pulled her towards the door.

'It's locked,' she said.

'How do you know?'

She gave him a withering look. 'You've obviously never had to live rough.' She pointed at the door. 'There's no handle. It will be bolted on the other side.'

He tried pushing it. She was right.

'Have you got a gun?' she was looking back over her shoulder.

'No,' said Lopes. 'I never carry one.'

'Great,' said Elena, raising her leg and kicking the door. It didn't move. 'Help me.' Lopes didn't hesitate, he stood alongside her and they kicked in union. The door stubbornly stayed where it was, it might look rickety but it proved to be well-built. Elena looked up. 'I can get over there if you give me a boost.'

'But...' protested Lopes.

'I'll open the door from the other side. Come on, they'll be here.'

'Alright,' said Lopes, bending down and putting his hands together. Elena put her foot in his hands and he lifted, marvelling at how light she was. Elena grasped the top of the wall and pulled herself to the top, giving Lopes a glimpse of a shapely, stocking clad leg.

Then she was over and out of sight.

A shout came from behind him, at the top of the alley.

'Elena, come on,' he urged. 'Open the door.'

But there was no sound of bolts being drawn. She'd abandoned him to his fate.

He turned and faced his pursuers.

There were half-a-dozen men, all armed.

He reached for his badge.

'PVDE, stop,' he said.

The first man didn't hesitate. He clubbed Lopes in the face with his revolver.

SATURDAY, 17TH MAY 1941

3.12 PM

Lopes had no chance to defend himself, he fell under a volley of blows, followed by kicks as he lay on the ground. All he could do was roll into a fetal position and ride it out, his hands over his head, his knees drawn up to his groin and stomach.

'Where is she? Where's the fucking Jew bitch?'

'Yid lover.'

'Leave him. They'll be hell to pay if we top another cop.'

Lopes listened with detachment yet most definitely with interest. He was pleased to hear his most vigorous assailant swear in frustration but was less happy when he received a final kick that got through his guard and into his guts, driving the breath from his body. He was left gasping, gulping down great gulps of air, unable to hear them leave but he knew they had — he was no longer being kicked after all — then he spent some time on his haunches trying not to retch.

It was probably a good five minutes before he was able to stand and take in his surroundings. Elena was long gone but had she got away from her pursuers? Who were they in any case? Lopes grunted at his stupidity "Yid lover". It was surely pretty obvious who they supported and what they'd done before, the reference to killing another cop made it even more certain.

But they were Portuguese not German, though one had an accent.

He was sure he had heard the voice before, but where?

He couldn't place him.

But, still, he was alive.

Lopes was guilty about feeling thankful for the young constable's demise but it was a fact; If he hadn't been sacrificed surely they'd have had no qualms about finishing him off. In a way though, this was the crime solved: this gang were the killers that he'd originally been tasked to catch, in his mind's eye he pictured the one man he'd got a good view of, the one who had pistol-whipped him, committing his features to memory.

'One day, you bastard,' he murmured to himself.

The case was not solved because the real investigation was of something else. And that something else clearly involved Elena. Had she got away? Lopes laughed to himself; despite the pain this caused him (he suspected he'd got at least one broken rib). Of course she'd got away, that woman was a survivor, she'd not have got this far if she wasn't. But how long could she go on surviving with killers like that after her? He needed to find her. And find out what she had.

He wasn't going to find her in this stinking alleyway. He needed to get home, clean up and get back to work.

MONDAY 19TH MAY 1941,

8.20 AM.

Costa's mouth dropped open when Lopes stepped into the office.

'I know,' said Lopes. 'Not a pretty sight, is it?'

His face was less swollen than it had been on Sunday but it was still bad and there was a livid bruise where the gun barrel had impacted on his cheek.

'What happened?'

Lopes explained, as well as letting Costa know his findings.

'A recording you think?' he said. 'Of the Duke?'

'I think so, though why it is important given how loose lipped he was I just don't know.' He nodded at the envelope that was on Costa's desk. 'Are those the evidence photographs?'

'Yes sir. Prints from the original negatives.'

'Are there any wax disks or cylinders?'

'No sir. Nor a *wire* reel. but...' Costa frowned.

'But?'

'There is something that might be to do with recording,' said Costa. He tipped out the contents of a buff envelope onto the desk, photographs, and sorted through them. 'Here,' he said, looking at one. 'I couldn't work out what this was but now it makes sense.' He handed a picture over. 'Could that be something?'

It showed a reel, like you'd get with a cine film but smaller and, wound on it, looking a little like exposed film, was a thin tape, some of which had been pulled out to demonstrate what it looked like.

'I've never seen anything like it,' Lopes murmured. 'But it could be a recording medium. With wire recorders, I believe that the sound is recorded by means of magnetism. Don't ask me how, I'm not that technical but I wonder...' He stared at the tape as if willing it to give up its secrets. 'I presume the PVDE has a surveillance section?'

'Yes sir.'

'It will be supported by a technical department,' he said. 'Let's go and find them and
show them this,' He picked up the photo. 'Come on Costa,' he said. 'We'll get to the bottom of this yet.'

*

.'Yes, I know who you are,' the head of the surveillance section glared at them. 'Everyone in the PVDE has heard of your ridiculous little section. We all think Oliveira has lost his mind.'

Lopes smiled 'If he has then Capitan Lourenço has too because he seems to be the one behind our appointment. I'm sure he'd be interested in your opinion.'

The section head visibly paled at this. 'There's no need for threats,' he muttered, 'I didn't say I wasn't going to help you.' He scribbled a. note and handed it to Lopes. 'Take that to our technicians. They deal with our equipment. They'll be best placed to help you. Down the corridor, turn right at the end.'

'Most kind,' said Lopes.

The section chief just glared at him.

*

The chief technician glanced at the note, sighed and gave it back to Lopes.

'Right,' he said resignedly. 'I'll drop what I'm doing, should I? Bloody hell, the old man is the first to complain if things are late but go on. What do you want?'

'We wondered if you recognised this.'

Costa passed over the photographs of the strange tape. The man's frown faded as his expression changed from surprise to deep interest.

'Hmm,' he said. 'That *is* interesting, where did it come from?'

'It was found in the possession of someone who tried to break into a hotel room. we think it could be something to do with recording.'

The technician nodded thoughtfully. 'Yes, it could be.'

'So, what is it?'

'It's magnetic tape. It records sound. I'd heard rumours that the Germans were developing it.'

Lopes and Costa exchanged glances.

'Germans? The state or private companies?'

'Aren't they one and the same now?' The technician smiled 'But, yes, private companies. BASF or Telefunken, I can't recall which.'

'Vogel worked for –' began Costa but Lopes cut him off.

'What are the advantages of this over normal recording methods?' he asked.

'Just about everything, if it works like it's supposed to. Clarity, Portability, the length of recording possible. There's nothing really like it,'

Lopes nodded to himself.

'This would need a special machine?'

'Yes,' said the technician.

'What would it look like?' said Costa.

'I don't know, do I? It's experimental.'

'Yes,' said Lopes patiently. 'But surely you could speculate. You are an expert after all.'

He made eye contact with Costa who gave a little nod. That was the way, massage the man's ego.

The technician gave this question some thought. He pulled over a pencil and a piece of paper from the desk behind him. 'Yes, I think I can work it out.' The pencil hovered over the paper for a few seconds then he started to sketch. 'This reel would run the tape to another, the tape running through a device that would both act as a method of recording the sound onto the magnetic tape and also reading it afterwards. That means that these reels would have to be driven, well one of them at least, possibly both, yes both to allow the tape to be rewound... ' The man tapped his teeth with the pen for a few moments then sketched in a rectangle round the two reels. 'You'd need a box like this one, possible the size of a gramophone or a small suitcase.'

Lopes and Costa looked at each other, then said together; 'The suitcase! Armstrong, damn and blast him!' much to be puzzlement of the technician.

MONDAY 19TH MAY 1941, 9.35 AM.

They sat, despondently, in their basement office.

'Armstrong,' muttered Lopes puffing hard on his pipe. 'Someone we can't touch. Of course.' He shook his head bitterly.

'Is it worth trying to track down MacDonald?' said Costa. 'We've got an address for him.'

'Somehow, I doubt he'll be there;' said Lopes. 'And the machine certainly won't be, that will be safely inside the British Embassy.'

'But –' began Costa. '

I know, we've got to do something. Let's go and check him out.'

*

MacDonald's apartment was only a few streets away from Vogel's in the same upmarket neighbourhood. It was easy to find but, as expected, MacDonald was not there.

'I'm sorry, gentlemen,' the concierge said. 'Senor MacDonald has not been here for home for many days.'

'Open it up,' said Lopes.

'But...'

'Do it,' said Costa.

The concierge did so. The results were both disappointing and eye-opening. Disappointing because it was obvious that the man was not there but eye-opening for the opulence of the fixtures and fittings. MacDonald lived in luxury, even more so than Vogel had.

Lopes caught Costa's eye. The younger man looked quite angry. 'This can't be legal,' he muttered.

'It probably isn't,' said Lopes. 'But he's got away with things, well, until now.'

'He should be watched,' said Costa. 'I'm sure we'd find something to take him down.'

'Maybe so, maybe so,' said Lopes. 'Whatever, neither our man nor our mysterious recording machine is here. So, we... wait, was that gunfire?'

There were a couple more sharp cracks.

They hurried out of the flat and downstairs. All seemed quiet. 'Perhaps it was firecrackers,' said Costa, frowning. 'I mean, shots in Lisbon? On the streets?'

'I know. But after the last few —'

There were more sharp cracks, followed by a scream.

'Come on Costa,' said Lopes, setting off towards where the sounds seemed to have come from. Costa, of course, being younger and not having damaged lungs, quickly overtook him.

There was something about this scene that reminded Lopes of the death that had started all this; he could picture Jorge, the sergeant, the older man, struggling to keep the young Constable, da Silva in view. A scenario that ended in death. It was all happening again.

'Costa,' he wheezed, 'Come back, please.'

But it was too late, Costa had reached the end of the street and turned left, out of sight, just as more shots were fired,

Lopes laboured towards the road end. It was like a nightmare, one where he needed to run but couldn't because his feet felt like they were made of lead. He got to the road end just in time to be showered by splinters of stone as bullets thudded into the wall just by his head. He threw himself down behind a parked car.

'Costa,' he called. 'Costa, where are you?'

There was no reply. Lopes peered around the car, trying to work out what was going on. He was on the edge of a small square, at the centre of which was a plinth surrounding a drinking fountain. He recognised it as the one outside Vogel's apartment. Of course, that made sense. A couple were hiding behind the fountain but whether they were involved or not or just bystanders caught up in the mess he couldn't tell. There was a body in the middle of the road, a large man in a bloodied, pale suit. So, there'd been at least one casualty.

But where was Costa? Who was shooting? At first he couldn't tell but then a new volley of shots started. He spotted at least two masked men on the far side of the street, one in a doorway, ducking behind the stonework as return fire came in, the other, like Lopes, crouching behind a car, the latter bearing the scars of at least a dozen bullet holes. Where was the opposing fire coming from? Lopes looked down the pavement on his side of the square. No one there but, in the far corner he caught side of a man sat with his back to a car. Lopes recognised him; it was Armstrong, the British diplomat.

He was armed with a small pistol which he was reloading. Once this was done, he turned and peered around the back of the car, ready to fire.

Immediately shots were fired at him from the other side, making him duck back.

Where was Costa? At first he couldn't see him but then realised that the couple behind the fountain were Costa and Elena. What was she doing here? Costa had his gun out and was firing back at the masked gunmen.

They were trapped, isolated. Lopes knew they'd be in deep trouble if and when Costa ran out ammunition, they were closer to the gunmen than Armstrong was. Unable to fire back they'd quickly be taken. Costa must know this, Lopes saw him looking over, it was clear he was looking for somewhere to retreat to on the far side of the street.

It was too open; they wouldn't make it. Unless there was a distraction.

Lopes stood up.

'Hey, over here!' he shouted at the gunmen, waving his arms, then dived for cover as a fusillade peppered the car. As he cowered he was sure he heard a cry and a grunt of pain.

When he risked looking again, Costa and Elena were gone. Had they reached safety? He couldn't see them.

A car engine started, Lopes spotted it, a Ford 10. It started to roll, swinging out from its parking place into the street. Instantly it attracted the attention of the shooters, the windscreen shattered and holes were punched in the metal of the bodywork. The shots seemed to be coming from all sides and whoever was driving was encouraged to get out of here quickly, even though they had ducked down out of sight and were steering blind. The throttle was floored and the car leapt forward, spinning its wheels, creating a smokescreen. The driver popped up briefly, to check the direction and Lopes was pleased to see it was Costa who then ducked down as the car exited the square, followed by more shots. It turned a corner and disappeared.

Another volley of shots rang out, followed by answering ones from Armstrong. One of the masked shooters was creeping up on him, using the cover of a van. 'Look out!' Lopes yelled. 'Armstrong, behind the truck! '

The Englishman reacted to the danger just in time, spinning round and firing just as the masked man levelled his pistol. The man staggered away and slumped against the rear wheel of an Austin car, his automatic clattering pistol by his side. He was clearly dead.

Sirens could now be heard; the police were coming. Lopes hoped they were armed otherwise this could be a massacre. How could he warn them? He was looking for somewhere that might have a phone when he noticed that the shooting had largely died down. Peering around the car confirmed it, the shooters were withdrawing Two, on the far side of the square were attempting to drag their fallen companion away but were discouraged by both the arrival of the first police car and some parting shots from Armstrong, though Lopes was sure he was firing over their heads. Moments later they had gone.

Cautiously Lopes got to his feet. About 50 metres away, Armstrong did the same, white-faced and shocked, standing over the dead man, holding onto the car for support. Lopes went over to him.
'Are you alright?' he said.

Armstrong nodded, the coolness and confidence he had displayed at their previous meeting had gone, his hands were shaking.
'Bastards.' He kicked the corpse.

'What happened?' said Lopes.

'They were waiting, they jumped us,' he muttered.

'Us?' said Lopes.

'MacDonald and the girl.'

'The girl? Elena Katz?'

Before Armstrong could answer he looked over Lopes' shoulder. 'Damn and blast,' he muttered.

Lopes saw he was looking at the first policemen who were now edging cautiously into the square.

'You'd better give me that,' he said, nodding at the gun. 'I can't imagine it would go down well with my government if they found a diplomat was involved in a shootout, whether it was self-defence or not.'.

Armstrong didn't argue. He passed the gun to Lopes, the latter making sure the exchange was done out of sight of the policemen. It felt almost toy-like in his hands, but he knew only too well that it was a deadly weapon, a Walther PPK, a preferred concealment gun favoured by, amongst others, the Gestapo.

'Where's MacDonald?' he said.

Armstrong nodded towards the body in the road.

Lopes walked over to it and, with difficulty as the man was heavily set, rolled it over. It was, indeed, MacDonald, he'd been hit in the right cheek, throat and chest and was not a pretty sight. Armstrong turned away.

'Stop! Step away from the body and put your hands up. Now!'

A young policeman had advanced towards them, his trembling hand outstretched was holding a revolver. Others stood back, letting their bolder companion take the risk, Lopes couldn't blame them, Lisbon had its fair share of crime, but gun battles were mercifully rare.

'Wouldn't you like me to put the gun down instead?' Lopes said.

'Yes, yes, do it! Slowly.'

He waved the gun around alarmingly.

'Easy, son,' said Lopes. 'We're no danger to you.'

He put the gun on the road.

'Kick it over to me.'

The young policemen had obviously been watching Hollywood gangster movies but Lopes did as he was asked.

'Look, lad, I'm on your side. I'm PVDE. To prove it I'm about to reach into my pocket and take my badge out so I'd be grateful if you could keep your finger away from the trigger. Police issue revolvers are notoriously variable in quality. it would be just my luck if you had one with a hair trigger.' He smiled to reassure the young man. 'Is that okay?'

'Yes, alright but no sudden movements.'

'I wouldn't dream of it,' said Lopes, very slowly and carefully reaching into his pocket and extracting the badge. There was an audible sigh of relief from the young constable and an easing of tension from the other policemen. 'And this man is a British diplomat, he has immunity.'

'But I should —'

'He just got caught up in all this.' He nodded towards Armstrong who seemed to be recovering his composure. Armstrong showed the young constable his papers.

'Thanks, sir, sorry sir.'

'Can I have my gun back?'

'Yes, of course. Please.'

The young policeman picked up the gun and passed it back to Lopes, then looked round, showing some confusion. 'Er... what do I do and... what happened?'

'There's been an assassination. It seems that man,' Lopes pointed at MacDonald's body. 'Was the target, though why he was I have no idea. For now, you should seal off the square, let no one in or out, the murder squad will, no doubt, want to interview all the witnesses. Armstrong, I'll escort you out of here, is that alright?'

'Er, yes, of course.'

The young constable looked confused 'But sir, you said —'

'I meant don't let anyone in or out except for myself and Mr. Armstrong.'

Despite the situation, Lopes couldn't resist a smile. This faded when he saw the unmasking of the slain gunman by the Austin. Lopes recognised him; he was one of Da Souza's cronies, one who'd been with him in the canteen.

The alleyway, the man's voice who he thought he'd recognised. Now he knew where he had.

Now he knew who the killers were; his own so-called colleagues in the PVDE.

'Mother of God,' he muttered.

'What is it?'

'Nothing. Come on Armstrong. Let's get you out of here.'

MONDAY 19TH MAY 1941,

10.36 AM

As soon as they were out of the square, Armstrong swore loudly in English then held his hand out. 'Give me my gun.'

Lopes stopped. 'Who the hell do you think you are, giving me orders?'

'Come on, Lopes, haven't you worked out who's giving you your instructions? Surely you realise that your little department was set up at our request?' said Armstrong.

'You mean…?'

'Of course. The whole idea was to have someone to help us solve our little problem, someone who could help us find out who had the, er, object we sought and work for us actively on our side inside the PVDE. So, hand it over.'

Lopes stared at him for a few moments until the anger that had been building within him erupted. He pulled out the pistol and jabbed it into Armstrong's ribs. 'Listen, Armstrong and listen well; I don't work for you. I don't work for anyone except the people of Portugal whatever Lourenço or Oliveira or anyone else might expect of me, so don't try and give me orders because it won't work.'

'You're making a mistake, Lopes. Don't be stupid.'

'It's you that are being stupid, Mr. Armstrong, because it's you that's on very thin ice. You carried a gun on the streets of Lisbon, something that is expressly forbidden for diplomats. Furthermore, you fired it —'

'In self-defence!'

'Whatever, you fired it and you killed a member of the PVDE. Yes, the man you shot was up to no good, you know, and I know that it won't be presented that way if it comes out. The story will be about the slaying of an officer of the state going about his legitimate duties. If it came out that it was a British diplomat who was the culprit, it would prove an immense embarrassment for your government and a victory for the Nazis.'

'There's no proof,' muttered Armstrong.

'Are you sure of that? Remember *I* witnessed it.'

'You wouldn't…'

'Wouldn't I? Believe me, Mr. Armstrong, unless you start giving me answers I will do, without hesitation.'

Now it was Armstrong's turn to stare in amazement. At last, he sighed and nodded. 'There's a cafe over there,' he said. 'I could do with a coffee. I'll answer your questions. At least as much as I'm able.'

*

Lopes ordered for both of them, and they found seats as far away from anyone else as possible.

'Right, let's get this over and done with. Ask away. It doesn't matter anyway, it's all over.' Armstrong raised his cup in a mock toast. 'Here's to Hitler and his cronies. They've won again.'

'What do you mean?'

'It's over. The woman's gone. The Jerries must have her. That means they also have the…er…the object.'

Lopes doubted this, although he hadn't seen her, he was certain Costa had her in the car with him which was why he'd left Lopes in the square but he wasn't going to tell the Englishman that if he hadn't witnessed it. For once he knew something that others didn't. 'You saw her taken?'

Armstrong shook his head. 'No but she's gone. They must have her. So, fire away.'

'I know quite a lot already,' Lopes said.

'Do you?' said Armstrong. 'Bully for you.'

'Yes, I do.'

'Go on then, enlighten me.'

Lopes could not disguise his irritation. 'Vogel recorded the Duke of Windsor during his visit to Lisbon last year on the instructions of the German intelligence agency, the Abwehr. This was done using experimental technology developed by Telefunken, a company Vogel used to work for, that used magnetic tape to record the voices. What the recording is I don't know, what I do know is that the recording was never delivered to Vogel's masters, though I don't know why. I also know that whatever is on it is so damaging that both sides are desperate to get hold of it.' He scrutinised Armstrong's face. 'How am I doing?'

Armstrong looked shocked, much to Lopes' delight. 'Alright,' he muttered. 'Keep your voice down,' he looked anxiously around the café in case anyone was listening.

'Would you prefer to talk in English?' said Lopes, switching languages. 'I learned it in Flanders. It might be a little more secure.'

'Alright,' said Armstrong. 'But what is there to talk about? She's gone and so, in that case, will be the tape.'

'It may not have.'

'What do you mean?'

Lopes mentally kicked himself for his carelessness.

'She wouldn't have had it on her, would she?'

'No but…'

'There's still a chance. And you have what I suspect is the only machine in Lisbon able to play it on, don't you?' Again, Armstrong looked surprised.

'There's probably one in the German Embassy too,' he said quietly. 'But, yes, we have one.'

'You took it from Vogel's apartment, didn't you?'

'Yes.'

'But Elena didn't know that did she? If she wanted to play the tape to someone, she'd need the machine, which is why you and MacDonald were waiting for her in Vogel's apartment, yes?'

Armstrong gave a little laugh. 'First name terms, Lopes? That's the way the land lies, is it?'

'What do you mean?'

'Oliveira said you had a weakness for the ladies. Miss Katz is easy on the eyes; I'll grant you that. But be careful, those dark and dusky looks are the cause of all this.'

Lopes chose to ignore the suggestion of his attraction to Elena. 'How do you mean?'

'Because, according to MacDonald, she was the reason Vogel hid the tape in the first place. He let her listen to it after he recovered it, she was shocked about what was on it. She begged him not to give it to his masters, to say that the recording had failed, that the tape had broken. We know he handed something over; it would have been too suspicious otherwise, Vogel was too good to have made a mistake in setting the kit up. He told MacDonald he gave them the first minute and a bit of the recording, then faked a break and handed over the rest of the blank tape.' Armstrong refilled his coffee cup from the pot. 'I suppose we should be grateful to her for doing that, otherwise the shit would have come out last year.'

'What's on it?'

Armstrong just shook his head. Lopes accepted that this was a step too far.

'Do you know why she persuaded Vogel not to hand it over?'

'That is s silly question, Inspector. I expected better of you.'

'Of course,' Lopes nodded in agreement. It was stupid; Elena was a German Jew who'd suffered at the hands of the Nazis. Of course, she wasn't going to give them a propaganda coup. 'So, you intended to grab her when she came looking for the machine.'

'That's right. And it worked like a charm. Until it all went wrong.'

'What happened?'

'I was careless. I hadn't counted on the opposition using *their* PVDE assets so openly. I'd checked the street to see if anyone was watching the flat but it looked clear. Obviously, I hadn't considered that there was a PVDE surveillance unit watching from somewhere concealed, probably across the street in another building. Whatever, we caught her all right but they were waiting for us when we took her outside. They jumped us, we were caught cold.'

Lopes frowned. 'I'm surprised they started shooting,' he said. 'If there were Germans involved. That's a good way for a quick expulsion from the country.'

'They didn't, at first. They just held us at gun point. It was Katz that caused it.'

'How?'

'MacDonald had a Webley in his pocket, he'd used it to frighten her in the flat. Outside, in the confusion she grabbed it and started shooting. God knows why.'

Lopes couldn't help smiling, Armstrong noticed. 'Why are you looking like that?' he said.

'Because it's your turn to be foolish. I understand her; she's not a victim, she's not some little girl who'd be cowed into accepting her fate, she's a survivor. She'd always fight.' Armstrong continued to look puzzled. 'Her family fled the Nazi's as a child, then they were uprooted by the invasion of France, she lost her parents and her home and future because of them. She hates them, she wouldn't let them take her.'

Armstrong shrugged, 'Maybe so but they've got her now, haven't they? And if she wanted to fight the Nazis, she should have brought the tape to us. It's the British Empire who's standing alone fighting the bastards, she knew that yet she was willing to sell it to the highest bidder.'

Lopes sipped his drink. 'She wasn't doing that. She was negotiating with the Americans, presumably for passage out of here to the States,' he said.

'I know that,' said Armstrong, 'And so what?'

'So what? The Americans are hardly unfriendly to the British, are they? Alright, they are not fighting alongside you yet but they are sending arms, yes?'

'Yes.'

'And Roosevelt wants to be directly involved as a co-belligerent.'

'Probably, yes.'

'So, selling the tape to them is hardly a hostile act, is it?'

Armstrong gave a snort of derision. 'God, Lopes, you can be naïve, can't you? Not all the Yanks want to be in the war, in fact a large minority, maybe even a small majority want to keep Uncle Sam well out of things. You might want to check who at the embassy Miss Katz was negotiating with.'

'Patrick Connolly?'

'That's the chap. He's a crony of that bastard Kennedy. He might have been the British ambassador, but he was hardly a fan of ours.'

Lopes nodded 'I see,' he said.

'Good,' said Armstrong looking at his watch. 'Are you satisfied, inspector? Have I done enough for you not to report I was on the streets of Lisbon armed?' He stood up.

'Almost,' said Lopes.

'Oh, for God's sake. What do you want, money?' Armstrong folded his arms. 'Is that what this is? A shakedown?'

'Of course, I don't,' snapped Lopes. 'I want more answers. Please, sit.'

Armstrong did, though with considerable bad grace.

'Go on then,' he said.

'This tape. It's damaging to the British, yes?'

'Obviously, yes.'

'What's on it? I mean what does the Duke say that's so bad that he didn't say around the dinner table or on the golf course? I've talked to our local head of security. The Duke wasn't exactly careful with what he said, was he?'

'No, he wasn't. He behaved like a total arse. But I don't know, I've not heard it, have I?'

Lopes nodded to himself. 'When did you find out the tape existed?'

Armstrong pulled out his cheeks, took a deep breath they exhaled through pursed lips. 'We never knew it actually did, not until a week or so ago.' he said. 'But fear that something like it might rear its ugly head? Basically, every day since he arrived in Lisbon last July.'

'How did you find out?'

'I can't tell you that,' said Armstrong, 'We have sources to protect. Sorry, if that means I get expelled so be it. Lives are at stake. That's a line I can't cross.'

'Alright, I won't push you.' Lopes frowned. 'One last question; why now?'

'Sorry?'

'Why is this so important now? Isn't what the Duke said last year ancient history? Surely with every day that has passed since last August what he said is less and less important. He's been tucked away quietly in the Bahamas since then, hasn't he?'

Armstrong's gaze flicked to another customer on the other side of the cafe. Lopes wondered if Armstrong was worried the man was listening to their conversation but that seemed unlikely as he was absorbed in his newspaper, though not, apparently the front page which still had Rudolph Hess's picture on the front, the man captured at a Hitler rally, staring up as if in worship at his leader through his mad-looking eyes.

'Yes, he's in the Bahamas,' said Armstrong. 'But he's still the King's brother. It doesn't matter when something like this comes out, it's always an embarrassment. Now, may I go?'

'Yes.'

Armstrong smiled. 'Very well, inspector. Oh, and thank you.'

'Thank you?'

'Yes. You saved my life back there.'

Lopes nodded.

It was only after Armstrong was long gone did he realise he still had Armstrong's gun.

MONDAY 19TH MAY 1941,

11.55 AM

Lopes was expecting to find Costa waiting for him back in the office but instead it was Da Souza.

'Damn you, Lopes,' he yelled. 'You and your little darkie have gone and done it now. One of my men is dead and that bitch has escaped, all thanks to your interference.'

Lopes took it all calmly.

'Your man brought that all on him himself,' he said. 'His starting shooting was all down to him and his colleagues, it had nothing to do with us.'

'It had everything to do with you. We'd have got her by now if it wasn't for you.'

'What's the matter, Da Souza? Are your German paymasters getting restless?'

'No more than your British ones are with you.'

'I don't serve any master except the Portuguese state.'

Da Souza's nose wrinkled like someone had put something rank under it. 'Yeah, right,' he said. 'I forgot that you were both naïve and stupid, so much so that you can't recognise when you are being used and who by.'

Lopes knew there was more than an element of truth in that. 'Just get out of my office, Da Souza.'

'Not before you tell me where she is.'

'Where who is?'

'That bitch Katz. Your man was seen with her, they escaped in a car. Where are they?'

'Frankly, I have no idea,' said Lopes. 'Now, as I said, get out of here.'

'Or what?'

Lopes could feel the weight of Armstrong's pistol in his pocket and, momentarily, was tempted to thrust it into Da Souza's fat face. He resisted though, it was one of the reasons he didn't like to carry one; it gave the holder too much power, too much of a temptation to resort to violence first and bypass rational argument.

'Or nothing because I know your type. You're a sad, scared little man, a bully who hasn't got the courage to do the dirty work himself. So go away, Da Souza, run off back to your Nazi friends where you can feel big and powerful.'

Lopes briefly thought Da Souza might explode but, instead, he pushed past the inspector and out of the office.

Trembling slightly, Lopes went and sat behind his desk.

Almost immediately the telephone rang.

'External line, sir,' said the operator.

'Put them through.' He waited. 'Who is this?'

'I'd rather not say who I am.'

The voice was a man's, American. Connolly? Lopes was pretty sure it was.

'What's going on? Where's Costa?'

'I believe he's safe.'

'Where is he?'

'I won't say where, not on here. It's not secure.'

'But how…'

'They'll find you,' the man said. 'Five minutes,' he added and then rang off.

Lopes stared in puzzlement at the instrument for a few moments then swore, grabbed his hat and headed out.

Thirty seconds later he was out on the street. Which way? It probably didn't matter, he set off walking towards the river. He looked behind him, as he'd expected he'd been followed. It would be one of Da Souza's men. He had a good 150 metres head start over him. He might need more.

Lopes increased his pace, just as a Citroen swung alongside him. The door was flung open, Elena was driving.

MONDAY 19TH MAY 1941,

12.15PM

'Get in!' she yelled.

Lopes did, Elena flooring the throttle even before the door was closed. He glanced back to see Da Souza's man briefly give chase on foot before realising the futility.

Lopes looked in confusion at her.

'Elena,' said Lopes. 'Where's Costa?'

'I'll tell you in a minute, when I'm sure we're not being followed.'

Lopes frowned at this but looked over his shoulder out of the back window of the car. The coast looked clear. He turned back to Elena. For the first time he saw that she had blood on her, on her sleeves and the front of her blouse.

'Are you hurt?' he said.

'No.'

'Whose blood is that? MacDonald's?'

'No. Will you be quiet?' She was looking in her mirror whilst manoeuvring the car through the narrow streets of the old town.

'Where are we going? Wait, this is the way to the British Embassy. What are you...?'

Abruptly, Elena swung the car into an alley and pulled up. When she turned to him she had a gun in her hand. He recognised it. It was Costa's service weapon.

'What are you doing with that?' he said. 'How did you...? Wait, the blood. It's Costa's isn't it? Where is he? Is he dead? Did you –' He started to reach for Armstrong's gun, still in his jacket pocket but she pushed the barrel of Costa's gun against his belly.

'Sit still and listen for once,' she said. 'If you want to see him again.'

Lopes froze. 'All right, I'm listening. Where is he?'

'Safe. He's hurt but he's safe – for now at least. No, I didn't shoot him, he caught one in the back as he drove away.'

'He's been shot? Elena, Costa's got a young family! How bad –'

'Bad enough,' she shrugged. 'He could die, I guess, frankly I don't care. He definitely will unless you get what I want.'

'Elena! You can't let him die.'

'I can and I will, believe me.'

'How do I know he's not already dead?'

'You'll have to trust me that he isn't, won't you?' She jabbed the gun into his chest. 'Look, I'm a lot of things but I'm not a liar. I stopped the bleeding. He's somewhere safe but his time his running out and you're wasting it. I suggest you start listening.'

Lopes nodded.

'All right. I suppose I've got no choice but to believe you. What do you want?'

'I need that machine, the one the British have.'

'What?' said Lopes. 'How…how exactly am I going to get that for you?'

'That's not my problem. That's yours. That British diplomat, Armstrong, he said you were his man.'

Lopes shook his head. 'But I'm not. Whatever he said, I'm not. I work for the state. I've no power over Armstrong. He's a diplomat. The machine is in the embassy.'

'As I said, that's your problem. Come on, inspector, your country need to keep the British sweet. Just do the deal.'

'This is for Connolly?'

She said nothing.

'Did he get this car for you?'

'I can steal my own cars, Lopes.'

'But he wants to hear the tape before he gives you a visa, doesn't he? That's why you are doing this, isn't it?'

'None of your business.'

'Do you know who he is? What interests he represents?'

'I don't care. All he represents to me is a way out.'

'Well, you, as a Jewess, should care. Connolly is part of a group wanting to keep America out of the war.'

'So? He's getting me passage and a visa; I don't care about anything else. I don't have anything else now. It was all taken from me when Uwe died by those vultures. I've got no money, nowhere to live. All I have is the tape. What Connolly does with it is up to him, all I want is out of this shit hole.'

'Elena, you persuaded Uwe not to pass the tape onto his masters at the Abwehr because of what was on it, didn't you? Because it would help the Nazi's and damage Jewish people, wouldn't it? That's why you did it, isn't it?'

'Yes,' she muttered. 'So?'

'So why throw it away now? Don't pass it to someone who will use it against you and yours.'

'What else am I supposed to do?'

'Let me do a deal with Armstrong for you. That I *can* do. I'm sure he'd get you passage out of Lisbon.'

She shook her head. 'Armstrong? No way. I'm not dealing with him.'

'Why?'

'Because the British are liars, they'd say anything to get the tape. I heard what their former king said about...' Despite the situation Lopes found himself holding his breath in anticipation at, at last, hearing something from the tape itself, something to justify all the death and violence it had initiated, but Elena seemed to regain some control and think better of it. 'Well, said what I heard him say. So just get me the machine.'

'And then you'll take me to Costa?'

'Yes.'

'Right. Forget the Embassy then, they'll not let me in. I'll go through my commander. He set all this up. If anyone has a direct line to Armstrong, it's him. Take me to my office.'

Elena thought about this for a second but then nodded. 'All right.' She started the car, and reversed it back out onto the road. Lopes looked at the gun. 'Don't even think about it,' she muttered. 'Even if you got it off me, I wouldn't talk. Costa would die. And remember, I know you don't carry a gun. You told me that yourself.'

Armstrong's automatic seemed to grow heavier in his pocket but he forced himself not to think about it.

'Alright. I won't do anything.' Lopes' mind was racing. 'How long will you give me?'

'Two hours. That should be enough time for you and Costa should live that long.'

'Will you call me with where we'll meet?'

'What and have the German lot ambush me? I'm guessing your phone is tapped, Lopes so even if you're honest, the Nazi lovers won't be. I'll give you a place to meet me. One where I can see whether you've kept your word. The slightest hint that you haven't and that's it. I'll put a bullet in my head and Costa dies with me.'

Lopes nodded.

'All right,' he said. 'I'll do as you ask. Where are we meeting?'

MONDAY 19TH MAY 1941,

1.35 PM

Lopes had been offered a seat but found that pacing up and down in Oliveira's outer office helped to work through his nervous energy. He'd got plenty of it; he'd been there over ten minutes. He went back to Oliveira's secretary to make another appeal.

'Please,' he said, 'I need to see the Tenente. It's a matter of life and death.'

She looked up frowning.

'I told Tenente Oliveira that, you heard me,' she said. 'He's a busy man.'

'Please. Try again.'

She tutted her displeasure but reached for the telephone. Lopes heard its brother ring muffled by the closed doors of Oliveira's inner office. 'Hello, sir, yes, he's still here. Yes, I told him that but…Inspector! No, you can't…'

Lopes ignored her. He strode to the door and opened it. Oliveira was at his desk, the telephone receiver to his ear, a look of surprise on his face.

'Sir, I'm sorry, I told him…'

'That's all right, Isobel, the inspector here is clearly upset about something. I'll see him.' He nodded at the chair in front of the desk as the secretary left, closing the door behind her. 'Let me just finish this call,' he said. 'Yes,' he said into the instrument. 'He's here now. I will call you back.' He put the telephone down. 'So, what's so urgent? I understood the item is lost.'

'No, it's not. I know who has it but that's not the point, they've got Costa, he's been shot, he's seriously –'

'Not lost? Of course that's the point. Where is it? We must get it.'

'No. We must get Costa back.'

Oliveira shook his head. 'I'm sorry, the priority is the recording, yes, I know what it is now. So, who has got it, this Jew woman, Katz? Where is she? I'll get a raid organised.' He reached for the telephone.

'No! You can't.'

Oliveira looked puzzled. 'Has she got the recording or not?'

'Yes, she has got it but she's got Costa's gun. She could kill Costa if we try to take her. If he doesn't die from loss of blood before.'

Oliveira looked puzzled. 'So? We still get the recording.'

Lopes stared at Oliveira in disbelief. 'But…Costa. He's your man, isn't he? He reports back to you on me?'

Oliveira smiled 'Of course he does. So what? Now where is she?'

Lopes shook his head. 'Costa has a wife and children.'

'You have a wife and a child too, inspector,' said Oliveira, 'Though in different places.' He gave a twisted smile. 'It doesn't mean you or any of us affect the bigger picture. We are all expendable, the Estado Novo's survival and needs trumps everything.'

Lopes felt a chill pass over him.

'Is she trying to do a deal with the Americans?' said Oliveira.

'Yes. She wants passage to the States.'

Oliveira gave a snort of laughter. 'I don't care what she wants.'

'Don't dismiss her like that,' said Lopes. 'She's a fighter. A survivor…'

'And also expendable. Let me guess, she sent you here to negotiate the passing over of the tape machine held at the British Embassy? Why do you think we'd ever agree to do that - even if I did have that sway with the British?'

'Well, you do, don't you? Have say with them? That was who you were on the telephone to, wasn't it? Armstrong? That's why my role was created, wasn't it, to do Britain's bidding, to counter the Nazi sympathisers within the PVDE?'

Oliveira smiled. 'You really are naive, aren't you, Dinis Lopes? Naive and imaginative. Nazi sympathisers? A British plot? Come on.' The smile vanished. 'Now, enough, where is she?'

'I don't know.'

'But you are meeting her?'
Lopes didn't answer.
'Where?'
'I don't know that either.'

Oliveira shook his head. 'You mean you are going to wait for her to call? Here? I don't believe that. You know every call is monitored…'

'Yes, and not just by friends.' Lopes couldn't help snapping.

Oliveira gave a little smile and nodded. 'Not just by friends, indeed. Thank you for the confirmation. Now, where are you meeting her?'

Lopes maintained a stony silence, his face set.

'Don't be stupid man. We'll find out. We'll follow you. Come on, this is your precious Costa's best chance, taking her means we can get him back.'

Lopes found himself weakening. Oliveira was probably right; this was Costa's best bet. But it was also a risk, a huge one in fact. He'd promised himself he'd get Costa home. What Elena wanted was impossible so…

'Enough!' Oliveira picked up the phone. 'Get a security detail to my office now. Have Inspector Lopes escorted back to his and tell them to wait with him.' Oliveira put the phone down. 'You see, things will work out how I want them to whatever. We'll just wait for you to go to your meeting. That will make things worse for Costa because we won't be able to prepare properly for the ambush so last chance, you stubborn, stupid man. Where are you meeting her?'

Lopes gave up. He'd tried. He opened his mouth to tell Oliveira where the meeting place was.

Then the telephone rang.

'Olivera answered it. 'What is it?' His voice was testy. 'Oh, right, yes of course. One moment.' He put his hand over the mouthpiece. 'I must take this. Your escort are in the outer office. Go with them.' Lopes rose and has he opened the door and stepped out he heard Oliveira say into the instrument; 'Capito Lourenco, sir. Yes, there is progress…'

Two typical PVDE men complete with their raincoat uniform were waiting with the secretary. One, who towered over Lopes strode across and grabbed him roughly by the upper arm. 'Come with us,' he said and dragged Lopes out of the door.

Lopes' mind raced as he was half-dragged, half-pushed through the corridors of the Headquarters' building, only a little conscious of the eyes on him and the knowledge that the news of his arrest would quickly be the talk of the PVDE. He had decided before he was whisked away but now had doubts again. Was what Oliveira was proposing, a coup to take Elena and recover the tape, the right thing for Costa? Was that it was his best chance for survival? A deal with Armstrong, the recovery of the tape machine was, he'd always known, impossible.

Yet…

Yet the cavalier and callous dismissal of Costa showed a total lack of care by Oliveira for him. An unplanned ambush increased the risk of his young assistant perishing in the crossfire.

So, it needed planning. Which meant Lopes had been right on what he'd decided; he had to tell Oliveira where the meeting was to give them some chance of preparing the ambush. It was the only way now.

They'd reached the entrance hall.

'Wait,' he said to his guards. 'I need to go back to Tenente Oliveira. I'm going to cooperate.'

To his surprise the guards ignored him and pushed him out of the door into the street.

'Hey, wait, what are you doing?'

There was no answer. A car drew up, the rear door was opened and Lopes pushed inside, the guard following.

Da Souza was sitting in the front seat, a gun in his hand which he pointed at Lopes' stomach.

'Sit still,' he said, and the car drove away.

MONDAY 19TH MAY 1941,

2.10 PM

'I've not had chance to search him, sir,' said the guard, twisting round to begin the pat down.

'Forget that,' laughed Da Souza. 'This is Dinis Lopes, the famous unarmed cop. He hates guns.'

Lopes almost blushed; he still had Armstrong's Walther in his pocket but wasn't going to tell anyone that.

'Where are you taking me? We're running out of time. Costa —'

'Be quiet,' said Da Souza. 'You are a fool, Lopes. You should never have taken this job. You have no idea what you're involved with.'

'But…'

'A man like you has too many secrets. You've too many skeletons in the cupboard, Dinis. Well, now you will find out what that means in our game. The birds are coming home to roost.'

Lopes shook his head in disbelief. What was Da Souza talking about?

Then he saw where the car had taken them to. He recognised the suburb.

'No!' he said. 'No, you can't! Leave them –'

The guard alongside him swung his fist into Lopes' midriff, driving the breath from his body.

'Shut it,' his assailant said.

Lopes fought for breath, thankful that the confines of the car had reduced the violence of the blow. His damaged lungs appreciated that they did not have to work as hard as they might have had to do.

The car pulled up outside an all-too-familiar address.

'Bring him,' said Da Souza, getting out of the car.

Moments later they were inside the apartment.

The moment she saw him, he got the reaction he'd expected. Margarida flew at him, her long, elegant nails clawing at his face.

'You! What have you done? This is your fault!' she screamed. 'They've got him. They've taken Joao!'

There were more of Da Souza's men in the apartment. They dragged Margarida away and pushed her roughly down onto the couch. She sprang up again and one of them slapped her in the face. She was flung by the force of the blow back onto the seat but then rolled onto the floor.

'There's no need for that,' said Lopes, hurrying to her. 'Control your men, Da Souza.' He put his arm around Margarida, helping her to her feet and then to the couch but, as soon as she realised who was helping her, she angrily pushed him away.

'Get off me! Don't touch me! This is all your fault.'

Lopes retreated a safe distance. He swung around to Da Souza. 'Where is he? What have you done with Joao?'

'He's safe. For now. And he'll stay that way…if you do what we say.'

'Which is to tell you where I'm meeting Miss Katz?'

Da Souza smiled. 'Exactly.'

He swallowed, mind racing. That would doom Costa, and Elena too. Two more people would die.

Or his son would.

But they'd kill him anyway. And Margarida. And him. They'd want no witnesses left alive. He had to find another way.

'How can I trust you?' he said knowing it was a hopeless question, but it gave him time to think. 'To bring him back safely?'

'You'll just have to, won't you?'

'Why should I? Your thugs have already killed a policeman. A young cop with his whole life before him.'

Da Souza smiled. 'My men got a little carried away.'

'Dinis!' said Margarida from the settee. 'Shut up! They'll kill Joao. Please. Do as they say.'

She was right. He seemed to have no choice. But still he had no illusions as to how this would play out.

But then an idea started to form.

'Alright,' he said. 'But on one condition.'

'No!' screamed Margarida. 'My son!'

'She's right,' said Da Souza. 'You're in no position to make conditions.'

'Still, I am going to make it. Too many people have died. I don't want any more. My way also ensures you actually do get the tape because I doubt whether Miss Katz will bring it to the meeting.'

'So? We only need her. Once we have her, we'll make her talk.'

Lopes stared at him. Oliveira's words came back to him to him again; "We are all expendable."

Indeed, he thought, and some are more expendable than others.

'She's expecting me alone. You'll spook her if you go in mob handed. She's armed and could just shoot herself if she sees you all. And then where would you be with your paymasters?'

He could see the cogs going round in Da Souza's head. 'All right. What do you suggest?'

'Where we are meeting it will be easy to block all the exits to if you have enough men, and I'm guessing you do. Let me go in, I'll disarm her and bring her out.'

Da Souza thought about this for a few moments.

'Very well,' he said, 'But no tricks.'

'All right,' Lopes swallowed, his mouth bone dry. 'It's at the São Pedro de Alcântara at 3 pm.'

MONDAY 19TH MAY 1941,

3.05 PM

Lopes looked at his watch, knowing that he was being watched albeit from a distance.

It was beyond time; they'd be getting jumpy. Well, let them. Hell, he himself was jumpy, this was one almighty gamble, one he'd pay for the rest of his life if it went wrong, and it could quite easily. Elena, Costa, Margarida and, above all, Joao, the son who didn't know his father could all be gone in the next hour if he made a mess of this.

There were lots of visitors at São Pedro, that was one of the reasons he had chosen it. This had always been the city's favourite viewpoint, the one where you could look out over the great city and see most of its highlights in one place.

But he couldn't be distracted by them. This had to be timed perfectly.

There were less people than before the war, of that was no doubt, but still they came, locals, people from the provinces, the better off refugees from lands riven by war and sailors from all lands taking advantage of a few, risk free days to enjoy themselves.

There was a group of them now, some of them Americans by the sound of it, being escorted by a guide, a local who haunted the viewpoint looking to make a few escudo by passing on their knowledge. He moved his group towards where they had the best view of the city, telling them as they did about the great earthquake and the terror it had brought.

Lopes moved with them using them as cover from the watchers.

He couldn't be seen. He needed as long a period of doubt as possible.

The entrance to the tunnels was there, right below him. Dark, forbidding.

The tunnels were not lit but he had his lighter. He hoped he had enough fuel to make it all the way through.

Now was the time.

Shielded by the American tourists he walked swiftly into the dark opening, holding his lighter out in front of him. He waited only a few seconds for his eyes to adjust then set off.

Alia Jacta Est.

The die was cast.

*

Lopes emerged from the tunnel after first cautiously checking the street. It was clear, no sign of Da Souza's men.

He could imagine the chaos and confusion back at the so-called meeting spot. He'd gambled that his watchers were the wrong age and wrong background to know about the tunnels, too young to have children to amuse by exploring the city's sites and from the rough side of the streets unlikely to have been exposed to anything but football, fighting and fornicating in their formative years. Lopes wouldn't have known about them either but this had been part of his beat as a trainee policeman. Whilst Da Souza's thugs were learning to spy and break heads, Lopes had been chasing pickpockets through Lisbon's narrow streets, alleyways and, more importantly, the ancient tunnels that dated from the city's founding.

It was useful knowledge even though then, as now, the exertion was not good for his gas damaged lungs. He was wheezing heavily.

He checked his watch; just under thirty minutes to get to the real meeting place. There were trams but, hopefully, there would be a taxi.

One thing needed doing first.

He headed into the nearest café.

'I need a telephone!' he gasped.

The proprietor pointed to the end of the counter. The phone was in use. Lopes didn't hesitate.

'I need to use that,' he said to the man who was making a call.

'Sod off. You'll have to wait.'

Lopes pulled out his badge. 'No, *you* sod off or I'll arrest you.'

The man went white and handed over the instrument without another word.

Lopes swallowed his guilt and called Oliveira.

*

He checked his watch as he stepped off the tram; 3.42 pm. He'd be a little late and out of breath; it was a good five minutes' walk uphill to the Rúa Nossa Senhora dos Milagres to the entrance to the English Cemetery. He was sure that Elena would be on edge but she would wait. She had to.

Another gamble. Like the fact that Costa was still alive.

The English Cemetery, unlike São Pedro de Alcântara, was surrounded by high walls, with a single main entrance through hefty wooden doors, and its grounds were dotted with mature trees, hedges and monuments, perfect for concealment and dreadful for an ambush which was exactly why Lopes had suggested it in the first place.

He went inside and made his way to the Boer War memorial. There was no sign of her. That was no real surprise; she would be checking that he was alone and had not brought unwelcome guests with him. He waited, steeling himself for what he was about to do.

She stepped out from behind a tree. She was alone and wore Costa's jacket. Her hand was in the pocket, presumably holding Costa's revolver. She stood facing him a couple of metres away.

Too far.

'Where's Armstrong?' she said.

'Where's Costa?'

'He's in the car like you said. Don't worry, he's still alive.' She stepped a little closer. 'Now, answer my question; where's the Englishman? I need that machine.'

Lopes made a show of looking around, as if he was checking that the coast was clear. He gave a little gesture inviting Elena to come closer as if he wanted to whisper something to her.

She fell for it. She came within a short step.

He took that step, pulling Armstrong's pistol from his pocket and jamming it into her ribs. She gasped and her eyes widened. He took advantage of the shock to use his free hand to dive into her pocket, grab her hand and twist it and the revolver to one side so the barrel was no longer pointing at him.

'Enough,' he said. 'Let go of the gun or I fire.'

Briefly she twisted, struggling to free herself but he was much stronger and he made sure she knew it. He ground the barrel of the Walther into her ribs.

'Stop it,' he said. 'I'll put a bullet in you if you don't stop struggling, don't think I won't.' She continued to fight him, he gripped her hand tighter and twisted it. She gasped in pain. 'Look into my eyes. Go on do it.' Reluctantly she did. 'They've taken my son so I've got no choice. You can see I mean it, don't you? Don't you!'

The fight went out of her. She nodded, sighed and stopped struggling.

'Let go of the gun,' he said.

She did. He took it out of her pocket and put it in his own.

'They'll kill me,' she whispered. 'If you hand me over, they'll kill me.'

The confidence had gone. For the first time she sounded like a lone, terribly vulnerable young woman a long way from home.

Lopes swallowed down his self-disgust.

'I know,' he said. He waved her on with the pistol. 'But this has got to stop. People are dying and now they've taken my son too.'

'I'm sorry about your son...I didn't –'

'Forget the apologies. Come on, take me to where you left the car.'

Meekly she turned. He didn't think she would run but still he took hold of her arm with his free hand and walked just behind her, the pistol concealed behind her back, the barrel still thrust hard against her.

'Please, inspector. Don't do this. Let me go.'

'Quiet. Keep walking.'

She led them through to a side entrance and out onto the street, the car was about 50 metres away down a side street.

'Where is he?'

'In the back, under a blanket.'

'Is he...?'

'No, he's alive. At least he was when I left him.'

Lopes opened the passenger door. 'Get in, then shuffle across. You're going to be driving.'

She did as she was told. Lopes got in next to her. Keeping the Walther pointed at her, he reached into the back and lifted the blanket up. He breathed a sigh of relief. Costa looked white but was still breathing though he'd been gagged and his hands were bound.

'Untie him and get that gag off him,' he said. 'Do it!'

She did. Costa briefly opened his eyes and looked at Lopes. He smiled then closed them again.

'Right, now drive. Do you know where the hospital is?'

Elena shook her head.

'I'll give you directions,' he said. She started the car. 'Turn around and then go left.'

She did as she was told. The evening traffic was starting to build. 'Come on, come on,' Lopes muttered as they were held up at a junction. He glanced at Costa. Elena immediately made a grab for the door handle, getting it open but, before she could escape, Lopes grabbed her and jerked her back. He pushed the gun against her. 'No,' he said. 'Shut the door and drive or the next time…'

She did as she was told. Behind them horns were blaring as the road had cleared. Elena let out the clutch and the car jerked forward.

It took another six minutes to reach the hospital.

'Drive straight in. To the main entrance,' said Lopes.

She did.

'Now sound the horn.'

She did as she was asked.

A puzzled looking porter came out. Keeping the gun on Elena, Lopes lowered the window. He pulled out his badge and showed it to the porter. His eyes widened when he saw it and then did further when he saw the gun. 'I'm escorting a dangerous foreign agent to custody. There's a wounded man, one of my colleagues, in the back seat. Get a doctor here and a stretcher and take him inside.'

'Yes, sir. Of course, sir.'

The man ran off.

A minute later Costa was being lifted gently from the rear seat, a doctor taking his pulse then listening to his chest through a stethoscope.

He'd done all he could.

'Look after him,' he said to the doctor, then turned to Elena. 'Drive. I'll guide you.'

She nodded glumly.

'Head north.'

'North? But the police station is…'

'We're not going to any police station, or anywhere near the PVDE. It's too dangerous for both of us, and for my son.'

'I don't…'

'I'm gambling, Elena. I'm not normally a gambling man but I am making a huge wager now, with my son's life.' He was too weary to explain further. 'Head out of town. I'll tell you where when we get closer.'

*

Some four hours later the car was labouring up steep, twisty gravel roads.

'Is this right?' said Elena leaning forwards and peering through the windscreen. The trees on both sides of the road cut out the late evening sun and the last farmhouse had been a couple of kilometres before.

'Yes. In about a kilometre there will be a turning to the right. There's no signpost but take it.'

Elena didn't say anything but kept going. The turning appeared ahead, Elena steered the Citroen into it.

'There's a village in a short while. It's not big, just a few houses, a small bar and a church,' said Lopes. 'Drive through to the far side and there will be another lane on the right, It's quite narrow.'

Elena did as she was told. The lane was rough, even worse than he remembered it and even the Traction Avant with its famed excellent ride bounced and crashed from pothole to pothole.

The little farmhouse was ahead.

'Take the car behind it, in the yard. It will be out of sight there.' Though, he thought, the car's arrival would be the talk of the village. There was no escaping the gossip here.

'Alright,' he said. 'Switch the engine off.' She did as she was told. 'Elena, listen to me, it might save your life. You can escape from here if you want but I really suggest you don't try. There's nothing around here but a few rough fields with goats and sheep in them. The fields are surrounded by woods, hills and scrublands. They are treacherous if you don't know them, it's easy to get lost, easy to fall and they are full of wolves, particularly close to the village because they often try and pick off the odd goat. Because of that everyone has a shotgun or a rifle and they don't hesitate to loose off at any odd sound they hear.' He smiled. 'Now you're not going to try are you because I'm not exaggerating. Portalegro is not for the faint hearted.'

'I don't think you are,' said Elena. 'No, I won't try. Who's this?' she added.

Lopes turned his head and smiled again. He opened the door.

'Hello, mother,' he said. 'How are you?'

MONDAY 19TH MAY 1941, 8.05 PM

Lopes watched his mother as she lit the first of the oil lamps with a taper lit from the stove. She had got old and stooped since he had last seen her, her hair now completely white. He was reminded how long it had been.

'You could have told me you were coming,' she said, turning up the wick, filling the room with the flickering, yellow light that took him back to childhood.

Lopes had been expecting the complaint.

'Mother, how? We've only got letters to stay in touch. I did say I could get you a telephone line run down here.'

'A telephone? What would I want with one of those contraptions?'

Lopes sighed. 'I don't know, mother, so I could call and tell you when I was coming at the last minute?'

His mother gave a grunt of disagreement. 'If you were a decent son you'd keep in touch more. I hardly hear from you. I blame that woman you married. She thinks she's far better than the likes of us.' Lopes didn't feel it necessary to defend her. Whatever, his mother's gaze switched to Elena who sat quietly on a chair by the fire. 'So, who's this then? Your latest conquest? She doesn't look like your usual type. She's skinny, no meat on her bones. I thought you went for the big busty ones.'

'She's…' Lopes began but Elena got there first.

'We're not lovers,' she said. 'I'm being hunted for something I've got. Your son is protecting me.'

Lopes stared at her in surprise. He thought she was sure to consider herself a prisoner but she sounded genuine.

'Well, yes, he is a good boy. When he wants to be. Watch out for him though, he likes the ladies a bit too much for his own good. It was when he went off to France, those damned flighty mademoiselles, that's what changed him,' His mother turned back to Lopes. 'How long are you staying?'

'I don't know,' he said. 'A few days anyway.'

'Alright,' she said. 'I'll put the young lady in your room, Dinis. You'll have to sleep down here. I'll get some blankets.'

She went upstairs.

'Sorry about my mother,' said Lopes. 'She's a bit direct.'

Elena gave a little laugh. 'I think she knows you only too well, inspector.'

'Dinis, please.'

Her face darkened. 'What you said before, about gambling, what did you mean? Was it about your son?'

He nodded. 'He was taken by some Nazi sympathisers within the PVDE. There's a man called Da Souza who's their leader. They've taken him to make me give you up into their hands.'

'But…you didn't? What about the boy?'

'That's the gamble. I know about pressure, about leverage. It can only be exerted if someone is there to put it on. Here, we are out of touch. There is no lever. They can also only use the threat to my boy up to a point; harm him and their power over me is lost.'

Elena looked shock. 'But at some point, we have to go back.'

'We do. It will all have to be resolved by the time we do, one way or another.'

Elena shook her head in disbelief, 'You're a cool one, inspector… Dinis. What does your wife think about this?'

'My wife doesn't know.'

Elena frowned. 'But surely, with her son missing…?'

Lopes looked at the floor. 'João is not her child. He's the son of a lady I know.'

'A lover?'

'A former lover, yes.'

Elena gave a little laugh. 'Your mother was right, you do like the ladies, don't you?' She glanced upstairs where Lopes' mother could be heard moving about. 'Does she know?' Elena continued; her voice lower. 'About João?'

Lopes shook his head. 'No, but she's always longed for grandchildren. She would be heartbroken to find out she's got one that she's never seen.'

Elena nodded. 'It will be our secret then. One that I promise I'll keep.'

'Thank you.'

'So, what's your plan? By bringing us here?'

Lopes looked up. He smiled.

'I haven't got one,' he lied. 'Yet.'

TUESDAY 20TH MAY 1941, 7.07 AM.

Lopes opened his eyes and was transported back in time.

It was 1917. He was 16 again, skinny, undeveloped, raw, knowing nothing but this house, the village, the forest, helping his father make a living on the small holding, sometimes working in the sawmills when they needed extra bodies because of an order from Lisbon or some other place that only existed, for him in schoolbooks. It seemed like this would always be his life but, in fact, it was all about to change, and change for ever.

The army called, and that led to a whirlwind of training, seeing Lisbon and the sea for the first time, going on a ship, a train, travelling through France to Belgium. And then to war, a conflict that neither Lopes nor Portugal was truly prepared for.

The trenches. Death. Comradeship. Cold, hunger, tiredness, lice, rain. And mud, so much mud.

He'd never been the same afterwards. It had been a turning point in his life. He'd never come back, other than on the briefest of visits, home. He'd found he couldn't face it.

Yet, this was still home. Home was always here; this ramshackle house, the tumbledown barn, the pig sheds, this was what he thought of when someone mentioned the word to him. Perhaps this truly was what home was to most people; an illusion, a dream, an idealized memory.

He was in his room, in his childhood bed, still sleeping under the self-same blankets he'd slept in years before, His mother's thrift and poverty meant that nothing was thrown away.

It had been a last-minute change of plan and Elena's insistence that had brought him to his old room.

'I can't turf you out of your old bedroom,' Elena had said. 'I'll take the couch.'

'I don't think so,' Lopes had said.

'Don't be stupid, Dininhno,' his mother had said. 'The girl's right. You should be in your own bed.'

'But...'

'Oh sort it out yourself, son,' said his mother. 'I need to turn in. I need my rest. Guests don't look after themselves. I'll need to get some food in. I wish you'd told me you were coming but, no, of course you didn't...'

She was still grumbling as she went up the stairs to bed.

'You're not sleeping down here,' said Lopes once her door was shut. 'I'm not having you slipping away in the night and heading back to Lisbon.'

She shrugged. 'I'm not going anywhere. You told me about the woods.'

'There's the car.'

'Disable it then if it makes you feel better, I'm sure you can make it so it doesn't start. I want to be here,' she lay on the couch and pulled the blankets over her. 'I like it in front of the fire. It reminds me of...'

Abruptly she stopped. Lopes was about to ask what it reminded her of but caught a gleam of moisture on her cheek. She was an actress, a schemer, a survivor, she had to be to have survived this long but he knew this was not put on.

'Alright,' he'd said, sure that she meant what she said about not escaping.

He'd still gone out to the car and removed the distributer cap from the Citroen.

And so, here he was, waking up in his bed and time travelling.

He'd woken to a murmur of voices. Not his mother and father, the influenza brought back from France had carried him off before Lopes, himself, had returned. No this was the two women talking. It sounded like his mother was giving orders, he braced himself from an explosion from Elena, a reaction, a response, resistance to being told what to do, the fight that he'd seen in her time and again. But it didn't come, instead he was sure he heard...laughter, yes laughter and not just from Elena but from his mother too.

There were smells too, good ones. Coffee. Toast. The pangs of hunger followed. He had to get up.

'Ah, here he is at last,' said his mother. 'Rip Van Winkle has risen. Now the work has been done, of course.'

Elena was sat by the fire which had been rebanked and was roaring strongly, holding the toasting fork near the flames loaded with a thick slice of bread. Next to her was a plate loaded with golden slices.

'Morning, inspector…or should I say Dininhno?' she said.

'Ah, look at his face, he doesn't like that. He's a man, Lena, he doesn't like his authority questioned.'

Lopes sighed. 'Good morning, mother. Morning, Elena.'

'Sit yourself at the table, son,' said his mother. 'And we'll wait on you in the time honoured way. I'm sure you're used to that with that wife of yours. Oh wait, no, that's beneath her, isn't it?'

Elena laughed. Lopes guessed that Maria Sofia had been one of the things the women had talked about since they'd got up. Mothers tended to dislike their son's partners and their failure to measure up to the standards they'd set in bringing up their son but the mutual enmity between mother-in-law and daughter-in-law was deep and the main reason why Lopes had seen little of his mother over the last decade.

However long their stay here was going to be, the last few minutes suggested that it would feel a lot longer for Lopes.

Meekly he sat at the table. His mother put a cup in front of him along with a coffee pot. He reached for it but had his hand slapped away. 'Wait, I'll do it. You'll slop it everywhere as usual, I know you.'

Lopes saw Elena grin to herself as his mother poured him a cup of milky coffee. He'd got the taste for strong, black coffee in France but this was the traditional way to have it in his homeland. Whatever, he wasn't going to ask for anything different here. He took a sip, it was too cloying for his tastes now and the underlying coffee was rough and bitter.

'Thank you. Lovely,' he said.

Elena put a plate of toast in front of him.

'There you go,' she said. 'Now can you manage to butter it for yourself?'

'I doubt it. His servants will do it for him at home.' His mother picked up a knife and reached for the butter pot.

'Oh for goodness' sake,' Lopes snapped. 'Stop it both of you. Give me the knife, mother.'

'Manners, Dinis. Manners.'

'Please, mother…thank you.' He took the knife and buttered a slice of toast. 'Elena, mother, please sit.'

His mother muttered something to herself but ignored him. Elena did, however join him at the table. She was still smiling. She reached for a piece of toast and buttered it.

His mother came over and put a pot down next to her plate. 'There's some honey for you, Lena. Or would you prefer jam? I've got some quince preserve left over from last year.'

'Honey is fine, thank you, Mrs. Lopes.'

'Beatriz, please.'

'Beatriz.'

Lopes watched this scene with astonishment. Elena had made more progress in being accepted by his mother in the last few hours than Maria Sofia had managed in the previous 15 years. But then his mother had always wanted a daughter; she had, in fact, had one but his younger sister, always a little sickly, had succumbed to measles at the age of 9 when Lopes himself was 14. Things had never been the same since and he'd always felt that, somehow, his mother blamed him for being the one that survived.

Well now it seemed he'd inadvertently made amends by supplying his mother a substitute daughter.

And, as he ate his toast, he realised that this could also explain the change in Elena. The sharp, bitter, edgy, somewhat ruthless woman in the city had been replaced by a gentler, more relaxed, humorous young lady. She'd lost her mother on the road fleeing from France. Lopes may have found her a substitute.

This was all a bit unexpected.

Whatever, a friendly, relaxed Elena was an advantage. She was more likely to work with him rather than fight.

'Elena, after breakfast, we need to talk,' he said.

Elena opened her mouth to reply but his mother got their first.

'That will have to wait, Dininhno,' she said.

'But…'

'No buts, Lena has no clean clothes left. We're going up to the village to the wash pond.'

Lopes' mouth opened and then shut again. The communal washing place was where the women of the area came together to do more than clean clothes, it was in many ways the heart of the community, a switchboard more effective than any telephone exchange to spread and hear news. And to show off new members of the family.

'Mother, you can't. Elena is…'

'Lena,' said Elena. 'I like that name. I prefer it. And if you're worried about news spreading about me it will have anyway judging by the fact there are virtually no cars here and you drove through the village yesterday evening with me in the passenger seat. People will be gossiping, won't they?'

'Well, yes, but…'

'Then it's better to nip that in the bud. Spread the story that we want them to think about who I am.'

'Which is?'

The newly renamed Lena grinned. 'Who knows? A relative from Lisbon. Or Dinis Lopes' new lover who's replaced his wife? I'm sure we'll think of something between us, won't we Beatriz?'

His mother laughed. 'She's a bright one this one, boy. If only you'd chosen brains rather than, well other things.' She sighed.

'Anyway,' said Lena. 'I really don't have any clean knickers left. I've been living out of a suitcase since Uwe died.'

'There,' said his mother. 'It's decided. Dininhno, you can make yourself useful by splitting some logs. We're going to need them, I'm going to do some baking later.' She put her hands on her hips. 'Come on boy, eat up. We've got jobs to do.'

Lopes gulped down his coffee. This was not going as he expected. Not at all.

Perhaps it wasn't going to be easier.

TUESDAY 20TH MAY 1941, 6.12 PM

Lopes stacked the last of the logs he'd chopped then put his hands on his hips and leaned back, stretching his aching muscles. He was getting old, this was one of his teenage chores, one that was satisfying and that he could do all day if given the chance. Not now. Now he'd be paying for this in the morning.

He checked his watch. It was nearly time.

He took his shirt off and pumped some water into the bucket beneath the house's only source of water. There was a hunk of near solid soap next to the pump as there had always been in his youth, he did have a strange notion it was actually the same one that had survived since then, like everything in the mountains things had to be hard and tough to survive, but laughed that off. Again though, as he washed, trying to raise some lather from the brick, reluctant to give up any, he had memories from his youth. When in Lisbon, when he'd thought or dreamed of home, it was always the home of his teen years, unchanged and unchanging. It was a bit of a shock to find out the imagined was, indeed, true. Things had not changed, the farmstead still had no running water, no electricity, the toilet was an earth one, the remains once rotted down used as fertilizer still.

Surely, at some point, change would come to the mountains. But there was no sign yet it ever would.

He gave a little laugh to himself. That was how Salazar wanted it, that was what everyone said. Portugal uneducated, unchanging, rural, the people not wanting what they never learned about.

Until refugees with a totally different outlook flooded in from abroad. People like Elena. No wonder the good doctor was worried.

He dried himself off, put his shirt back on then took a basket of split logs into the kitchen.

It was hot inside and full of the aroma of baking and roasting. His mother and Elena - sorry, Lena - had been preparing a feast though whether this was in his or Lena's honour he wasn't quite sure.

Lena smiled at him as he came in. She was at the kitchen table slicing tomatoes. His mother was basting a chicken.

'It smells good in here,' he said, putting the basket down next to the stove.

'So it should,' said his mother. 'We've been working hard.'

'I can see,' said Lopes. He reached for his jacket.

His mother scowled at him. 'Where are you going?'

'I need to go into the village,' he said.

His mother's frown deepened. 'Why? Dinner will be at eight.'

'Because I need to, mother,' he said. 'Don't worry, I'll be back in time.'

'You'd better be. Don't get talking and drinking like you used to. We won't be waiting for you, will we Lena?'

'No, Beatriz,' said Lena. She raised her eyebrows at Lopes, an amused gesture but one that he found charged with something else; allure. Lena was, he thought again, startlingly attractive.

He swallowed. That wouldn't do.

'Right,' he said. 'Won't be long.'

His mind raced as he trudged up the hill. This was not what he had in mind when he brought Elena here. It had been for self-preservation, removing himself from the ability of Da Souza to control him by threats to his flesh and blood and to take Elena away so the end game could run itself out, an outcome that would see all loose ends; him, Elena, Costa probably, his son and Margarida all silenced. The move had been to buy him time, time to regroup and work out an exit strategy. It had not been to transform Elena the difficult into Lena the sweet and desirable.

Sweet, desirable, pretty and yet still dangerous with the potential to be deadly.

That was the perfect combination he'd found elsewhere and been unable to resist.

But now he had to.

He reached the bar and went inside.

The proprietor, Hector, was still the same man Lopes remembered from his late teens, albeit both he and Lopes had aged somewhat.

'Dinis Lopes,' smiled Hector. 'Someone said you were back and you've brought a pretty young thing with you.' He chuckled. 'Not your wife, eh, you old devil? Anyway, what can I get you?'

The rumour network had clearly worked well.

'Just a glass of wine, I'll be eating soon. Oh and I'll need the telephone.'

Hector nodded towards the end of the bar. No privacy here so he'd have to keep his voice down. But what choice did he have? He checked his watch. Still a few minutes really but it would have to do otherwise he'd attract attention.

He picked up the instrument and waited for the operator. When she came on the line, he gave her the number he needed to be connected to.

'Oliveira. Who is this?'

Lopes breathed a sigh of relief. As arranged, Oliveira was at home waiting for this call. The last thing Lopes wanted to do was go through the PVDE switchboard. At least this way there was a chance that the call would not be overheard.

'It's me,' he said.

'Good. Have you got the woman?'

'What's happening with my boy? Have you found him?'

There was a brief pause at the other end of the line. 'We've managed to free the boy's mother,' Oliveira said at last. Lopes waited but nothing more came.

'His mother? Is that it? What about Da Souza? Have you arrested him?'

'Look, Lopes, you know the situation, Everyone, and I mean everyone has their protectors higher up. We can't move against him. It would create...problems.'

'Problems? Oh, for God's sake!'

'This is why it's so important for you to recover the object, Lopes. Until it's under our control people are going to suffer. Including your son.'

Lopes felt his face redden as his anger grew.

'You've not tried to find him, have you?' he said. 'It might as well be you holding him, it's just saving you a job, isn't it? Anything to manipulate me.'

'Enough, Lopes!' roared Oliveira. 'How dare you!'

'Well, it's true, isn't it?'

'Where is the object?'

Lopes ignored Oliveira's question. 'How's Costa?'

There was an irritated sigh at the other end of the line which Lopes could not let pass.

'Look, Oliveira, I don't care what priorities you, Capito Lourenco or Salazar himself has but Costa is mine. He's made sacrifices for you, major ones, and he's paid the price. How is he?'

'Be careful, Lopes. I warn you –'

'And I warn you, I can ring off and you'll never find me.'

'Of course we can find you. How long do you think it will take? For us and for the others? We can trace where this call came from by one visit to the central switchboard.'

Lopes knew he was right but wasn't going to back down.

'Whatever, I'm armed. Come for me and I'll fight back. It won't be easy to take us. It would be a bloodbath.'

'That's mutiny. You wouldn't dare to —'

'When my son's life is at stake, I would.' Lopes waited for a response then gave up. 'Look, sir. This is how it's going to be. You'll just have to trust me that this is the right way.'

After a few moments he heard Oliveira give a low curse before saying, more clearly, 'Very well.'

'Good. So, how is Alvares?'

'He's doing better. He's not completely out of danger but he's had a blood transfusion. His wife is with him.'

Lopes nodded to himself. 'Good. Then, yes then, I have the women.'

'Then why are you talking to me now? Where is the tape?'

'She hasn't got it with her. I'm pretty sure of that.'

Lopes saw the barmen raise his eyebrows at this. He was obviously listening. Lopes scowled at him and was pleased to see him move away a little. Still Lopes turned his back on him.

'So where is it?'

'I don't know as yet.'

'Find out. Interrogate her, in fact use torture if you need to. We need it, Lopes, urgently.'

'There's no need for violence. I will get it.'

'When? It cannot be in play. The future of the Estado Novo may depend on it.'

'Yes, I know.'

'Your son's life absolutely depends on it.'

Lopes gripped the counter with his free hand otherwise he'd have had to use it as a fist to punch the wood. Pain to quell pain.

'Yes,' was all he said.

'Do whatever it takes, Lopes, but get the tape.'

Lopes nodded to himself.

Whatever it took.

'I do have a plan,' he said. 'But it will take a little time.'

TUESDAY 20TH MAY 1941, 8.03 PM

'You're late. we almost started without you.'

The admonishment was familiar, and the threat an empty one as each party knew but Lopes still had to acknowledge the transgression. That was always the rule.

'Sorry, mother.'

He smiled at Lena, who returned it with interest.

With interest. Was she interested? Was he? Of course he was, just look at her but... she was half his age and involved in this case. 'Whatever it takes,' Oliveira had said.

'Stop staring at Lena and take your seat, Dininho.'

His mother never missed a trick but, judging by the look on Lena's face, neither did she. Meekly, and feeling like his face was glowing, Lopes did as he was told, as the women started loading the table with food. His stomach rumbled. The log chopping had taken a lot of energy, he hadn't realised how hungry he was. He'd forgotten what it was like to do physical work and breathe good, clean country air. His shoulders and arms ached but it felt good. Maybe this was what he needed; no pressure, a life in the country without someone wanting to kill him. Absently he reached for the bread, only for his mother to slap his hand away.

'Manners!' she said. 'Wait for the grace.' She took her seat. 'Lena, will you do the honours?'

Lopes looked up sharply straight at Lena, then back at his mother.

'But...' he began.

'Blessed are You, Lord our God,' said Lena. 'King of the universe, who brings forth bread from the earth.'

There was a moment's silence, which Lopes quickly ended by intoning; 'Amen.'

'Amen,' said the two women.

'Right,' said Lopes' mother. 'Now we can start.'

They tucked into the food. Lopes was watching his mother carefully; whilst antisemitism wasn't a major issue in Portugal and never had been, that was mainly because the Jewish population, pre-war, had been so small. Growing up around here, particularly he'd known no Jews, it was only by leaving and going to France and Belgium that he'd met any at all. No, the issue was the church, always the backbone of the community and quite strong on the 'the Jews killed our Lord' idea. Lopes, whilst he ate, glanced at his mother. She looked deep in thought. This could go wrong. He had counted on staying a few days at least. The way his mother and Elena - sorry, Lena - had bonded was a bonus. Would that continue if his mother realised that she was Jewish.

Perhaps she hadn't noticed.

'That was an unusual grace, Lena,' his mother said. 'It was nice though. Is that what your pastor at home taught you?'

Lena looked straight at Lopes who flashed her a warning glance back.

One that Lena completely ignored.

'My Rabbi, Beatriz,' she said. 'I'm Jewish, I thought you realised.'

Lopes held his breath. Here lay the end of the nascent mother/daughter relationship.

'I see,' said Lopes' mother, her face stern.

Here it comes, thought Lopes, some variation on 'Your people killed our Lord.'

But instead his mother smiled, leaned across and squeezed Lena's hand. 'My poor dear,' she said, 'No wonder you're a refugee. You're in safe hands now.' She looked at Lopes. 'You could have told me,' she scolded. 'Look, I've served pork. I even got the poor girl to prepare it.' She rose, reaching for the pot of stew. 'I'll take it away.'

Lena reached across to stop her.

'There's no need,' she said. 'My parents were strict but I never was and, in the last year, well, niceties about what is kosher and what isn't have taken a back seat to survival. Anyway,' she added, reaching for the spoon. 'Pork is really tasty and this stew is delicious!'

Lopes' mother settled back down and he breathed a sigh of relief.

He still had some time

TUESDAY 20TH MAY 1941,

11.20 PM

Lopes was waiting for his cue.

The dinner things had long since been cleared away. He'd offered to help with the washing up but had been told, in no uncertain terms by his mother that that was none of his business and that she and Lena would be quicker.

Now it was just a waiting game. Surely his mother would tire soon and head for bed? This was much later than her normal bedtime and she was yawning. But she was also enjoying herself, recounting anecdotes about the scrapes the young Lopes had got into whilst growing up and adventuring on and around the small holding. He was surprised at her memory, surprised by what she did know and somewhat relieved that some of the more lurid secrets he had had seemingly remained that way.

It was with guilt that he realised that this was Christmas, Easter and Birthdays all combined for her. She'd been alone for too long, he'd neglected her and for what? Marital peace, certainly. That had worked out so well, hadn't it?

At last she seemed to flag all of a sudden. She said less, her head kept nodding and her eyes closing, but still she made no move to retire.

'Mother, you're asleep,' he said.

He had to repeat himself slightly louder before she jerked awake.

'I was just resting my eyes,' she said.

'And snoring,' said Lopes. 'Please go to bed, mother.'

'What, so you can have your way with young Lena? I don't think so.'

Elena, curled up on a chair across the other side of the room, smiled at this.

'Mother, really,' said Lopes. 'Even if that was my intention, I wouldn't do anything like that under your roof and I'm sure Lena would have a say in that. Whatever, anyway, it's not, I'm a married man. You're tired, go to bed, please.'

'Honestly, Beatriz, I'll be fine,' said Elena. 'I trust your son.'

His mother gave a snort of derision but did struggle to her feet. 'Many a young lady has trusted him in the past and it's not helped them.' She swayed slightly. 'All right,' she said, waving away Lopes who had risen too and stepped to support her. 'I can manage. I'm not an old lady, I'm just tired.'

At that moment, to Lopes, she looked exactly like that; a tired old lady, one whose time was running out.

After she had gone upstairs Lopes reached for the bottle of de Medronho he'd brought back from the village and held it up questioningly to Lena.

She nodded. 'Why not?' she said. 'Oh, unless it's to get me tipsy to have your wicked way with me?' She smiled as she took the glass. 'Although that wouldn't be the worst thing in the world.'

Lopes ignored the obvious and ploughed on with his true intentions of getting Lena alone.

'We need to talk,' he said.

The smile vanished. 'About the recording?'

'Of course, that's the key to everything.'

'Yes it is; it unlocks the door for me to get out of this country and to the States.' She sipped her drink. 'You can't expect me to give it up.'

'I don't expect you to give it up for nothing. You can still use it as a bargaining chip.'

'You're asking me to negotiate with the British? I don't think so,' she shook her head. 'That's who you're working for, isn't it?'

Lopes shook his head. 'No, it's not. I work for the Portuguese state.'

She shook her head. 'It's the same thing.'

'It's not. Salazar keeps Portugal neutral. We favour neither side.'

'Have it your own way. Both you and I know the truth.'

Lopes pulled a face and sipped his drink. 'Even if that was true, and it's not, is it so bad to deal with the British?'

'I don't trust them. Not in the slightest. Not after what I heard.'

'Heard? On the recording?'

'Yes. It would be like giving it to the Nazis. They're both the same.'

They're both the same? Lopes puzzled over this.

'But the Americans you're wanting to give it to…'

'Want to keep the US out of the war, yes, you said.' Lena drained her glass and let Lopes refill it.

'Don't you care about that?' Lopes said. 'That can't be good for your people…'

'My people? Look, Dinis, I have long since stopped believing I could do anything for anyone else but me. Connolly has offered me a ticket out, he can use the tape to decorate the tree at the Irish American Christmas party for all I care as to what he does with it as long as I get that and the visa.'

'Elena…Lena. People have died over this thing. They'd have quite happily killed you and me, and they still might kill my son.'

Lena shrugged. 'I don't care,' she repeated.

Lopes shook his head. 'I don't believe that,' he said. 'You're not mercenary.'

'Believe what you like. You don't know me.'

This was getting nowhere. Lopes took a deep breath. Setting Lena against him was not going to help.

'Fine, I won't press you,' he said.

'Good.'

'But it's safe, isn't it? You haven't got it on you, have you?'

'I'm not that stupid,' she said. 'It is safe, don't worry about that.'

'In Lisbon?'

She gave him a withering look. Lopes puffed out his cheeks and slowly exhaled.

'You didn't expect dealing with me would be easy,' she said. 'What did you think, you'd use your dark Hispanic charm on me, get me in bed and I'd hand over the tape to you?'

'No, of course not.' Lopes was sure he was blushing.

'Good because I may have done some soul-destroying things in the last year but I'm not some cheap whore or a helpless little girl in search of another protector.'

There was something deep in Lena's eyes that told him that, at times, she'd thought herself all of those things. Lopes actually felt a prick of tears, an emotional, protective wave that he struggled to suppress.

'I never thought of you like that,' he said, surprising himself that his voice had not displayed his true feelings. 'The truth is I admire you.'

'Admire me? Oh really? So it's flattery now, is it?' She got to her feet. 'God, Lopes you're pathetic.'

Lopes rose too. 'Hey, where are you going?'

She tried to step past him, heading for the door. He grabbed her arm and she swung the other one and slapped him hard in the face.

'Get off me! Let me go!' She struggled to free herself as he grabbed her free arm too, the pain and shock from her slap beginning to register. She dug her nails into his hand as she fought, so much so he let go on that side. She immediately went for his face with her nails. Quickly he took hold again and, with some effort, got her in a bear hug. She struggled against him, her tiny and lithe, him twice her size. Her body was warm, firm, she was wearing some light, flowery perfume, her hair smelt of…

She suddenly stopped struggling.

'Don't hurt me,' she said, her voice low and dull. 'Please. When you…don't hurt me.'

For a moment he didn't know what she meant. Then he realised; her body held tight against him had aroused him. She had felt his erection pressing against her.

He let her go.

'No, no, I wouldn't do that. Lena, I wouldn't.'

She didn't run. Didn't move. She just stared at him. He felt a wetness on his cheek, instinctively he raised his fingers to it then looked at the moisture on them in some bemusement. He knew it was not the aftereffects of the slap.

The next moment she was back in his arms, her head buried against his chest.

They stood silently there for what seemed like an age. Then Lopes kissed the top of her head.

'It's late Lena,' he said. 'We need sleep. Well I certainly do. We'll talk in the morning.'

Still she didn't step back. At last though, she nodded and let her arms fall away from him.

'Do you want me to come up with you?' she whispered.

Hell, yes, he thought.

'No,' he said. 'We'll talk tomorrow. Goodnight Lena.'

'Night, Dinis.'

As he laboured up the stairs he had a definite lump in his throat.

'Shit,' he muttered.

WEDNESDAY 21ST MAY 1941, 7.20 AM

Lopes woke with the sun on his face.

He didn't feel at all rested. His mind had raced when he'd turned the light off, his thoughts jumping from his son, to Costa, to Margarida, the recording, the dead policeman but, frequently, to Elena - Lena - to her scent, the darkness of her eyes, the curve of her chin, her nose, her mouth, lips and the feel of her body against him. Time and time again he found himself aroused, but then he forced the other thoughts to the forefront, reminding himself of the desperate situation he and those he loved were in, and that this sojourn was not a solution, it was a temporary refuge and one that would not stay secure for long, he had no time for…distractions.

But the distraction returned again. The thoughts and feelings were as stubborn as the woman herself. When he did finally fall asleep, she returned and his libido and imagination filled in the gaps in his knowledge.

No wonder he felt tired.

The murmur of voices downstairs ceased and he heard the creak of the stairs as someone came up. He caught the clink of spoon on china and the faint aroma of coffee and realised, to his surprise, that he was being brought a morning drink. This was puzzling as it was totally out of character for his mother. There was a light knock on the door.

'Come in,' he said.

The door opened to reveal Lena. She smiled at him.

'You look a bit big for that bed,' she said, putting the cup on the nightstand. 'It would have been a squeeze for two,' she added in a whisper.

He couldn't find any words in response and just watched her as she left. She was wearing a men's shirt and slacks, he was not normally a fan of women in trousers but, on Lena, it suited her, showing off her petite curves, again not his usual type but it was enough to bring the same feelings back.

'You've been too long without a woman,' Lopes muttered to himself and for the first time, thought about his wife and their loveless marriage. Something needed to happen, but in the Estado Novo? Divorce? It was frowned on, more than frowned on. Maybe now he was in the PVDE it would be allowed?

He suddenly felt sick. The PVDE? He didn't belong there either. And a divorce from them was likely to be as impossible.

Sighing, Lopes swung his legs out of the bed and took a drink of his coffee.

*

As he finished the last of his toast, he noticed that the women were packing bread and cheese into cloth and wrapping them carefully.

'What are they for?' he said.

'For you and Lena, of course,' said his mother.

'But she and I have to talk. About work.'

'Well, you can do that on your hike. She wants some fresh air and to see the Tagus at its most beautiful. I thought you could take the car to Outeiro and do some walking along the river there. Your father and I used to cycle there when we were teenagers.' She smiled. 'We had a lot of energy then.'

That explained Lena's choice of trousers but there was something about the way she said this that Lopes found uncomfortable.

'But mother, we're trying to keep a low profile…'

'Oh don't give me that police talk, the girl needs some exercise. You're taking her and that's an end of it. I need you both out of the house anyway. I need to do some cleaning.'

Lena smiled at him. 'You've got your orders, inspector,' she said, 'You'd better follow them to the letter.'

Lopes scowled at her.

*

'We do need to talk, Elena,' he said as he drove.

She had the car window open and had her face out in the air. Her eyes were closed as she soaked up the morning sun. 'Oh hush,' she said. 'There's plenty of time for that.'

'There isn't,' he snapped. 'Time is running out. For all of us. My son…'

'…is safe for the time being. You said so yourself. They can only put pressure on you if they can get at you.'

Lopes shook his head. 'For now, maybe but we can't hide here forever. They'll find us.'

She didn't reply immediately. He wondered if she had chosen not to or whether she was thinking things over.

'I know it can't last, I'm not naïve,' she said. 'I like it here though. I've not felt like this for so long. Let me have today at least.'

So it was thinking. Good, thought Lopes.

'Alright,' he said.

*

Lopes was struggling, he couldn't hide it.

The path by the river was far from level. It ran like a switchback along the bank, rising and falling at each rocky outcrop. Every assent was short but steep, in places it required scrambling, then it plunged downwards again to the next low spot. The top gave a moment's respite with the bonus of affording views of the heavily wooded, steep sided river gorge. He'd forgotten how beautiful it was here, he hadn't been here since his teens, before France, before the gas, before the years of relative sloth in Lisbon had eroded his fitness.

Hence his struggles.

He stopped at the top of the latest climb, hand on hips he gasped for breath. Lena, lithe and light, looked barely affected by the exertion.

'Are you all right?' she said. 'Come on, old man, what's the problem? What are you, forty? You look 60 at the moment.'

Lopes sank to his haunches, fighting back the nausea. 'The problem is…my…lungs. The…war…gas.'

'Oh, God, me and my big mouth.' Lena knelt next to him. 'I'm sorry, I didn't know.' She put her hand on his shoulder.

'You weren't to know,' he said.

'I know, but…' She puffed out her cheeks. 'Why don't we stop here for lunch. It's as good a place as any.'

'Yes,' said Lopes but then saw where they were. 'Actually, I think we're near a better place. There's a spit of rock out into the water, it makes a sheltered bay. It's a nice spot for lunch.'

Lena smiled. 'Okay but take it easy. You're too big for me to carry.'

Lopes laughed.

*

It was further than he remembered but, twenty minutes later, they were sat on a grassy area with their backs to a rock facing out over the river. The sun was shining, glinting off the water, insects buzzing and birds swooped as they hunted. It was idyllic.

Lena looked blissful as she munched her bread and cheese, her face raised to the sun. She was not wearing much make up and her scar was more prominent than he'd seen before. It was definitely made by a blade, though whether it was a knife or a razor Lopes couldn't tell.

She seemed to feel his gaze. She didn't look at him but said 'It's not pretty, is it?'

'No. How did you get it?'

'A Spanish border guard did it to me.'

'Why.'

'To stop me fighting him off. He was trying to rape me. He said the next cut would be right across my face if I didn't stop.' She looked pensive. 'Of course, you can see that I did stop.'

'And he didn't? Stop I mean.'

She shook her head.

'I'm sorry, Lena.'

She shrugged. 'It wasn't the first time,' she muttered.

Lopes thought of the previous night and her whispered "Don't hurt me." It all made sense now.

Abruptly she stood and looked around. 'It's very quiet around here.'

'Yes, it's usually pretty much deserted on a weekday.'

'In that case I fancy a swim.' She unbuttoned her shirt. 'Join me?'

'But I haven't got a costume.'

Lena took her shirt off. 'So? Neither have I.'

She took her shoes and socks off, then her trousers, and started walking to the water's edge. He thought she was going in in her underclothes but, at the water's edge she stopped and took these off too. She turned, and stood naked, Lopes taking in her pale slim body, firm small breasts and the dark triangle of her sex, things that he'd dreamed about the previous night now made real.

The reality was better than his imagination.

'Coming?' she said and turned back to the water, wading in until it was deep enough to swim. She gave a little squeal. 'It's so cold!' she giggled. 'Come on, Dinis!'

He nodded and, in less than a minute he was naked too and stepping into the water. He gasped as the cold hit him.

'It feels okay after a few moments,' she said, pushing over onto her back and pushing her head into the water.

Lopes forced himself to go deeper and then plunge in, getting the shock out of the way. It was intense for a few seconds then his body adjusted. He came to the surface and swam a few strokes out into deeper water, the years since he'd been in water like this dropping away as his muscle memory of what to do came back. He then turned back and swam towards Lena.

'This is lovely,' she said. 'I haven't been swimming since…' Her face darkened momentarily but then she seemed to push the memory away as she swam to Lopes. 'Thanks for bringing me here,' she said and wrapped her arms around him. He stared into her eyes for a moment, conscious of her breasts pressed against his chest, the small nipples hard, then leaned forward and kissed her. She didn't resist, in fact she responded passionately, then wrapped her legs around him too. He was instantly erect.

This was only going to end one way. Whether it was sensible or right was immaterial now, the Rubicon had to be crossed. There was no turning back.

He carried her back to the shore.

*

Afterwards they lay together, skin against skin, in the warm May sun as their breathing returned to normal. It had been too long since he'd experienced this, the intoxicating pleasure of intimacy but, underlying it all, was the feeling, all-too typical for him, that his life had just become even more difficult.

He shook his head.

Lena noticed. 'Regretting this already?' she said.

He found the lie easily. 'No, not at all.'

The look on her face told him that she did not believe him in the slightest. 'I've learned to trust my instincts as to what's right and what's not,' she said. 'I've got no doubts about this. It's what I needed and I could tell it was for you too, wasn't it?'

The woman was too perceptive.

'Yes,' he said. 'It was.'

'See, I'm always right,' she said and they kissed again.

When they'd finished he couldn't resist asking; 'Always?' He knew she'd know what he meant.

She laughed. 'Alright, not always. I do have doubts about the recording. Not about keeping it out of the hands of the Nazi's, which was obviously the right thing to do, and it was easy to persuade Uwe to do it, he could see that too even if it was dangerous for him.'

Lopes thought instantly of the body on the slab, grey, flabby and had a picture of him and Lena lying like this, naked together.

As if she could read his mind, though she'd probably detected some slight change in his body, she raised herself up on her elbows and stared at him, eyes wide open. 'Really, Dinis? Jealousy? Already?' Abruptly she grinned and settled back into his arms again. 'Nice to know I've still got it.'

He couldn't help but laugh. 'I'm sorry,' he said. 'I'd no right.'

'Of course you do. No one likes to think about your lovers' former lovers.'

'No. They don't. So you do have doubts about passing it to Connolly?' For once the recording was safer ground.

'Yes. I do. In a way. But in a way not.'

Lopes tried to process this. 'Because you get your ticket out? That's the upside?'

'Yes, of course. That's become more important now.'

'Important?'

'Yes, now Uwe's gone…oh, no, don't get all jealous again, you really don't understand…' She sighed and sat up. Despite the sun Lopes suddenly felt cold without her pressing against him. 'It's hard to explain. I didn't love Uwe but then also, in a way, I did. Yes, I know that makes no sense but it was how I felt. But, whatever, we had an arrangement. I'd give him a year and then he'd get me papers and a ticket. It was a business deal.' She paused, her head bowed. 'We never got to a year of course. The bastards came and got him and then the vultures swooped and took all he had.' She lifted her head briefly into the sun then lowered it again. 'It was my fault,' she whispered.

Lopes sat up and put his arm around her. 'No it wasn't. It wasn't at all. Don't blame yourself.' He kissed the top of her head. She responded, turning her head to rest against his chest.

'Thanks,' she said. 'But I know the truth. After I heard what was on it, I made him tell a lie, that the tape had broken. Uwe was like you, a lousy liar. They didn't believe him but I didn't care.'

'It was that bad, was it?'

She nodded. 'Not so much the words but just the sheer…deceit. And that it was all discussed so casually by two powerful men who seemed to have no qualms about wielding the power of life and death over people like me and you, little people who don't apparently matter to them in the slightest. I was so angry that I threw my pencil across the room and tossed the paper in the fire. I had to start again, which meant I had to listen to it all over again. I'm still angry now.'

Lopes' mind reeled as he took all of this in. Was she saying what he thought she was saying?

'You transcribed the tape?'

She raised herself up. 'Yes. I used to transcribe my father's lectures. He was a Chemistry professor. I'd take them down sitting at the side of the stage then typed them up later. I offered to do it for Uwe.'

'You typed them up?'

'Yes, I said.'

'Where is the transcript? With the tape?'

She smiled. 'One copy is but I took a carbon. That's in the lining of my case.'

Lopes swore softly to himself. Lena looked puzzled.

'What difference does that make?' she said. 'It's the tape that's important, isn't it?'

'Yes, but I've been chasing something that seemed like a myth or a mirage. At first I didn't even know what it was I was looking for, getting to know about it felt exactly like trying to squeeze a stone to get an atom of blood out of it and, now, I find that you could have told me what it was all about, in fact let me read what was on it.' He shook his head. 'We could have got here earlier.'

Lena stared at him for a moment then laughed and rubbed her body up against him. 'I don't think we'd have got here exactly any sooner, Dinis Lopes. I'm not that easy.'

Her movements had an instant effect on him. 'I know you're not,' he growled knowing that he was not going to stop. Even though one particular thought swirled in his head, so much so he had to push it out of his mind as it was too much of a distraction.

Sometime later, when they ended up panting in each other's arms again, it came back.

'Lena?' he said.

Her reply was muffled by her face being buried in his chest.

'Before, when you told me about the transcript, you said something.'

She raised her head and looked into his eyes.

'What?' she said.

She'd been on top and had been rather energetic so her hair adhered to her face with the perspiration, something Lopes found so erotically distracting he almost forgot his question.

Almost but not completely. He loved women but he was still an investigator.

'You said two powerful men?'

'Did I?'

'Yes. Obviously, one was the British King...'

'Ex-King, Duke.'

'Yes, the ex-King. But who was the other one? Espirito Santo, the banker? Or the German ambassador? Who was it?'

She smiled and shook her head. 'No, someone far more important. Someone that a senior person in the British establishment absolutely should not have been meeting in July of last year when his country stood alone and on the brink of defeat. Given what's happened in the last week I'd thought you'd have guessed who it was. Someone who seemed to have made a habit of flying himself to places on his own.'

Lopes was briefly irritated by her, he wasn't in the mood to guess.

But then it all fell into place.

'Hess?' he said. 'The Duke of Windsor met with Rudolf Hess?'

Lena nodded. 'Yes, the deputy Fuhrer of the bastard Nazi state himself flew himself down to talk over with Edward or David or whatever he was calling himself how they'd run Europe and the British Empire when the war was over and Germany had won. Nice, eh?'

WEDNESDAY 21ST MAY 1941,

3.42 PM

Lopes glanced across at his travelling companion. She was curled up, cat-like on the front seat, apparently asleep. It all now seemed so unreal, Lopes almost doubted that their love making had happened, yet he knew it had, most definitely.

He silently berated himself. He should never have allowed himself to get so vulnerable, to be without a woman for so long. Yes, his relationships were a mess but he had other choices, didn't he? Yet here he was again, complicating his life again.

But the truth was he gained no satisfaction from sex without feelings. It was the connection he craved, the closeness, the emotional bond. That was why he didn't seek out prostitutes, that held no appeal however pretty the girl might be. It just didn't work for him.

But was this genuine? Was it a real relationship? How could it be? He was 41 and not a fit man whilst she was, what, 20? 21? Young, pretty, vivacious even though she bore the scars of her recent past on her face and body, including a series of cigarette burns and signs that she'd suffered a couple of broken ribs at some point that hadn't healed properly. Whatever, what could she see or want with Lopes? A burnt-out ex-soldier, ex-policeman, ex-except-in-name-husband with damaged lungs and enough personal baggage to fill a wagon. The answer was obvious; although Lopes had little in the way of wealth, he had his position with the PVDE. He was Uwe Vogel Mark II. A protector. Useful.

He sighed, too loudly apparently.

'What's wrong?' she said, opening her eyes.

'Nothing…well, apart from the obvious.'

'Us you mean? Or rather, me?'

He shook his head. 'No, the recording. The transcript. My son. The fact that so many people want it and don't care who they kill to get it.'

Whether she believed him or not, this did, at least, cause her to be silent for a few minutes.

'What we did doesn't change anything,' she said at last. 'I still want to use it as a ticket out of here. I want to go to the States.'

'But…what about us?'

She smiled. 'Dinis, us? Really? How can there be an 'us' long term? I don't want to be a mistress but that's what I'd be, wouldn't I?' He was trying to frame a response to this but was interrupted by her laugh. 'Come on, Lopes, I can read the signs. You never mention your wife, I don't even know what her name is, yet I know you've had a lover that you stayed with long enough to have a son with. You clearly don't love your wife, you showed no guilt or remorse for making love to me, yet you haven't divorced her, have you? So if you haven't done it by now, you never will.' She untucked her legs and sat looking straight ahead out of the windscreen. 'That's the truth, isn't it?'

He opened his mouth to speak, then swallowed back the words. He was going to put the argument he had always made to himself, not about the money, not about not wanting to break the promise he'd made to his wife in their vows but about divorce and the Estado Novo, about Salazar's belief in the Catholic Church and upholding the sanctity of marriage and the importance of that to the state.

It was a lie he told himself that he'd chosen to believe for his own comfort.

'Yes,' he said. And then, after a long break, he asked. 'But why then? Why did you - we - do that?'

She turned her head and smiled. 'Just because, Dinis. Because you're honest enough to answer the way you just did. Others would have lied but you didn't. It's just one of the reasons I like you, you're a nice, honest, fundamentally decent man.' She turned to look ahead. 'The fact you're nice looking and a more than decent lover is a bonus. And I do enjoy sex.' She looked at him again. 'You look shocked. But, yes, Lopes, it's true. Women like it too.'

Lopes swallowed. What had he got himself into? He knew that many in Lisbon had been shocked by the fashions and looks of the more well-to-heel female refugees, particularly the chic French who sported both short hair and short skirts, and the tut-tutting had got louder when the younger local women had started to follow suit. He hadn't viewed Elena - Lena - the same way, she was more demure, less showy, more of an intellectual in making, still unusual in Portugal, still intimidating, at a Margarida level but in a different way. Margarida's came from her temper, from pure emotions whilst Lena was just so quick, mentally agile and clearly very bright. Now he found that behind that also lay a quite shocking attitude to relationships.

But then, wasn't she just like him for that? Why should he judge her for behaving in the same way he did? But, then again, he couldn't get pregnant.

Pregnant. My God they'd taken no precautions.

'Lopes, don't look so worried!' Lena laughed. She shook her head. 'Honestly, what we did today is the least of your worries. Live for the moment, Dinis, tomorrow we could all be dead. Yes?'

'In our case that might be true,' he muttered.

'Then concentrate on that, not anything else,' she said. 'Mind you, it was very nice. Wasn't it?'

'Yes, it was.'

'Good, that's all that matters.'

'All right.'

'And,' she added, her tone changing. 'If you're worried about babies don't. When things…happened to me, well let's say they did some damage. I'm pretty sure I can't.'

He couldn't help it. He had to stop. He braked hard and pulled the car to the side of the road.

'Lena, no, that's awful. I'm so…'

He reached across but she turned away. He sat back.

'Why sorry? I'm not. Who'd want to bring a child into this world?' He glanced across. She'd shut her eyes. 'I'm sorry. You have a child. One that's in danger. I'm sorry, I was talking generally.'

'I know,' he said. He sat, thoughtfully, looking at the road ahead.

Abruptly she turned and embraced him. He could feel a wetness on his skin. He held her close. It didn't seem right to say anything.

At last she pulled away, but not before kissing him. 'You're a lovely man. Lovely, but a mess.'

'And I think you're the same. Lovely and a mess.'

'Totally,' she said. 'Come on, let's get back. Oh, and before you ask, I won't tell your mother about us.'

He put the car into gear and set off again. 'Thank you,' he said.

'There's no need,' said Lena after a few minutes. 'She'll know anyway.'

WEDNESDAY 21ST MAY 1941, 5.12 PM

She *did* know.

Lopes' mother didn't say anything but the expression on her face, part-amused, part-smirk, part-exasperated told its own story. But one thing was obvious; the affection she showed towards Lena was clear. She certainly wasn't blaming her for anything.

It was the closest thing to approval they were ever likely to get.

There were other issues more pressing for him to worry about. He had arranged to call Oliveira again at 6 pm and was running out of time.

'You want to go out again?' said his mother. 'You've only just got in.'

'I don't want to go out, I *need* to, mother. It's work.'

She gave a huff of displeasure.

'If you must,' she said.

'Yes, I must,' said Lopes testily.

'This is what you've got to put up with this one, Lena dear,' said his mother. 'I'm not sure anyone can, to be honest.'

'He's not so bad,' said Lena, smiling.

Lopes ignored them both, 'Lena, can I have the document?'

The smile vanished from her face. 'Have it? No. It's not leaving my sight.'

'Please, Lena, I need to know what they said. I don't want to talk to Oliveira without knowing.'

Lena folded her arms and lifted her chin defiantly. 'I said no and I meant no.'

'But…'

'Dininhno, you heard what she said.'

'Mother, keep your nose out of my business.'

His mother stepped over from the stove and slapped Lopes hard across the face as she had done so many times as a child.

'Don't you talk to your mother like that,' she said. 'You may be a grown man, you may charm the ladies but you're not too big not to have your ears boxed.'

Lopes, his face smarting and blood pounding, moved towards his mother but Lena stepped in between him. 'Dinis, no,' she said softly. 'There's no need. You've got plenty to tell Oliveira, you won't have time to read the transcript properly before anyway. I really don't want it to leave here…'

'Don't you trust me?' He hadn't intended that to sound hurt but that was the way it came out.

'As much as I trust anyone,' she said, raising her hand and stroking his face. Lopes enjoyed her touch, he almost reciprocated but then remembered his mother. 'Dinis, you're welcome to read it tonight, after dinner but with me there so I can see it.'

'So what's the difference then?'

'The difference is that it leaves my sight and my control.'

'So you *don't* trust me?'

'I'm just being cautious. I may never be able to get the recording itself back. Yes, it's safe but I'm not and neither are you. We may never be able to go to the…to where it is kept and retrieve it. At least with the transcript I've got something, something that might still get me a ticket out of Lisbon.'

For a moment he almost pushed things further because she'd said the dreaded words about leaving Portugal and he wanted to remove any chance of that. Then he reminded himself of who he was and who she was, he had to stop acting like a lovestruck teenager.

'All right,' he said. He looked at his watch. 'I need to go, and, yes mother, I will be back in time for dinner, before you say.'

His mother smiled. 'I never thought you would be. Not tonight when you've got something you want to come back to.'

He stared at her. He hoped she meant the transcript. He knew she didn't.

*

Hector pushed the phone over to Lopes as soon as he walked into the bar and followed this by pouring a glass of wine and placing it next to the instrument.

'I hear you've been out driving with your lady friend,' he said. 'Why don't you bring her in sometime? This place could do with brightening up.'

'Thanks, Hector. Perhaps I will. But she's not my lady friend.'

Hector smiled and raised his eyebrows but said nothing, instead going back to drying glasses and stacking them back on the shelves.

Lopes thought about saying something, denying things more but what was the point? This was what life in a small rural community was like. It was why they didn't need telephones, there was no need, everything spread, every bit of news, every tiny scandal went through the community and was common knowledge almost before it had happened. It was suffocating, disturbing to Lopes even when he knew no different, when he knew nothing about the outside world. That was perhaps the biggest shock that came to him when he went to camp for his basic military training; the world was huge, everyone didn't know everyone else, people kept secrets and, above all, were *able* to keep them. It was intoxicating, this freedom to have mystery, to meet people, to have affairs without anyone else knowing, was refreshing. Then he found another benefit; when people didn't know all about you, where you came from, what you knew, who your mother and father were, didn't assume what your skills were then, in that big world you could be anyone. You could invent a whole new you.

This was what Lopes had done. It had taken him a long way. He'd never wanted to come back to this.

Until the real Lopes, the simple, generally honest, country boy started to come back out and the lie within started to crack the facade he'd created. Then he'd started to lose control.

Lopes puffed out his cheeks. This was no time for deep introspection. He had to remember the situation. He had to be Inspector Dinis Joao Matos Lopes not young Dininhno, son of Alfonso Lopes.

Also, he knew what Hector had said about Lena was true. He couldn't lie to himself.

He reached for the phone and waited for the operator. He gave her the number.

'Tenente,' he said. 'Hello?' The line clicked and buzzed for a second, but then connected.

'Lopes,' said Oliveira. 'What news? Do you have it?'

'No,' said Lopes turning away from Hector and keeping his voice low. 'But I do know a lot more about it. But first, what news from you? Have you got my boy?'

*

Twenty minutes later he was trudging down the hill towards his mother's house, Oliveira's words still echoing in his ears.

There'd been no fresh news about his son and Da Souza was still at large and active around PVDE headquarters. Oliveira had only grudgingly given up this information, anxious to move things back to what he was concerned about.

'Come on, Lopes, I'm being pressured on this, from the highest authorities and I mean the highest. I have been told that we *must* bring this to a conclusion.'

'Tenente, I'm trying to do that.'

'Well, from here it doesn't seem like it. It seems more like that you're having a vacation in the countryside whilst the fate of the state teeters in the balance.'

Lopes tried to put the image of the naked Lena standing at the water's edge from his mind.

'Sir, I resent that. This is no holiday. My son –'

'Progress, Lopes. What progress have you made?'

'A lot, sir. For one thing I know something about what was on the recording. And who the Duke met.' He'd told Oliveira about Hess and the transcript.

Oliveira had sworn. 'Hess? Good God, so he *did* come over.'

'You knew about it?'

'No, not for sure. There was a rumour last summer but the German embassy assured us that it wasn't true. Damn them, they were lying through their teeth.'

'They may not have known,' said Lopes. 'Lena said that Hess flew himself down and held papers in the name of Alfred Horn. Apparently, Vogel told her that this was the way the Nazi's operate, not as a whole but in distinct cells. They almost consider their colleagues as enemies.'

'Hmm,' said Oliveira. 'I suppose so. It makes sense that it's Hess though, that might explain why this has come to a head now.'

'You mean given Hess's flight to Britain?' said Lopes.

'Yes,' said Oliveira. 'I believe he originally gave the name Horn when he was arrested by the British.' Lopes heard Oliveira sigh. 'But why did Hess's capture trigger this?'

'Maybe the transcript will tell us.'

'That's why we need it. Why haven't you got it?'

'Lena is a bit reluctant to let it out of her sight.'

'Why should what she wants matter?' snapped Oliveira. 'She's an illegal, a refugee, an undesirable. A nothing.'

'But sir…'

'And what's this Lena business?'

'Sorry, Elena, Miss Katz.'

'Christ, Lopes, Lena? You're getting too close to her, aren't you? Mind you, that's you all over isn't it? A whiff of perfume, a shy glance and you go to jelly. That's what your record says, Lopes. I hoped it was wrong, that you'd learned your lesson but it seems not. No wonder you haven't got the transcript yet.'

'Tenente! That's not fair. I object.'

'Object all you like, it's the truth. I shouldn't have trusted you to take her on your own. With you it's too risky.'

'But- '

'Just get it, Lopes. Get it and then get the recording.'

'But –'

'Do it, Lopes. Don't let whatever your feelings are get in the way. You're a man, not just a man, an agent of the state, and she's a mere woman, a woman on her own with no family to protect her, no one to step in and object. So just do it, Lopes. This ends in the next 24 hours.'

Oliveira had rung off. Lopes had stood by the telephone for a few minutes whilst his temper eased. His reverie was only interrupted by Hector pushing another glass of wine in front of him.

'On the house. It looks like you need it.'

Lopes gave a rueful nod.

'Trouble with the boss?'

'You might say that.' Lopes had downed the glass in one. 'I'll have to go,' he'd said.

Hector had muttered something and had turned to one of the other customers.

Lopez had started to leave but turned back. 'What was that, Hector,' he said?'

Hector laughed. 'I said he was just jealous. Your boss probably wants to shag her himself. Mind you he's not alone, everyone around here I've talked to, every man anyway, thinks you're a lucky bastard.'

Lopes didn't smile.

'Hector, I need a word.'

'Of course.'

'Outside.'

'I'm busy with –'

'Now, Hector.'

Reluctantly Hector followed Lopes outside.

'What is it Dininho? I've…'

Lopes pulled out his badge and held it in front of the barman. 'You see this, Hector?'

The barman nodded.

'What does it say.'

He saw Hector swallow. 'PVDE,' he croaked.

'Which means?'

'Secret police.'

'That's right, Hector, so what you've got to do is to keep your mouth shut.'

Hector had gone pale. 'But…'

Lopes ignored him. 'If you heard anything about that call then forget it. You don't repeat it to anyone. This isn't about me and the woman, it's bigger and more dangerous than that, more dangerous than you could know. Rumours, gossip about me and her could get people killed.' He'd paused for breath. 'One of them could be me,' he added. 'But also could be you. So, keep it to yourself, understand?'

Hector nodded.

'Good,' said Lopes. He had almost let him go then but the memory of the cracks and buzzes on the line to Oliveira when it had first connected came back to him. Was that normal? Had he heard it before? He couldn't be sure.

'Hector,' he said. 'There's one thing you can do to help.'

'Of course, Inspector,' said Hector, now eager to please. 'Anything.'

'If any strangers come to the village, or anywhere near it, don't, whatever you do, or whatever they say, like their old colleagues or something, tell them that you've seen me or where my mother's house is.'

Hector now went even paler. 'What? Thugs might come here?' He looked inside the bar, at the telephone. 'Because you used that?'

'Yes,' said Lopes. 'Hector, I'm sorry, I didn't think they'd work it out so quickly.'

Hector had delivered some choice swear words and had gone inside without another word.

So now, here he was, ten minutes later, heading back to Lena, burned bridges behind him and ahead…what? Betrayal?

"You're a man, not just a man, an agent of the state, and she's a mere woman, a woman on her own with no family to protect her, no one to step in and object…"

She was all that. That and more.

'Fucked it up again, Lopes,' he said as he got to the door. He hesitated briefly, took a deep breath, then stepped inside.

WEDNESDAY 21ST MAY 1941, 9.25 PM

'I'll leave you two to your business,' said Lopes' mother rising with some difficulty from her chair.

'There's no need to go on our account, Beatriz.' Lopes mildly cursed Lena for this but it was unnecessary.

'It's not, I'm tired. I'm not used to having visitors any more I suppose.' She did look weary and Lopes again realised his mother's frailty. The cottage had been cleaned top to bottom whilst they'd been out at the river, she was clearly trying to make an impression and Lopes knew it wasn't aimed at him. 'I'll see you both in the morning.'

'Goodnight, Mother,' said Lopes. After she had gone, he turned to Lena.

'It's alright, you don't need to ask, I'll get it,' she said.

She went over to her case, a battered but clearly once expensive small leather affair, and lifted it onto a chair. Opening it she took out a small make-up bag and retrieved a pair of nail scissors. She then pulled at the lining of the lid, exposing some stitching. It looked untouched from when the case was made but Lopes guessed this wasn't the case and it had been deliberately done this way to disguise a hiding place.

Lena glanced at him. 'Uwe realised what we had was dynamite and asked me to hide them. I did this months ago. Those sewing classes my mother made me do came in handy after all, though not in the way she expected.'

She used the scissors to snip at the stitches. It took a few minutes as they were so small and tight but, at last, there was enough of a gap for her to slip her hand inside the lining. She had to then work the board stiffening inside away from the leather and Lopes realised that the papers had to be the other side of this, against the thick hide. Clever, he thought, even if the lining had been torn free in a search the papers wouldn't have been revealed. At last Lena succeeded and extracted half a dozen flimsy sheets. She passed them over to Lopes before putting the case back where she'd got it from.

He started to read. Lena sat next to him, resting her head against his shoulder. The memories of that afternoon were distracting but, given how long he'd waited to read what was in his hands, he managed to concentrate.

> DOW *'I say, when is this chap we're meeting getting here? I want to get 18 holes in this afternoon, dash it.'*
> UNKNOWN *'He'll be here shortly, your highness.'*
> DOW *'He'd better look lively, damn him.'* [inaudible] *'Look, just get the car. I'm not waiting a minute longer.'*
> UNKNOWN *'Sir, please…ah, here he is now.'*
> DOW *'About bloody time. Who is it anyway? You said someone important but that could be anyone.'*
> *[Inaudible]*
> *[Sound of door opening, chairs scraping]*
> HESS *'Your Royal Highness, apologies for my tardiness. My driver took a wrong turn.'*
> DOW *'Good God, my dear Rudolf. Don't worry yourself. It's dashed good to see you after all these years. How is Ilse?'*
> HESS *'She is well. And your lovely wife, she is well too?'*
> DOW *'She is. Worried about our things in Paris of course, and what Winston is demanding of us. Have you heard, the governor of The Bahamas. What a dump that is. It's exile, nothing more nothing less. Our treatment is damnable. It's intolerable. I don't blame Winston though, it's my brother and that wife of his.'*
> HESS *'Indeed, your highness…'*
> DOW *'David, Rudolf, call me, David. No need to stand on ceremony.'*
> HESS *'Thank you, David. Yes, the Fuhrer wishes to send his sympathy to you about your treatment, as well as his disappointment that our two countries are at war at all. It is unnecessary. As he often says, Britain is not out natural enemy.'*
> DOW *'We need someone like the Fuhrer in charge in Britain.'*

'They are chatting like old friends, aren't they?' murmured Lena. 'Rather than what they should be, two bitter enemies.'

Lopes nodded. He could understand the British wanting to suppress this, the embarrassment of their former king meeting at all with the deputy Fuhrer of the enemy their country was locked in an existential conflict was enough. The fact that it was happening on such friendly terms made it worse. But why were the Germans so keen to get it too? Sure, it would make excellent propaganda even now, but the impact would not be as great as it was in July or August of 1940 when the Nazi armies had swept across Europe and stood, ready to invade, across the English Channel. That had to be the reason for the recording, certainly made without the duke's knowledge but, probably, also without Hess's either, otherwise he might have been more guarded about what he said and been more formal in his delivery.

So why now? Why had the Nazi's instigated the search for it the day after Hess had flown to Scotland.

There had to be something else in it.

Something that Hess said, not the Duke.

He carried on reading.

Ten minutes later he found it. After the blatant antisemitism, the petulant complaining about his family's treatment of him and his wife, about the annoying interruption of his life caused by the war and grumbling about his exile came what Lopes realised had to be the key passage.

'This is it,' he muttered, pointing at the page and showing it to Lena.

HESS 'Your highness, David, it is indeed unfortunate that you were replaced on the throne. The Fuhrer is sure that, if that had not happened, friendly relations would have been maintained between our two countries.'
DOW 'Possibly, Rudolf, possibly. But put yourself in my position. I cannot be seen as any puppet ruler. I won't do that.
HESS. 'We would not do that…'
DOW 'But then the whole country's gone to the dogs. Mark my words, we'll have the Bolsheviks taking over. I don't wish my brother physical harm but, if that happens, it will be like what happened to poor Nikki and his family in Yekaterinburg all over again. Those damned commissars won't hesitate. Perhaps that damned woman deserves it but his

girls…dash it, it doesn't bear thinking about. Stalin must be laughing to himself whilst he watches the west tear itself apart.'
HESS 'Indeed, David, indeed. He must be stopped. Bolshevism must be put to the sword and consigned to history.'
DOW 'Indeed, indeed. More brandy, Rudolf? Oh, of course you don't, do you?'
HESS 'No David, I am fine with water.'
[Clink of glasses. Sound of a lighter clicking.]
DOW '[Unintelligible] …made it worse by doing a deal with that monster.'

Lopes was momentarily puzzled by this then remembered, the Molotov-Ribbentrop pact, the Nazi/Soviet pact. That was what the duke must be referring to.

[Laughter]
HESS 'That is an illustration of the Fuhrer's brilliance.'
DOW 'I say, what do you mean? That the pact was a ruse.'
HESS 'Of course it was. It was a deal that allowed us to act without fear in dealing with the Polish question and then with France without fear of being stabbed in the back by Stalin. He even provides us with vital war materials. What a fool. He is providing us with the coal, bullets and grain to provision our invasion of his own country.'
DOW. 'Good God. Well, that is good news. We need to deal with those monsters.'
HESS. 'Indeed. But, of course, fighting your country has stopped us acting, or at least, delayed us. The Fuhrer is still determined to act. This is why the current position is so unfortunate.'
DOW. 'Too true, Rudolf, too true. We should be standing shoulder-to-shoulder against the real enemy.'
HESS. 'Indeed. Perhaps if and when you're restored to the throne and Churchill and his war party have been removed things will be different.'
[Clink of glasses, sound of liquid being poured.]
[Inaudible]
HESS. 'Sorry, David, I did not catch that…'
DOW. 'I said, we're no threat, are we? All our equipment left in France, our army beaten. Yes, we have the navy but that can't sit in trenches. I don't see why you don't walk into Russia right now.'

HESS. 'Patience, David, patience. The Fuhrer knows that the myth of the Russian bear is just that, a myth. Stalin's purges have destroyed the leadership of the army. The Fuhrer says Russia is rotten to the core. All we need to do is kick down the door and the whole rotten edifice will collapse. He will act, it is only a matter of time.'
DOW. 'Good, about bloody time.'
HESS. 'But I am concerned. The Fuhrer will invade whatever, he is committed to that path. England will not stay weak forever. It may be that we have to invade and smash your country, there is nothing to stop us, even though the Fuhrer does not want that.'
DOW. 'The channel and the navy are still formidable obstacles. Whilst I agree with you about the invasion, it won't be easy for you.
HESS. 'Exactly. Whatever the outcome we would weaken the forces of both our countries. Then Stalin really would be the victor,'
DOW. 'I agree. But what do you suggest?'
HESS. 'It would be far better if your country was out of the war completely. This is why my mission to see you is so important. To destroy Bolshevism forever we must first make peace between our two countries.'
[Clink of glasses. Sound of liquid]
DOW. 'This is a damned fine brandy. Rudolf, I totally agree with your thesis but what can I do? I'm not king anymore - damned Baldwin and that woman - and Churchill and my brother are sending me to this damned flea-bitten back of beyond island.'
HESS. 'You still have influence, sir. You are in contact with those more enlightened people in your country who have power and can work behind the scenes to avoid this mutual disaster for our countries.'

'This is it,' said Lopes again.

'You sure?' said Lena.

'Absolutely. That's why the Nazi's were so keen on getting the tape. The second in command of the German regime being heard to admit that the pact with Russia was a sham and that Hitler always intended to invade.

'They must be scared shitless that Hess is saying the same things to the British. That might not be enough for the Soviets, they would put it down as western propaganda. But...'

'But if they hear Hess himself saying it...'

'Yes, Lena, exactly. It would carry far more weight than if it's just an intelligence report.' He closed his eyes and sighed 'Yes, the Germans were not able to invade Britain last year. I think Hitler has decided that now is the time to move onto his main target. My guess is that the invasion is imminent. Perhaps in the next few months, weeks or days but it's going to happen.' He looked down at Lena and kissed her head. 'Lena, you're in more danger than ever I thought. Both sides are desperate. They need the recording. They are not going to stop.'

WEDNESDAY 21ST MAY 1941,

11.20 PM

Lopes lay in the narrow bed of his childhood wide awake. There was no way that sleep was going to come any time soon.

They'd argued, him and Lena, quietly so they did not wake his mother but argued, nonetheless.

'You want me to give it up, don't you?'

'Lena, you have to. This won't stop until you do. My son…'

She pulled away from him. 'Don't blackmail me, Dinis, just don't. That's not fair.'

'I'm sorry but…'

'I didn't take him, did I?'

'No but…'

'And you said yourself they are trying to pressure you. They can only exert that pressure if the recording is still theirs to get. If that chance is removed, if the tape is taken out of their reach forever, what can they do?'

'They can still kill him out of revenge.'

'But why should they? And might they anyway even if you give them the tape?' She shook her head. 'No, Lopes, you're not blackmailing me. Even if I do…'

Her voice had trailed off. What had she meant to say? About what she felt for him? Maybe he'd never know.

And how real could any feelings be? He hardly knew her and ten days ago she was in a relationship with a man now dead. Could anyone move on that quickly? Alright, she'd said it was a business relationship but he'd seen her reaction to the news of Vogel's death when they were in the cafe. There were genuine feelings there.

So was she using him, pretending?

He was normally a good judge but, in this case, he couldn't tell. Maybe she was the best liar he'd ever met.

He knew how he felt.

Like a smitten teenager. That feeling, the heady combination of desire, excitement, connection, was addictive.

He was an addict. He always had been,

'You old fool,' he muttered to himself but the image of the naked Lena stood by the river like a pale, dark-haired Venus came straight to the front of his thoughts.

And that was the point, wasn't it?

He knew women. He knew the effect women had on him. She must have seen that in him, had found his vulnerability and had arrowed in with unnerving accuracy on it.

He was being used.

'Do it, Lopes. Don't let whatever your feelings are get in the way. You're a man, not just a man, an agent of the state, and she's a mere woman, a woman on her own with no family to protect her, no one to step in and object.'

That was what Oliveira had said.

He'd have to do it. But how? How was he going to get out of this with all he cared for intact? It was overwhelming, he was on his own.

Like Lena. She was on her own too.

He pushed the thoughts of her away. There was a plan forming, an idea, rather nebulous as yet but an idea, nonetheless. He could see a possible ending but not yet the route to get there.

The stairs creaked. Someone was coming up them, treading carefully. For a moment he was on edge but then relaxed. There was only one person it could be.

Moonlight was coming in through the thin curtains, not a great deal as it was in a waning phase, but in the darkness of the country sufficient for Lopes' eyes, adjusted as they were to the low light, to see Lena step into the room and quietly close the door behind her. She had a thin silk robe on which she slipped off to reveal her nakedness beneath. She appeared like a living alabaster statue and, once again, he felt the electric jolt of arousal.

'Budge up,' she whispered. 'It's cold.'

'Lena, we can't,' he said. 'Mother is…'

'I just need to be held. Please.'

He moved over and the animated statue revealed its true state, warm, vital, and very, very alluring. The bed really didn't fit them both so they had to hold each other to stop themselves falling out; this, of course, increased the intimacy of the moment. To Lopes it seemed that that they were clinging together like survivors of some shipwreck cast on some flotsam onto the stormy sea.

'I don't want to fight with you,' she whispered. 'I really don't. I do understand about your son and I want to help but…'

'I know, Lena. I think I understand you too.'

She gently stroked his chest as she rested her head on his shoulder.

'I've been set on getting to the States ever since my mother and father died. It gave me hope, it gave me a reason to keep going. I could focus on a future rather than the blackness, the loneliness, the horrible things that were being done to me.'

He kissed the top of her head.

'That was why I did the deal with Uwe. One year, then he'd pay my passage.' She sighed. 'We only made it to ten months.'

'I know.'

'But then there was the recording. It was obvious that was why they took Uwe, why they killed him. It was important. And that made it my ticket out. It was easy. Then you came along.' She was silent for a few moments. Lopes waited not wanting to break her chain of thought. 'I love your mother, I love…this…it feels like a family. I know it's stupid, you're married, you work for the state, it's been five minutes. And you've got to think about your son.' She paused again. 'It's unbelievable, I know, but strange things happen in wartime. Things speed up, they have to. Maybe here, in Portugal where you're neutral, you're insulated from it, from this world upended, shaken, broken but I'm not. I'm part of the debris.'

'Lena, I…'

'Come with me.'

Lopes was rarely floored by anything but this came out of the blue.

'What?'

Lena raised herself up and looked into his eyes.

'Come with me,' she repeated. 'To the States. Help me get it to Connolly, let's negotiate a deal for both of us.'

Lopes stared at her.

'But my…'

'But your what? Your wife? Dinis, if your marriage was any good you wouldn't have a former mistress and an illegitimate son, would you? You wouldn't be laid here with me, would you?'

'No,' he admitted. 'But, my son…'

'A son you don't see. But forget that, I know you care about him, it's horrible that he's being held. Yet you provided the answer to that by bringing me here. He's only in danger if you're in their hands, when they can put pressure on you.' Her stare intensified. 'You said it yourself, didn't you?'

'Yes, I did.'

'So, if you're completely out of their hands, safe in another country, and the recording is out of play, then that is doubly true, isn't it?'

Lopes didn't answer.

'And what else is there to keep you here? Your job? Really? I've seen the way you are, you hate being part of those bastards. I don't know why you work for them. It's not you, is it?'

Lopes shook his head. 'No,' he admitted. 'I never wanted to work for them. I was a policeman, a proper one, until I was sacked for arresting the wrong person. Everything the PVDE does goes against what I believe in. I was blackmailed into doing this job.'

Lena's eyes widened, then she nodded. '*This* job. They recruited you just to do this?'

'Yes.'

'So what happens afterwards?'

'I don't know,' he gave a little shrug. 'Let me go, probably. I'm not exactly popular with them.'

'You see,' she said. 'What have you got to keep you here? Really, what is it? Your mother? Yes, okay there is Beatriz but when was the last time you came up here? Five years?'

'Nearer ten,' whispered Lopes.

'Exactly.' Lena laid her head back on his shoulder. 'Dinis, there's nothing to keep you here, nothing but the mess that is your life. You could make a new start, with me, in a whole new world.'

Lopes' mind was swirling, his thoughts were a jumble, not at all helped by Lena's lithe, firm, naked body pressed hard up against him.

'I know this seems too fast,' Lena said, interrupting his confusion. 'You've only known me a few days, we only became lovers today and Uwe is hardly cold in his grave but one thing I've learned over the last year is that time is short, far, far too short. Things, people, you love can be taken in the twinkling of an eye, this world, this old world, is changing from day-to-day, minute-to-minute, moment-to-moment. If you find something good, something that you feel is right, it doesn't matter about time, there isn't the luxury of waiting. It has to be seized, you have to go with it or it may vanish like the morning mist.' She raised herself up again. 'This feels right, Dinis. It feels good. To me at least. Do you feel the same?'

'Yes,' he said without hesitation. 'I do.'

She kissed him.

'Then do it. Help me. Come with me.'

The plan which had been nebulous, a vague idea, suddenly became real.

'Yes,' he said. 'I'll do it.'

THURSDAY 22ND MAY 1941,

7.20 AM

Lopes woke alone, confused and unsure.

Had last night happened? Had he just dreamed it? If he had then it was a very vivid one.

He smelled coffee and toast. They had the usual effect. This time he didn't wait, he started to wash and shave, using the jug of water and basin that he'd habitually taken to bed here in his teens and which he'd started doing again as if he'd never been away. He was just washing the soap off his face when the door opened and Lena stepped in carrying a coffee cup.

'Morning,' she whispered. She put the cup down and embraced him. 'I thought I'd better be downstairs before Beatriz woke,' she added.

So it had been real. All of it.

'Thank you,' he said.

'Should I pack?' she said. 'Are we going today?'

Lopes bit his lip. In many ways, for many reasons, he wanted to delay. At least one of the reasons was personal; he had discovered a rare thing, an idyll, a Garden of Eden where he could play Adam to Elena's Eve. An aging Adam to a lithe and vital Eve.

'Where are we going to?' he said, delaying the moment.

She smiled. 'You mean "where's the tape?" don't you, Mr. Policeman?' She gave him a playful little punch. 'Don't look like that, I was joking. Estoril. Uwe loved the place. It's at a bank there, in a safety deposit box.'

'You've got access to it?'

'I may need to be accompanied by my supposed husband, thanks to Portugal's strange laws but I'm sure you can help out there.' She gave him a little kiss. 'Now hurry up or your mother will think we're at it up here. See you downstairs. Then you can tell me whether we should pack or not. Deal?'

'Deal,' said Lopes.

He was left with just the memory of her perfume.

Was this too early? Possibly, there were calls that he wanted to make first. On the other hand these could be made from Estoril, in fact it might be better to wait until he knew he had the recording, and, anyway, the longer they stayed here the greater the risk that Da Souza and his men would find them. It was better to keep moving.

Estoril also had other advantages; hotels, a beautiful beach, a lively nightlife, restaurants, bars, discrete desk staff (as far as that was possible in the Estado Novo). A lovely place to take a young woman.

To have one more night, in comfort, in a bed, under crisp white sheets with his young lover.

Lopes closed his eyes and sighed.

'One more night,' he muttered.

A few minutes later he was dressed and headed downstairs.

'Morning, mother,' he said, kissing her on the cheek. 'I'm afraid it's time. We have to go.' He nodded at Lena, who turned away.

There was an odd atmosphere at the breakfast table. Unlike the previous mornings no one spoke. Both Lena and his mother were quiet, both looked subdued. Lopes himself, never naturally talkative, had retreated further into his own thoughts.

This was an ending.

THURSDAY 22ND MAY 1941,

9.26 AM

Lopes lifted the two bags into the car, his and Lena's. He looked across at the house. His mother and Lena were stood close. There was clear affection between them, they were exchanging words, nods passed from one to the other, both looked to be supporting and encouraging each other. Lopes shook his head in disbelief; how had this happened so quickly? It really was like they'd known each other for years or, indeed, that they were mother and daughter.

No, he thought, they were a daughter who'd lost her mother too soon and a mother who'd mourned a daughter for so long.

Two souls that fate had brought together.

He looked at his watch. They should go. It was a long drive to Estoril, they'd be lucky to make it before dark but, still, he didn't have the heart to separate them. Not yet.

The sun was well above the trees. He raised his face to it, enjoying the warmth, enjoying the birdsong and the hum of insects and the myriad scents of the countryside that he's probably not noticed in his youth but now were so evocative. Flowers, sawn wood, a slight hint of smoke from the cottage's kitchen fire. It was enchanting, he hadn't realised how much he missed this. Maybe he should come back.

He dismissed that thought. He couldn't ever go back. There was Lena to deal with first.

He turned back to look at the women.

His mother had prepared food for them, bread, cheese and olives, some salt cod acquired from God-knows-where, and fruit and had put it all in a sack. Lopes recognised it; it was the one his mother had made for his father and him when they'd be out working all day somewhere. It was lined with a fine cotton and slightly padded to keep the food fresh. He'd assumed it was long-since gone but, it seemed, it had been put carefully away somewhere, kept safe with other secret, treasured memories. Now it was being willingly passed on.

Lopes smiled and nodded to himself as his mother gave the bag to Lena.

He puffed out his cheeks and checked his watch again.

They really *must* be going. He'd give them a few more minutes though.

He turned to look up the lane to the village. That was odd, someone was coming down it. He squinted, trying to make out who it was.

Hector. The bar owner was hurrying and looking back over his shoulder.

What was he doing up so early? Unless…

'Lena,' he yelled. 'We've got to go.'

'But…'

'Now!' Lopes opened the car door and tried to start the engine. It turned over but didn't catch.

Hector had broken into a near run, difficult for a man of his age and bulk and Lopes could now see why. Two men were following him.

Two armed men.

'Dinis,' gasped Hector pointing behind him. 'They came, looking…'

One of the men raised his weapon and fired. Once, then paused, crouching to aim more carefully. The first bullet missed the bar keeper but hit the Citroen, thudding into the bodywork. The second found it's mark and Hector crumpled into the dust.

Lopes tried the engine again, it had started perfectly yesterday, why not now when they needed it?

More men had appeared, there were now four — no five — all armed and heading down the lane towards them. One had a rifle. Shots rang out from the first two men, now no more than fifty metres away, as Lena, ducking, dived into the passenger seat, still clutching the bag. It would need a lucky shot from a small revolver to hit them from here but Lopes had his eye on the rifleman. He was something different. As Lopes watched, the man knelt and brought the weapon up to his shoulder.

Lopes tried the engine again. It roared into life and a cloud of smoke, courtesy of the lousy spirit they'd bought yesterday no doubt.

There was another volley of pistol shots, aimed at him, he noted, not towards Lena. They wanted her alive. The screen was holed in front of him but he ignored it and crashed the car into gear. There was a bigger thump as a rifle round found its mark somewhere. Lopes had been a rifleman himself, after running, the first shots were always wild until you got your breathing under control and adjusted your aim. If this was a marksman, they had moments at best before he'd find some accuracy.

As the car lurched forward there was a huge report from behind them. Out of the corner of his eye he saw his mother. She'd got the old shotgun out from the kitchen, an ancient single-barrelled thing and had fired it at the nearest gunmen. The one who'd shot Hector spun back as he caught a load of pellets in his shoulder. His mother had split the gun and was loading another cartridge into it.

He'd got the car into second now and, engine screaming, it lurched onto the lane, gathering speed. The wounded gunman, holding his right shoulder, tried to stagger out of the way but the Citroen's wing caught him and flung him to the side. His companion had jumped clear and, in the rear-view mirror, Lopes could see him trying to regroup and take aim at the car. Lopes was more concerned about the rifleman, who was crouched, taking a bead on Lopes himself as the car sped towards him. Despite the trauma of the situation, Lopes was able to process what was happening almost as if it were a film being shown in slow motion. The rifleman definitely had the calmness of a marksman, he was taking his time. He wouldn't miss.

Lopes braced himself for the impact.

Instead the roar of the shotgun was followed by the rifleman jerking his head to the right, taking his hand off the trigger and bringing it to his face. It was only momentary, he recovered, resumed his grip but swung the weapon across, now aiming it past the car.

Lopes knew what the target was.

The movie continued.

The man fired. The rifle's muzzle jerked up. Lena screamed.

'No, no, Beatriz!'

The rifleman swung back to resume his aim, pulling back the bolt in the same movement. Lopes could see in his eyes the knowledge that it was too late but still he didn't move.

For all the hatred he felt for what he'd just done, Lopes admired the man for his devotion as the Citroen hit him full square at perhaps 40km per hour. There was a spray of blood, the already holed windscreen shattered as something came through it. The car notably slowed at the impact, bumped and lurched over the man's body and then was away, Lopes ducking as the three remaining gunmen fired their pistols at the retreating vehicle.

A slight bend gave them respite, the men behind no longer had line of sight, but Lopes guessed this would be temporary, there'd be more men in the village. It's what he'd have done, if he had tracked down a potentially dangerous target. Once they'd traced them, he'd have sent a full team to make sure his quarry did not escape. He'd seen five men, that was at least two cars worth.

There'd be more.

As they raced into the village his suspicions were confirmed. There were three cars parked near Hector's bar in front of the church and more of Da Souza's men stood by them, guns drawn, forewarned by the sound of gunfire. Their car attracted a fusillade of shots, more glass shattered, Lena yelped next to him and clutched her face, plumes of steam came from the radiator and it lurched to one side as a tyre burst. Fortunately, being a Traction Avant, this wasn't fatal, the Citroen hardly lost any of its poise as it swept past the gunmen.

Wrestling the damaged car, they left the village behind. Lopes knew that they'd be followed and, with the damage, there was no way that they could escape. He looked in the rearview mirror only to find it had vanished, presumably shot away. He briefly looked over his shoulder, yes, one of the cars was pulling away.

He glanced at Lena.

'You alright?'

'Yes, it was just glass. Nothing serious.'

She was crying. Lopes knew it wasn't from fear.

He turned back to look at the road. The steam still streamed from the holed radiator. With the puncture he could only get the Citroen to just over 30 kph. They had a few hundred metres on their pursuers, maybe 800 at most, that was all.

Not enough. It was over.

Then he saw what had come through the windscreen and now lay between him and Lena. It was the gunman's rifle.

That gave them a chance.

He looked ahead. There was a bend in the road. He recognised it, it was a sharp one, more than 45 degrees to the right. He knew what was beyond, another track, also on the right side of the road.

He'd have to be quick. He'd also have to go back in time twenty-something years and be a soldier again.

He took the bend as quickly as he dared, catching the slide, then pulled onto the track, slamming on the brakes. The car slid to a halt, its nose in the undergrowth.

'Lopes! What are you doing?'

'Keep down,' he said, grabbing the rifle and opening the car door. He went to the back and crouched down. He half pulled back the bolt. One in the chamber. How many in the magazine? More than one he hoped.

He put the bolt back into the firing position and readied himself. His breathing was all over the place but there was familiarity in what he was doing; he was a marksman, the sniper again.

The first car was nearly at the bend. Lopes mentally calculated where he would start to track the vehicle, how much of a lead he'd have to give it, and where he would fire.

He'd only have one chance.

What he'd rehearsed became real. The car appeared and Lopes was the man he'd hated again; a battle-hardened 18-year-old killer with no conscience. He fired, the rifle's barrel rose and the recoil thumped back into his shoulder like it had all those years ago.

He hit his target, the driver's head. Of course he had; the range was only, what, fifty or sixty metres, how could he miss? Whatever the result was as sickening as he'd remembered from all those years before. No little hole, no slumping back as they showed in the movies, real life wasn't like that. Instead the powerful steel-clad lead slug impacted the flesh, bone and brain, fragmented inside and blew the man's skull to bits as it exited.

The car careened on, the dead man's foot still hard on the throttle, and disappeared into the trees. There was an almighty smash as it impacted something solid but Lopes paid no attention to it. He still had work to do.

He pulled back the bolt, ejected the spent cartridge and prayed that the magazine would deliver at least one more bullet into the chamber.

It did.

He resumed his stance, taking aim again.

The second car appeared slightly further to the left than the original. He had to adjust his aim. He was ashamed at how natural it felt, how good he was at it. For all the years, for all the regret, he was still the same.

He fired. His aim was true again but this time the dead driver must have been thrown away from the pedals and knocked it out of gear for the car slowed and trundled to a stop, its nose in a bush, engine still running. The passenger door was opened, a man got out, revolver in hand. Lopes pulled back the bolt, ejected the cartridge and knew instantly that the rifle was empty. He closed the chamber as if it was loaded and stood, taking aim at the gunman.

'Drop it,' he said. 'Now, or you get the same.'

The man hesitated.

'Do it! Now!'

The man dropped the gun.

'Good, kick it towards me.' Lopes was aware that Lena had got out of the Citroen. 'Go and get it,' he said. 'Then cover him.'

She did as she was told though the gun was held in a very shaky hand. That would be the shock and the adrenalin wearing off, he'd be the same in a few minutes. He kept the rifle up as he walked towards the pair. 'Hold it in both hands,' he whispered in her ear as he passed her. 'Shoot him if he moves,' he added more loudly.

He lowered the rifle from his shoulder and headed over to the car, a black Ford.

'You're a dead man, Lopes,' said the gunman. 'When the boss finds out, you're dead.'

Lopes laughed. 'And what were you lot trying to do before, just tickle me with lead. Go fuck yourself.' Lopes was actually shocked at himself; he rarely swore. Now it seemed appropriate. He got to the car door, laid the rifle down next to it, and steeled himself for what he'd see inside.

He was taken back to the last time he'd done this; September 12th, 1918. Two days after his 18th birthday. It was the big push, the Kaiser's army was in full retreat. They were fighting alongside the

British, but they'd been held up by a machine gun nest, manned by a lone, lonely, left behind private. Their officers had called up the snipers. He'd made the kill, not surprising, he was the best shot. He'd done it dozens of times before. He'd like to say he didn't know the number but the truth was, he did, they were represented by 24 notches carved into the stock of his rifle. This was number 25 but he'd never add this one, the last one. After this he let others fire first or shot to scare, not to kill. The difference; this was the first one where he'd seen the results, the officer had brought him forward after the troops had advanced to congratulate him. What he found was a boy even younger than him, Lopes' bullet had removed the top of his head. The boy's hands were still on the machine gun's trigger and his face showed pure terror. Not surprising as he was facing down an army on his own.

He had soft blue eyes. Lopes never forgot that. An artist's eyes.

He pushed that memory away and tugged open the driver's door of the Ford. The driver rolled out. Lopes dragged him away, trying not to look at his head. The other car was all but invisible in the undergrowth but he could see it had hit a tree pretty much head on. There was no sign of movement but there was a lick of flame. Time to go before it properly caught.

He went back to Lena. 'Give me the gun then go and get the bags. We'll take the Ford.'

She did as she was told.

Da Souza's man spat on the ground. 'That's the Jew bitch, is it? She's the one who caused all this.'

Lopes stared at him for a few moments. He was tempted, so, so tempted, to shoot him then and there.

But he was better than that.

'Run off to your friends. What's left of them are back that way.' The man didn't move, perhaps afraid that Lopes would shoot him in the back. 'Go on! Go!' he yelled. 'Run!' Lopes encouraged him with a shot just behind the heels. Da Souza's man virtually sprinted away.

Lena was now stood by the Ford.

'Get in, we need to get away before the rest get here.'

Lopes got into the driver's seat. There was a neat hole in the windscreen and a spray of blood and brains on the seat and door. He ignored it. The engine was still running, he put the Ford into gear and lurched back onto the road.

It was five minutes before Lena spoke.

'Dinis. Your mother…'

'I know,' he said. 'I know.'

THURSDAY 22ND MAY 1941,

8.50 PM

'Thanks,' said the night manager, a man in his sixties dressed in a mauve jacket that had perhaps been part of a smart uniform twenty years before, as he took the money. He tossed the keys over to Lopes. 'Room's on the 3rd floor,' adding. 'There's no lift,' before retreating back to his office where the radio could be heard playing.

Lopes picked the keys up and collected his bag. 'Come on,' he muttered to Lena.

They trudged up the stairs side-by-side, not saying anything. It had been a long day and a long journey but Lopes knew that sheer tiredness was not the reason why they'd barely exchanged a dozen words. Each had been lost in their own thoughts.

They had been in the Ford for less than two hours, all the time checking behind them for pursuers as well as being on edge in every village or town they drove through in case the authorities had been alerted. The bullet hole through the windscreen was relatively neat, the high velocity slug had punched a neat hole in the glass that only had the slightest starring radiating from it, but it seemed to Lopes so obvious that everyone who saw it must know what it represented and that they surely must also catch sight of the bloody stains on the door and window to his left but no-one seemed to. Whatever, it was a relief when they reached the coast and were able to abandon the car in a side street and caught a train south. They hadn't risked going all the way into Lisbon in case the station was being watched (Lopes would certainly have done that if he was in charge of the search for them). Instead they got off at Malecas and caught the bus to Estoril.

And now here they were, checking into a hotel that had seen better days well away from the fashionable seafront. Those were favoured by the in-crowd and spies alike. Lopes had no desire to be seen and this establishment, although tacky and far from clean, had a reputation for asking no questions and not passing on their guests' details to the authorities as they were required to do.

As he let them into their room, Lopes couldn't help but imagine how he'd feel if the circumstances were different. He'd taken rooms with Margarida and others and had always experienced an electric frisson, a jolt of excitement and anticipation as he'd opened the door, knowing that once it was closed with them inside what would follow. He and Lena were lovers but the events of the day stood in the way. As he closed the door behind them this time there was no excitement but, instead, a mourning, not just for the dead but because he knew this was unlikely to be repeated in happier circumstances in the future.

'We should unpack and then go and get something to eat,' he said.

Lena sat on the bed. 'I'm not hungry,' she said.

'I am,' said Lopes.

'There's still no need to go out,' she said. She held up the lunch bag. 'Beatriz…' she began but then the dam he'd suspected she'd built broke, the tears flowing.

Lopes sat next to her and put his arm around her.

'It's all right,' he said.

'It's not! How can it be? She's dead…and it's my fault. It's all my fault, all of this.'

He shook his head. 'No it's not. Don't blame yourself. You didn't start this.'

'But I – '

'No, you didn't,' he said firmly. 'The blame is on a loose-lipped idiot and a megalomaniac madman and his cronies. You've just got caught up in it.'

She wiped her face with her fingers and shook her head. 'I don't believe that,' she said. 'And I don't think you do, not really.' She stared at him. 'Why aren't you angrier? Why aren't you more upset? You've just lost your mother.'

'I know,' he said. 'I do feel…something. It's just a numb feeling at the moment. Maybe it's not sunk in properly yet. Not like it has with you.'

She nodded and fresh tears started. 'Maybe it's because you've only lost your mother once,' she muttered. She got up and went over to the mirror. 'God, what a state,' she said. 'I'm going to find the bathroom,' she said picking up a towel and opening her case. 'Then I just want to sleep and forget today.'

Lopes just nodded. After she had slipped out of the room, he looked again at the lunch sack. It had already held so many memories, today had added many more. He reached for it, imagining his mother's hands on it, then reached inside and took out some of the contents. He smiled, the bread and cheese were as neatly wrapped in waxy paper as he remembered from his teens. He nodded to himself, then unwrapped it and started to eat.

Today had been long but tomorrow was another day. He didn't know what they'd face. He needed to be ready for it whatever it was.

FRIDAY 23RD MAY 1941, 7.50 AM

The morning started unexpectedly, perhaps to both of them. Lena had sought him out in the night, probably looking for warmth or security but it meant, when they woke, they were in sensuous proximity. They made love without exchanging a word which, somehow, accentuated the closeness. Afterwards they lay together in each other's arms, each lost in the sensations of the afterglow.

It was Lopes who broke the spell.

'Which bank is it, where the box is held?'

She told him.

'Ah yes, I know where that is. You have the key for the box?'

'Yes, and the account number. That's all I need. With you giving your approval, of course, as my male supervisor.'

There was no bitterness at the barb aimed at the Estado Novo.

'Good. Hopefully Da Souza won't have made any connection with Vogel and Estoril. We'll have to be careful though. There's a chance he'll have spread the word to look out for us.'

She nodded. 'I know.'

'And when you do the exchange with Connolly. That will be back in Lisbon I take it?'

Lena raised herself up and looked into his eyes, frowning. 'Why the interrogation, Lopes?' she said.

He laughed. 'I'm not interrogating you, Lena, honestly. I wouldn't dare. I'm just trying to plan ahead and keep us both alive. If we're going to the States, I'd like to keep us all in one piece.'

She kept up her gaze for a few more seconds then settled back down again.

'I'm to call him when I've got it. We'll arrange a time and place then, though he had talked about doing it in the Embassy itself.'

Lopes nodded to himself. 'It makes sense to do that. It's safe and puts us beyond the reach of everyone.' He checked his watch. 'Nearly eight,' he said. 'I don't know about you but I could do with breakfast.'

'I'd like a long soak in a bath first,' she said. 'I've missed doing that, and it might be a while before I can do it again.'

Lopes smiled and kissed her on the head. 'That sounds like a good idea. I'll go and see if I can organise some room service, and get breakfast sent up here. Better that than risk being seen in public. Let's play it safe.'

She raised herself up again, seeking out his lips. She did feel so good in his arms.

Ten minutes later, when Lena had gone to the bathroom and he'd quickly dressed he headed downstairs.

He handed some banknotes to the desk man. 'Have breakfast sent to room 317 in half an hour,' he said. The man quickly flicked through the money, counting. His eyes widened. Lopes knew it was overly generous. It was meant to be.

'Of course, sir,' said the desk man. 'Will there be anything else?'

'I need a telephone,' said Lopes. 'And I'd like to use it somewhere private.'

A few seconds later he was in the back office. A glare had been enough to encourage the desk man to go elsewhere. He picked up the instrument and waited for the operator. When she came on, Lopes told her the number he needed.

'Alberto?' he said. 'Sorry to call you so early.'

'Dinis, my boy, what is it?'

'There's something I need you to do, or rather two people I need you to contact. I'm pretty certain you'll know them. It's important and it needs to be done right now.'

'Is this something to do with what you came to see me about the other day?'

'Yes, it is. Which makes it potentially dangerous.'

There was a pause at the other end of the line. He knew that the old policeman, for all their friendship and years of service together, was weighing up whether he wanted to be involved. Lopes could understand why he wouldn't, Alberto was enjoying his retirement, a well-deserved retirement free from the politics and unpleasantness that came with the job. On the other hand, if he didn't help, Lopes had no other plan. For it to work, he needed Alberto.

'Alright,' said Alberto. 'Who do you need me to contact.'

Lopes gave a silent prayer of thanks and told him. Though he didn't need to he explained why.

Two minutes later he was back up in the room. As expected, Lena was still luxuriating in the bath. He had time now to shave.

Time to shave and reflect.

Not just reflect, doubt.

But he was committed now.

FRIDAY 23RD MAY 1941,

10.50 AM

The bank proved to be easier than Lopes expected.

He'd anticipated resistance, the Estado Novo had laid down restrictions on women's lives; the Constitution of 1933, although stressed that citizens were equal, went on to say, "except for the woman, the differences resulting from her nature and the good of the family". That meant restrictions on the professions women could do, on the rights of married women and on financial controls. This was one of the reasons the influx of refugees had been such a shock to straight-laced Lisbon, the women, relatively independent and fashionable had been something that the authorities had worried about. They provided a strong lead as to an alternative.

But here, in this Estoril bank, the teller had no issues in dealing with a woman. Perhaps it was because the resort had a long history of attracting a cosmopolitan clientèle from all corners of the globe. Whatever, as soon as Lena handed over the key and provided the account details she was accepted as the true custodian of the security box and she and Lopes were ushered into a private office where the box was brought to her and then the pair were left alone to carry out their business.

Lopes realised his heart was beating faster as he regarded the box sitting on the table in front of him. Lena seemed to share his near shock that the object he'd puzzled about, that had caused such violence, sadness and death was almost within touching distance. She, too, just stared at the box for a few seconds, almost as if she was afraid to touch it.

The tension became almost unbearable. Lopes almost got to the point of yelling at her to open it when she made her move to do so.

The box was metal, narrow, about 30 cm wide and perhaps 400 cm long, the lock being at one end, the lid hinging at the other.

Lena unlocked it, then he heard her take a deep breath and only then opened the lid.

She breathed a sigh of relief.

'Here it is,' she whispered, taking out a small box, almost as wide as the security box itself but quite shallow, no more than 3 cm deep. She opened it and showed Lopes the contents.

And there it was, looking so innocent but, in fact, so, so deadly. A spool, like you'd get with a cine film but the fragile looking tape on it had no image frames but was a ferrous reddish-brown colour. He reached out to touch it. Yes, it was real.

Lena had turned her attention to the rest of the box. There was some paperwork that looked like deeds to a property. She ignored those but didn't ignore the stacks of cash, some Escudos but also Francs, Dollars, British Pounds and Reichsmarks. She collected them and put them into her bag, along with a couple of jewelry cases.

She caught Lopes' eye and shrugged.

'So?' she said defiantly. 'Uwe would want me to have all this.'

For some reason, Lopes found the mention of Uwe's name wounding but he nodded.

'Of course,' he said.

There was no doubt that she would need the money in the months to come, but he didn't mention this.

'Right,' he said. 'Shall we go and find a telephone for you so you can call Connolly and tell him we're on the way to the embassy?'

She was putting the tape carefully into her bag, fortunately it was quite capacious. 'Yes,' she said. 'Let's get it done.'

'Whilst you're doing that, I'll organise a taxi for us. It's too dangerous for us to take the train into the city. Da Souza's men will be sure to be watching the station, probably the buses too.' He took out his wallet and checked the contents. 'But this might be a problem. I, of course, didn't bring my chequebook when I left.'

Lena nodded. She rummaged through her bag and took out the roll of escudos and peeled off some notes, handing them over. Lopes took them without displaying his emotions.

'It'll soon be over,' he murmured.

FRIDAY 23RD MAY 1941,

12.32 PM

They sat together in the back of the taxi. At first, they were like strangers, not speaking, a distance between them but, as the car reached the outskirts of the city, the spell that kept them apart seem to be broken. Lena looked across at him and smiled, then reached for his hand

'Sorry I've been so cold and distant since…well, since you know,' she said.

He nodded. 'It's all right, I understood. It was…hard.'

Lena leaned into him and he put his arm around her. It felt wrong but she felt good. He almost told her then and there but found the strength not to.

'I loved her, you know,' she said. 'I only knew her such a short time but I loved her.'

Lopes swallowed hard. 'I know,' he croaked, pushing the emotion away. 'And I could see she felt the same about you.' He kissed the top of her head.

She lay still for a moment then lifted her face to his, her lips seeking out his.

They kissed until Lopes became conscious of the taxi driver's eyes on them in the rear-view mirror. Lopes had paid him extra to stay silent but couldn't stop him eyeballing them. Lopes broke away, smiling slightly in embarrassment.

Lena saw where he was looking and grinned. 'Get used to the jealousy, Dinis,' she whispered, 'I'm aiming to make a lot of American men envious of you.'

Lopes swallowed but couldn't force an answer out of his lips.

The taxi drove on, Lena in his arms and, increasingly, on his conscious.

It was with some relief when, about ten minutes later, she noticed what he knew would be obvious. She had glanced out of the window, then straightened up, pushing away from Lopes.

'This isn't the way to the American embassy,' she said. 'We should have turned then. Hey, driver, driver.'

The driver ignored her, as he'd been paid to do.

'No, you're going wrong! Stop, turn around.'

'He's not going wrong,' said Lopes quietly. 'He's going to exactly where I told him to go.'

'What?' she turned, her face showing her bewilderment. 'Where you…? Why, Dinis, why? What have you done?'

'I'm sorry, Lena,' he said, pulling out Armstrong's pistol. 'I have to do this.'

FRIDAY 23RD MAY 1941, 1.10 PM

She stared at the gun, disbelief on her face.

'So…what? Where am I going? To the PVDE? Am I under arrest?'

'No. I wouldn't do that to you.'

She gave a snort of derision. 'Of course not, of course you wouldn't because you're such a nice a nice guy.' She sat back, looking straight ahead. 'Was this always the plan?'

'Pretty much so, yes.'

'I trusted you, Dinis. I love you. At least I did.'

The word hit him hard. Even though it had only been a few days, even though he'd once doubted her, now he believed her. It was all too late.

Far too late.

He had to believe this was the right way.

The taxi pulled up outside a familiar building but one that looked very different in daylight.

'Here you are, sir,' said the driver, eying the gun nervously.

'Thanks,' said Lopes. 'Out you get, I'll follow you.' He took a firm grip of Lena's right arm and, sure enough, she tried to twist free as soon as she got into the street whilst he was still shuffling across to follow. He was ready for this and jerked her roughly back, sharply enough to hurt judging by the yelp of pain.

'You bastard,' she whispered. 'You utter bastard.'

The side door opened and Alberto stepped out into the street. The old policeman nodded as Lopes gave him a questioning look; Lopes sighed in relief and gratitude. His old friend had come through.

'Inside,' he said.

Once in the building, Lopes saw her puzzlement grow.

'This is-'

'The kitchen of a Fado bar, yes,' said Lopez. 'It has the advantage of my knowing it and the proprietor. We can meet privately here. It was the best place I could think of.'

'For what?' said Lena. 'Who are you selling me out to? The British? The Germans?'

'I'm not selling you out to anyone.' Lopes waved the pistol indicating she should walk through to the bar area. Inside there were two middle-aged men waiting, sat at the same table as they had nine days before.

'This is Sir Simon Hazelwood,' he said nodding at the British diplomat. 'And this is Herr Von Wernsdorf, I'm sorry, sir, I can't recall your first name.'

The German diplomat rose, clicked his heels together, and bowed his head. 'Otto,' he said. 'I was named after Bismark.' He turned to Lena. 'Good afternoon, Miss Katz.'

'Sod off, you Nazi thug,' said Lena.

'Otto here is no Nazi,' said Sir Simon. 'He's not part of that crowd. If he was, I wouldn't have any dealings with him.'

'So what is this?' said Lena. 'An auction? You're going to go for highest and best bids for me?'

'No. Give me the bag and sit down.'

'No.'

'Do as he says, Miss,' said Alberto, who'd drawn his own weapon. There was a brief standoff then she, reluctantly, did as she was told. Alberto passed the bag to Lopez.

Lopes rummaged through it and extracted the tape and the transcript. He kept the former and passed the latter to the two men. 'You read English?' he said to Von Wernsdorf.

'Yes, I do.'

The two men moved their chairs closer together so they could read the transcript at the same time. They looked like two old men sharing a newspaper. They read in silence, the pages being turned by wordless agreement, waiting whilst one or the other finished or re-read a section.

At last they reached the end.

The two men moved apart and looked at each other.

'This can't get out. It's wrong to use this. It would embarrass your King and the Royal Family.'

To Lopes' surprise it was Von Wernsdorf who said this.

'I'm glad you agree, Otto,' said Sir Simon.

Von Wernsdorf turned to Lopes. 'I understand some of my countrymen have committed crimes in this country in pursuit of that.' He nodded towards the tape still held in Lopes' hand. 'Even if it was one of our countrymen who was the victim it shouldn't have happened on the streets of Lisbon. I apologise for that on behalf of my country.'

Lena gave a snort of derision. 'They've done a lot more than murdering poor Uwe,' she said. 'And not just to Germans.'

Von Wernsdorf frowned and looked questioningly at Lopes.

'She's right, at least three Portuguese citizens have been murdered, one a policeman, as well as one Briton,' he said. 'One of the Portuguese was my own mother.'

'I apologise for that, and my condolences,' said Von Wernsdorf. 'But, since the circumstances of the death of Herr Vogel came to our attention, certain members of the embassy staff were placed on restricted duties and had their movements limited. So these crimes cannot have been carried out by German nationals operating out of the embassy.'

The man was shrewd, Lopes gave him that.

'No they probably weren't. They were carried out by PVDE agents but they were acting on the orders of factions within your embassy.'

'Do you have evidence of that? Sound evidence?'

'No I don't.'

Von Wernsdorf smiled. 'Then it is just conjecture on your part, isn't it? We cannot be held responsible for what – '

'I don't care what the diplomatic niceties are,' said Lopes sharply. 'We all know the truth and I know how Salazar will view the situation when they get my report. There will be consequences.'

The diplomat suddenly looked uncomfortable. 'Indeed,' he said.

For all the respect Sir Simon might have had for his counterpart, he couldn't help but look smug at the German's discomfort. Lopes knew he needed to address this.

'Your agents are not without blame,' he said. He pulled out Armstrong's gun and showed it to the diplomat. 'I had to confiscate this from a member of the British embassy staff after he was involved in a gun battle on the streets of Lisbon.' Lopes paused whilst this sunk in. 'Again, there would be consequences for Anglo/Portuguese relations if this was revealed.'

Sir Simon nodded. 'I understand.' He looked at Von Wernsdorf. 'What I don't understand is what you want from us. You clearly need something.'

'I do. The rogue PVDE agents have seized my son and they are holding him to make me hand over the recording to them. I need him released and an undertaking that he and my family are not threatened again, from *both* sides.'

The two men looked at each other. 'And, in return, we get what?' said Sir Simon.

'My report will blame rogue elements primarily within the PVDE and stress your help in clearing up the matter.' He looked at each man in turn. 'It means that your access to Wolfram will be maintained,' he added.

Von Wernsdorf was looking at the tape. 'And that, what happens to that?'

Lopes looked at it too, then at Lena who glared defiantly back at him.

'I have a solution that suits all sides,' he said.

Mentally, he added to himself, all sides but one.

Von Wernsdorf rose. 'Is there a telephone here?' he said. 'I need to call the ambassador.'

'I'll take you to the proprietor's office,' said Alberto. 'Dinis, will you keep an eye on Miss Katz?'

'Of course.' Lopes still held Armstrong's pistol. He looked pointedly at it as Alberto guided Von Wernsdorf to the manager's office.

'Would you really shoot me, Lopes?' Lena said. 'Would you really sink so low?'

'I don't know,' he murmured. 'I've done things in the last few days I didn't think it was possible for me to do. It would be better not to test me.'

She shook her head, her face bitter. 'I trusted you,' she said. 'More than that…I…' He saw her glance towards Sir Simon who gave the impression of a dinner guest caught at a table unawares in the midst of a lovers' argument. He rose.

'I'll just…well, I'll get some air. Do call me when Otto returns. Excuse me.'

After he'd stepped outside, Lopes came and took a seat next to Lena.

'I had to do this,' he said. 'I had to.'

'Why?'

'Because it's my job. Because all this affects my country. And because of my son.'

She shook her head again.

'You're a fool, Lopes,' she whispered. 'Such a fool. More than a fool, you're something worse.'

Lopes nodded.

'I know,' he said.

They sat in silence for a few minutes, until Alberto and Von Wernsdorf came back.

'It's done,' said the diplomat. 'The ambassador was furious with those responsible. They will be disciplined. He too passes on his deepest apologies. But, above all, the boy is safe. He is being returned to his mother.'

'Thank you,' said Lopes. 'Alberto, Sir Simon has stepped outside. Would you mind getting him?'

Alberto did as he was told. When everyone was present, Lopes got up and retrieved the tape and the transcript.

'So who gets that?' said Sir Simon.

'No-one does.'

Lopes walked over to the fireplace, unused in the warmth of spring. He crumpled up the transcript and placed them on the old ashes, then put the tape on top.

'No Dinis, no, please. You can't do it, that's my ticket out of here.'

He ignored her. He reached for his matches, took one out, struck it, waited until the wood was properly alight then lit the paper. The fire started slowly but, when it reached the tape, it intensified abruptly. The reel was consumed in moments.

He looked at the diplomats who were apparently mesmerised by the flames.

'Well?' he said. 'Does that satisfy you both.'

The two men looked at each other and nodded.

'It does,' said Sir Simon.

'A most sensible outcome,' said Von Wernsdorf.

'Hey, where's she gone?' Alberto said. 'Damn it, Dinis, I wasn't watching her. I'll go – '

'Leave her, Alberto,' said Lopes. 'I was going to let her go anyway.'

'She's taken the bag.'

Lopes nodded. 'Good, that means she's got Vogel's money and the jewels. She deserves that.'

'We will take our leave,' said Sir Simon. 'Good luck, Otto,' he added.

The German diplomat just nodded. He clearly had a difficult path to tread whether he had the support of his superior or not.

Like, Lopes reflected, his own situation.

Alberto seemed to read Lopes' mind. 'So my boy, where do you go from here?'

Lopes smiled and shrugged. 'Who knows, Alberto, who knows?' He thought about his mother and the small holding. 'Maybe I'll go back to farming,' he added. He looked at his watch. 'But for now I need a drink.'

Alberto nodded. 'That's a damned good idea, my boy. Lead on.'

MONDAY 26TH MAY 1941,

11.15 AM

Lopes took one last look at the office. In his absence it had not turned it into a palace, it was still a basement storeroom and he had spent so little time in it that he had virtually nothing to pack up and take with him. It was a wrench leaving it though; he had shared it with Costa and Alvares had done a good job in turning it from a dump into a proper workplace.

He had little to show from the last couple of weeks, at least little that wasn't negative. His relationship with Margarida was already awful but from now on it would be totally hostile. His chances of ever seeing his son, the boy whose life he'd saved, had gone. He had found his clothes moved into the spare room, had spent most of the weekend in an empty house, his wife had gone to her parents. She had come back on Sunday evening as frosty as a January morning in the mountains.

'She came here,' she had said as soon as she had come in through the door. 'That woman. That whore you had a bastard with.'

'I'm sorry,' he muttered. 'I'll move out.'

'You will not!' She stood a foot away from him, bristling with fury. 'You will not put me through that shame, nor the ignominy of a divorce. You'll stay. We'll pretend to all outside. But here, in my house, keep out of my way. I don't want to see you.'

She had swept past him on the way to her room.

So that was over - no, not over, worse, continuing as a living death.

And, what made it more dreadful, his thoughts kept returning to Lena, Elena now he supposed. He remembered how she felt, how she looked by the river, how he felt inside when he'd let himself entertain thoughts that it could all be real.

And that terrible, nagging doubt that it could so easily have been made real and that he'd thrown it all away.

There was no respite at night. After struggling for hours to sleep in the spare bed, sleep had made it worse. She'd come to him in his dreams and he'd confessed his love for her.

She'd laughed and walked away.

The one highlight of his weekend had been seeing Costa in the hospital and meeting his wife and children.

Costa was on the mend, getting stronger every day and his family were delightful, the children lively and mischievous, the bond between Costa and his wife strong and loving. It was both wonderful to see and so, so hard for Lopes, a reminder of what he didn't have and probably never would.

'I'll be out soon, sir,' Costa had said. 'And then we'll be back together. I really enjoy working with you. I know you might not want to. I hated having to report back to the Tenente. That wasn't right.'

Lopes had nodded, said all the right things, easy because it was the truth, he had enjoyed working with Costa and had always known and understood that Costa had been made to spy on him. He knew too though that this would never happen again because his time at the PVDE was over. Whether he wanted to or not (which was a not), he'd have no choice. He'd disobeyed orders, he'd gone his own way, ended the affair of the disgraced King and his loose tongue on his own terms and in his own ways, not the way his superiors had wanted.

There was only one way this was going to end.

He was surprised he'd even been let into the building. He had only come here because he had nowhere else to go and because he still had enough strength of duty to face up to what he'd done like a good soldier.

He expected to be arrested but the doorkeeper had let him in with barely a nod.

The phone on the desk rang, making him jump.

He picked it up.

'Hello?'

'Inspector Lopes? Tenente Oliveira would like to see you in his office.'

'Of course, I'll be right up.'

He put the telephone down and sighed. So this was it. Wearily he got to his feet.

To his surprise he wasn't kept waiting but was ushered straight into the inner sanctum. His surprise increased when his superior got to his feet and came across to meet him, hand outstretched.

'My dear Lopes, I'm so sorry about your mother. It was an absolute tragedy.'

'Er, thank you, sir, yes, it was a shock.'

'Come, please, sit down.'

Lopes did, as did Oliveira.

'You will, of course, have as much leave as you need for the funeral and in dealing with your mother's affairs,' Oliveira went on.

Lopes just stared at him.

'Leave?' he said at last.

'Yes, of course.' Oliveira looked puzzled. 'Why, what did you expect? To be fired?'

'At least that.'

Oliveira gave a snort of laughter. 'That's one of the things we admire about you, your honesty and straightforwardness. It's not something we are used to in the PVDE.' He looked more serious. 'But although your methods were...how do I put this? Unconventional? Yes, that is the word, unconventional, the results were just what the country required. That was why you were recruited in the first place; you were known as a man who gets results.'

'But...' began Lopes but then bit his lip. He was going to protest that he wasn't 'recruited' he was blackmailed into a job, that it was strongly hinted that it was a one-off and, once completed, he would not be needed. It *was* complete and many of the things he'd been blackmailed over were now out in the open. But he knew that Oliveira knew this too so there had to be something else, something that gave him the certainty that Lopes had to stay.

Oliveira was smiling, Lopes knew he was watching the realisation sink in. After he had stretched these moments out into seconds, his superior at last opened one of his desk drawers and took out a slim manila folder, opened it and extracted the single page within, glanced at it briefly then handed it over to Lopes.

It was a hand-written note, the writing neat and somehow professorial:

To Inspector Dinis Lopes,

I have been informed of the service that you have recently given to Estado Novo and the deep, personal sacrifice that you have suffered. On behalf of myself and the state we offer you our deepest sympathy but also our heartfelt thanks for what you have done.

Portugal and I, as you know, treads the difficult path of neutrality. I know that you endured the terrible times that this country's young men and mothers suffered in the Great War and this must never happen again. We must and will avoid being directly involved in this conflict. Your actions in this recent affair, the details of which I have closely monitored, have resulted in a most desirable outcome and helped us to avoid this fate.

I know that you will continue to serve Estado Novo in the years to come and will closely follow your career as you continue your vital work.

Salazar

Lopes closed his eyes. This last line gave Oliveira the power as well as his instructions. Salazar himself wanted Lopes to continue and, in the Estado Novo, what Salazar wanted, Salazar got.

He handed the note back to Oliveira.

'When do you want me back?' he said.

Oliveira carefully replaced the note in the folder then put it in his desk. 'A week,' he said. 'That should be sufficient time for you?'

'Yes,' said Lopes dully. Oliveira rose, clearly indicating that the meeting was over but Lopes stayed stubbornly where he was. With a sigh Oliveira sank back into his chair.

'Yes?' he said.

'Da Souza. What has happened to him.'

Oliveira stared at Lopes. 'He has been suspended.'

Lopes waited, but nothing more was forthcoming.

'And?' he prompted.

'And what?'

'What will happen to him? Will he be prosecuted?'

'What for?'

Lopes' mouth dropped open. 'What do you mean, what for? For the murder of a young policeman. Kidnap, orchestrating a shoot out on the streets of this city, the deaths of my mother and another citizen of Portugal.'

Oliveira shrugged. 'There is no evidence that Da Souza himself was directly involved in any of these unfortunate cases.'

'He may not have pulled the trigger but he was the leader, the instigator and –'

'Lopes, stop!' snapped Oliveira. 'As Da Souza has pointed out that there are many rogue elements within the state, which is why the work of the PVDE is so vital.' Oliveira held up his palms to forestall Lopes' protests. 'I am, of course, aware that he is lying but he, too, has influential friends who protect him. We have to work within the system, Lopes. It is a delicate machine.'

Lopes stared at him, trying to control the anger that seethed within. At last he felt he was able to speak.

'I understand,' he muttered, then got to his feet and walked out of the office.

SATURDAY 31ST MAY 1941,

11.10 PM

Lopes stepped back into a doorway, the shadows hiding him from view. He watched the two men who had come out of the bar a little way down the street. He waited until they stepped under the light of a streetlight. No, neither of them was the man he was waiting for so he stayed hidden in the shadows until they'd passed by.

He was about to step out into the street again to resume his vigil but something, a feeling, one that he'd been having since he left his house a couple of hours made him pause. It was one he'd had many times on the beat, a sixth sense for danger that had saved him uncountable times. This time he could not pin down the source of his concern. Eventually, reluctantly, he dismissed the feeling that someone was watching him and moved out into into the place where he could see the bar better.

Of course he had that feeling, he told himself, it was because of what his mission was. It was inevitable.

His heart skipped a beat. Two more men had come out of the bar and stood talking in the street, sharing a joke. Lopes stepped back into the shadows. Yes, this was who he was looking for. Now he needed them apart... yes, the pair were saying their goodnights, going their separate ways.

'Perfect,' he murmured.

His quarry walked towards him as Lopes knew he would. This was his route home, a fifteen-minute easy stroll. He let him pass, though there was a moment of alarm when the man paused almost opposite Lopes to light a cigarette. If he'd glanced over, the light from the match would have been enough to reveal Lopes lurking in the shadows, but he didn't, he carried on. Lopes waited a few seconds then followed.

This wasn't the place to act, it was too well-lit. Lopes knew where he would. He'd planned this.

Five minutes, five long minutes later and they were there.

The man turned off the main street into the quiet alley that Lopes knew he must take. It headed straight uphill, only an athlete would be able to run up it and this man was far from that. This was the place. He pulled out Armstrong's pistol and followed.

Da Souza was waiting for him, his own gun drawn.

'Well, well, well,' he said. 'So it's you. You've got balls, I'll give you that. I never thought you'd have it in you to come for me.' He nodded at Lopes' gun. 'Drop it.'

Lopes ignored him. 'I was always going to come for you, Da Souza,' he said. 'After what you did to my mother and Hector.'

'Hector?'

'He was the barman your men killed when they came for me.'

Da Souza laughed.

'And for the woman your men pushed under a tram. I don't know her name but I know her husband is still mourning her.'

'You pathetic little man,' Da Souza spat on the ground. 'Don't come on all tough. You haven't got the guts to — '

Lopes shot him in the face.

'And Da Silva,' he muttered. 'A young man with his entire life in front of him. That's for him too.'

He turned and walked back out of the alley, not bothering to check for signs of life. He was too good a shot not to have killed. He put the pistol in his pocket. It would be rubbed free of fingerprints and in the Tagus before the night was out.

Elena stepped out of a doorway in front of him, a small gun in her own hand. It was pointed straight at Lopes' head. He stopped,

They stood in silence for a few seconds.

Then she smiled. 'I wondered what you were doing, sneaking about after dark,' she said. She looked beyond Lopes and into the alleyway. Lopes followed her gaze. One of Da Souza's feet was all that was visible, the rest of his body hidden in the shadows. 'Well now I know.'

'He was going to get away with it,' said Lopes. 'I couldn't allow that.'

'He was the leader of the Nazi faction? The one you told me about?'

'He was.'

She nodded. 'He was next on my list,' she said. ' But I wasn't sure how I was going to find him. I never thought you'd…' She smiled again. 'But you did, so…' She lowered the gun. 'You get to live a little longer, Dinis.'

They stood in silence for a few more moments. Lopes broke it this time.

'Lena, I —'

'No,' she interrupted. 'Lena's gone. She's not coming back. It's too late.'

He nodded slowly and sadly. 'Okay,' he said.

They stood for a few more moments.

'What will you do now? You've got the money for a ticket to the States.'

'Some good that did me. That bastard Connolly has blocked my visa. So, I guess I'm staying. What I'll do? I don't know yet.' She shrugged. 'I'm sure our paths will cross, Dinis.'

She turned and walked away.

Lopes stood and watched her until she turned the corner.

He sighed. At least he had the memory.

He turned and walked towards the Tagus. He hoped he had the courage to only throw the gun in and not follow himself too.

But he had to live with what he'd done.

It was the least he could do.

THE END

CATCH UP WITH INSPECTOR LOPES AND COSTA IN THE NEXT BOOK IN THE SERIES

'THE QUEEN OF LISBON'

An extract is included below:-

21ST OCTOBER 1941 - 2350 HOURS - THE SS NORMAN GIBSON AN HOUR OUT FROM LISBON

Edward Jenkins wished he'd gone with his gut instinct and worn his duffel coat; it was as cold as he'd expected and, even up on the end of the wing bridge some thirty feet above the water, he and the other duty watch were periodically pelted by spray whipped up by the strengthening breeze. It wasn't the done thing though, the other three watch members were dressed like him in shirtsleeves as if they were still out on the town. Edward was, at sixteen, the youngest member of the crew, the kid, the boy, the powder monkey, whatever that was, the butt of all the jokes, the ribbing, the pranks everything was fired towards him already. He wasn't going to give them any cheap shots.

A night on the town.

Like last night.

Edward couldn't help smiling; last night. What a town, what a night, the best of his life, the whole city lit up, like Liverpool used to be when he was a kid before the war and the blackout. But his hometown was never like Lisbon, fragrant, heady, a melting pot of peoples like any port city but far more exotic. And the women, oh the women, well one woman, Ana Maria, a Brazilian. His first, though no one knew that but him and Ana Maria, his teacher, his muse.

She was so beautiful. Perfect.

He looked across to the South-East, up the Tagus estuary, where there was a glow in sky, the lights of that wonderful city reflected on the clouds. She was there. When would he see her again?

How many men would she see whilst he was gone? Edward hated the sick feeling that thought brought.

'Ow! Soddin' hell! What you do that for?'

The blow to his head was more of shock than pain but still he turned, furious, to face the culprit. His anger instantly vanished. It was Ellison, the Second Mate.

'Stop daydreaming, boy!' Ellison yelled into Edward's face. 'You're on watch. Keep your fucking eyes on the sea.'

'Sorry, sir,' muttered Edward, putting his binoculars to his eyes and turning to look out over the blackness.

'I'll give you bleeding sorry if I catch you again. You'll be in the brig.'

'Leave the boy alone, mon, can't you tell the lad's in love.'

The rich, deep golden voice could only be one man; Swanny, the Jamaican. Laid back, languid, Edward had been scared of the towering black man when he'd signed on but Swanny - real name the magnificent Lancelot Lionel Earnest Swan - had become first a protector and then a friend, sheltering Edward from the worst of the teasing.

Ellison, all five foot three of him, now squared up to the six-foot four West Indian, 'And you watch yourself too, Swanny.'

There was a distinct chuckle in Swanny's voice when he replied with, 'Yes, mister mate, mon. I will be watching myself, mon.'

Edward saw the other watch members turn away and knew they were hiding their laughter.

Ellison was no fool, he could tell he was being mocked. He backed away. 'All right, all right, enough. This is no sodding pleasure cruise. There are U-Boats out there,' he pointed to the west, towards the Atlantic. 'And we've got a hold stuffed with Wolfram that Hitler's boys would love not to get back to Blighty, so all of you, keep your wits about you and your eyes on the fucking sea, understand.' He turned back to Edward. 'And you boy, you keep your thoughts off whatever cheap whore took your drinking money and filled your head full of lies and promises last night.'

Edward took the strap of heavy binoculars from round his neck and stepped towards Ellison who'd turned his back to step inside the shelter of the wheelhouse. He was going to smash the mate's head in with the binoculars, not caring what would happen to him afterwards.

He didn't get far. It was like being grabbed by an immovable force. Edward was skinny, no more than nine stone sopping wet and his Jamaican buddy was not only tall, he had the physique to go with it. Swanny, whilst holding Edward to him, took the binoculars from out of his hands as easy as picking the head off a flower.

'He's not worth it, Eddy mon,' whispered Swanny. 'Just leave it.'

'But Ana Maria is…'

'I know, I know.' Swanny's tone was like honey and a soothing balm all at once. 'I saw her, Eddy, she really was a sweet little lady. Ellison's just jealous, he's trying to get a rise out of you. Don't let him get to you.'

Edward stopped struggling. 'Alright, alright, Swanny. Let go of me.'

Swanny didn't release him.

'You sure? You looked to have murder in mind, mon.'

'Yeah, yeah, I'm fine. Let me go.'

Swanny did.

'Give me those back.' Edward held out his hand for the binoculars. 'I've got a job to do, ain't I?'

'Job?' muttered one of the other watch members. 'Some bloody job, the Jerries never come this close in.'

'That's right,' said Charlie, the fourth watchman on duty. 'It's out in Biscay where it gets serious.'

Edward brought the binoculars up to his eyes and started scanning the horizon. His ability to focus was limited by the tears that had come with his anger at Ellison's insults about Ana Maria but Charlie was right; there was nothing to see anyway. Everyone knew the U-boats never came in this close to the Portuguese shore, that's what everyone said anyway.

He let his binoculars track away from his assigned quarter to the glow of lights that was Lisbon. He missed her already, yes, he knew what she did, hell he'd handed over his money on that first night. But after that she was his, he'd taken her out for the next two nights. He'd told her everything, of Liverpool, of growing up, of his mum insisting he went into the merchantmen instead of the Royal Navy because she thought it would be safer, of her horror when she realised the truth. He also repeated proudly what Swanny had said about their cargo when he'd asked what the hell Wolfram was; that it was the stuff that would win the war against Hitler, that when added to steel it turned it into something that could punch right through tanks, that both sides desperately needed it. 'We've got our holds full of it, Ana Maria. I'm helping win the war,' he'd told her and she'd nodded and kissed him and then listened how he'd take her home to see his mum in Liverpool once the war was won but that he had to go because his ship, the Norman Gibson, was leaving on the next night's tide, but he'd be back, with a ring.

Him and Ana Maria. Forever.

That was going to happen. He'd make it happen.

Edward suddenly remembered the job he was supposed to be doing. Swanny was right, there was no point letting Ellison win. He'd do his duty, get his pay, buy that ring and then, one day soon, put it on her finger.

He swung the binoculars back to his assigned quarter.

At first he couldn't process what he was seeing. A white line in the water, filling the lens from top to bottom. Was it some spray on the lens? A crack in the glass. He dropped them from his eyes and tried to check, first the lens and then the eyepieces. Nothing. Which meant…

He looked out to sea again, without the binoculars this time.

He could see it. Clear and stark. Just like he'd been told to look for.

It was coming.

'Tor…' he croaked. His words wouldn't form. 'Torpedo.'

He managed barely a whisper.

Somehow, he was flying.

How could he be flying? He was though, he could see clouds, the lights of Lisbon, a large blaze, the waves that —

Red.

Black.
Pain.
Cold, cold so cold.
He gasped. He didn't take in air, it was water. Pain. Choking.

He fought, panicking, what was holding him?

Swanny again?

His scrambled brain started working again.

No, he wasn't being held, he was deep under water, drowning. He had to stop fighting to take a breath and kick up, like he did at New Brighton, when he jumped off the pier with his pals.

How far down was he? Too far, too far!

Might as well give up.

Take a lungful.

End it.

Suddenly he could see — and breathe, he could breathe.

Edward took in deep, luxurious breaths of air, glorious air, coughing his way back to life. Now to get back to the Gibson. Did they know he was overboard? Had they stopped?

Where was it?

He trod water, turning slowly.

And there it was. The bow at least, sticking straight up out of the water, illuminated by the flames that ran all the way up from the new waterline up to the forward anti-aircraft gun position.

Just the ship. No people. No sign of life. Where was Swanny, or Charlie or even the Mate Ellison or any of the other thirty-odd people in the crew? He looked around for a life raft, a boat, anything?

There was nothing.

A flash of light was followed by a rolling roar like thunder and the sea suddenly fizzed and hissed. The magazine!

Edward dived down, forcing himself deeper into the cold sea, anything to get away from the rain of bullets and fragments of steel. Only when his lungs cried for mercy did he kick back up to the surface again.

It was dark. Of the SS Norman Gibson, his home for the last two months, there was no sign other than the debris that he floated in.

Then, abruptly, something white shot out of the water next to him. A cork lifebelt ring, the ship's name in peeling black paint on the side.

Gratefully, he ducked under the water and came up inside it, letting it support him.

He was alive.

For now

AFTERWORD

I hope you enjoyed Lisbon '41. It's been great to plunge into the murky world of neutral Portugal and the somewhat strange dictatorship created by Salazar. It's a world I intend to revisit.

Even if you didn't enjoy the book could I ask a big favour? I'm an independent author, I don't have a massive budget for marketing and distribution. I rely on targeted advertising and word-of-mouth to reach new readers. What really helps them to find authors like me that may be new to them are ratings and reviews. If you could spare a few moments to rate Lisbon '41 I'd be very grateful. I will certainly be in your debt if you can provide a longer review. Good or bad, I don't mind, it all helps to improve my books.

So, thank you in advance.

MH February 2024

BOOKS BY THIS AUTHOR

LMF

On a bitter night in January 1944 one last RAF bomber struggles on to the target alone with one engine out and its crew terrified, driven on by its burned-out pilot who needs one last mission to complete his tour.
And all of them know that if they fail the RAF has the sanction of declaring them to be 'Lacking Moral Fibre'... essentially cowards.

Eleven Days: A novel of the Great War

In April 1917 the average lifespan of a British pilot posted to the Western Front is just eleven days.
Eddie Grenville is 19, young, keen, idealistic. He hero worships his brother Percy, follows him into the RFC.
Then he finds that Percy has committed a war crime...
Eleven Days looks at how war changes people. Set against the events of Bloody April, it drops the reader into the most dangerous part of the first global war.

The Honey Talker

May 1997. Election night. Blair's New Labour is predicted to win with a landslide. It feels like a new start for everyone, the grey days of sleaze are over. There's a new hope that things really are about to get better.

But not for Aidan. He's a reporter whose life and career are going nowhere, relegated to a backwater job within the paper, existing on a diet of fast food and with virtually every day starting with a stinking hangover. He's clinging on to his job by his fingernails.

Then, after a terrifying road-rage incident, the story of his life drops in his lap. It looks like the chance to make his name
and salvage his career.

But within 24 hours his best friend is dead, and he's forced to work with Suzie, a combative, abrasive, ambitious younger colleague whilst the most powerful gangster in Manchester hunts Aidan armed with a weapon no one can resist.

Printed in Great Britain
by Amazon